ISLAND
OF THE
SUN

THE DARK GRAVITY SEQUENCE

BOOK 1: THE ARCTIC CODE

—● BOOK TWO ●—
in the
DARK GRAVITY SEQUENCE

ISLAND
OF THE
SUN

Matthew J. Kirby

BALZER + BRAY
An Imprint of HarperCollins*Publishers*

Library of Congress Control Number: 2015947627
ISBN 978-0-06-222490-3 (trade bdg.)

Typography by Carla Weise
16 17 18 19 20   CG/RRDH   10 9 8 7 6 5 4 3 2 1
❖
First Edition

For my sisters,
Amy and Sarah

ISLAND
OF THE
SUN

THE ROGUE PLANET WAS UP THERE.

Though Eleanor couldn't see it, she felt its weight all the time now. An immense shadow come from the distant reaches of space to drain the life from her own planet. Her freezing, dying earth.

No one else could feel it. Eleanor was certain the only reason anyone believed her, including her own mother, was that Dr. Powers had proven the rogue planet was real. She stared at the thin strip of wild Arctic sky visible between the buildings on either side of her. The planet was lurking up there, hidden somewhere among the stars.

"Are you sure about this, Luke?" Eleanor's mom

asked. Her polar mask obscured her face and cast her voice in amorphous metal.

"I'm sure," Luke said, his voice similarly distorted by his own mask, a layer of protection they all needed or the cold would crystallize their lungs in moments.

They all huddled together in a snowbound alleyway—Eleanor and her mom; their pilot, Luke; her mom's coworker, Dr. Powers; and his sons, Julian and Finn—between two small warehouses in Fairbanks, Alaska, having fled Barrow and the clutches of the Global Energy Trust the day before. Outside the alley, across a narrow, empty corridor in the ice, lay a darkened dome not unlike those used by the oil companies back in Barrow. Everywhere in the Arctic, buildings bent their failing wills against an assault of wind and snow that would not relent until the structures—and any people left inside them—had been wiped away.

"But for all we know," Dr. Powers said, "the G.E.T. has placed a bounty on our heads."

"What're you saying?" Luke asked.

"Well . . . just how good a friend is this Betty?"

Julian and Finn looked from their father back to Luke. Eleanor had met Betty once before, after stowing away on Luke's plane, but didn't know her well at all.

"She's a good enough friend for me to suggest we hide out with her," Luke said, sounding irritated, and even a little angry.

"Keep your voice down," said Eleanor's mom. "And Simon, Luke is right. We're out of options."

"Then let's do this," Luke said. "But wait here till I give you the all clear."

He ducked away toward the street even as Dr. Powers began to protest, and scurried across to the airlock hatch. The informal Arctic Code dictated that air locks be left open at all times for emergencies, and this hatch was no different. Luke was able to open it with a turn of the lever and step inside.

"Dad?" Finn said. "You really think the G.E.T. put a bounty on us?"

"I don't know," Dr. Powers said.

"Couldn't we just tell them the truth?" Finn asked. "Dr. Skinner was the criminal, not us." Finn was twelve, like Eleanor, and in some ways much smarter than her and his older brother. In other ways, though, he wasn't.

"You really think anyone would believe us?" Eleanor asked, but Julian wasn't so gentle.

"Wake up, Finn," he said. "Dr. Skinner is dead. We totally destroyed the G.E.T. research station, and all the evidence of what they were doing with that alien . . .

whatever it was. To the rest of the world, we're the criminals."

Eleanor had to agree with that assessment.

"I'm afraid Julian is right," Dr. Powers said. "Bounties aside, by now they will have at least issued warrants for our arrest."

"So what are we going to do?" Finn asked.

"I'm not sure yet," Dr. Powers said.

"We'll hide here for now," said Eleanor's mom. "And come up with a plan."

The empty street bore not a trace of life, no other people outside at this time of night, and no animals, for nothing could survive unprotected in the Arctic. Fairbanks did seem slightly less hostile than Barrow had, less lawless city and more ghost town. Luke had said that before the Freeze, the borough of Fairbanks had a population of a hundred thousand, but based on the scattering of buildings and oil rigs Eleanor had glimpsed as they'd flown in, there were fewer than a thousand people left. Everyone else had been driven south by the cold, which had buried the old Fairbanks under an ice sheet that now covered half the Northern Hemisphere under a mile-thick glacier. The Alaskan refugees had fled with the rest of Canada and the northern states to cities like Phoenix, where Eleanor was from, or even farther, to Mexico.

"It's Luke," said Julian, pointing as the hatch opened across the street, and their pilot peered out and waved for them to cross.

"Let's go," Eleanor's mother said.

They crept from the alley, and once they'd stepped into the open, a gust of wind slammed into Eleanor's right side, trying to knock her down. She leaned against it and pressed ahead until she reached Luke and the open hatch. Once they were all inside the air lock, Luke closed the outer door, sealing out the wind, and waved down the short corridor at Finn.

"Give that other door a smack, would you, kid?"

Finn rapped on the door with his gloved hand, and the hatch opened. A woman stood there sleepy-squinting at them, her short gray hair pressed flat against her head on one side. She appeared to be a bit older than Eleanor's mom, and smaller, but harder, the way driftwood seems harder than a freshly cut branch, even though they're made of the same stuff. Eleanor hadn't seen beneath her mask the first time they'd met. The woman yawned, covering her mouth.

"Well, can't say you're quite the pack of dangerous terrorists they warned us about," she said.

Luke pulled off his mask, revealing his haggard face and a beard that had been only a coarse stubble when Eleanor first met him. "That's just the disguise," he said, and gestured toward the rest of them. "Dangerous terrorists, this is Betty Cruz."

Betty nodded and stepped aside from the opening. "Come on in."

They filed through the hatch into a large room that seemed to function as an office, a workshop, and a laboratory all at once. Near them, a battered wooden desk piled with papers and files squatted in the spotlight of a single lamp, while on the opposite side of the room, assorted tools hung from the wall above a workbench. A metal table nearby was spread with glass vials and instruments.

"You're a scientist?" Dr. Powers said, removing his mask. He was a handsome man, with darker skin than his sons and a narrowed gaze that swept the room. "A geologist, it would seem."

"Correct," Betty said.

Eleanor and the rest of them removed their masks as well.

"Dr. Powers and I are geologists, too," her mother said. "Who are you with?"

Luke answered before Betty could. "She's, uh, an independent contractor. So to speak."

"Meaning?" Dr. Powers asked.

"Meaning I analyze samples for folks who may not want the results on the books," Betty said. "I don't concern myself over what they do with my results once I hand them over."

"I see," Dr. Powers said, frowning. "I'm Dr. Simon Powers. These are my sons. The older is Julian, the younger is Finn."

Both boys nodded, and so did Betty. "Nice to meet you both."

"I'm Samantha Perry," Eleanor's mother said. "And this is my daughter, Eleanor."

"I believe Eleanor and I have met before." Betty smiled.

"She kept Luke from throwing me off his plane," Eleanor said, and Luke snorted.

"Damn right," he said with a crooked smirk. "Good thing for you she was there."

"Betty," Finn said, "you just mentioned 'they' had warned you about us. What did you mean?"

"The Global Energy Trust put out a bulletin yesterday," Betty said. "It was scarce on details but made it very clear that you all had destroyed a research station up in Barrow. If you're spotted, we're to call it in and make no effort to apprehend you."

So they were all wanted now, just as Dr. Powers had feared. Eleanor imagined her face on a wanted poster, calling her a terrorist, and her throat tightened.

Betty turned to Luke. "Where's *Consuelo*?"

"A hangar at the edge of town. Landed under false ID. It's so late, they haven't really checked us yet."

"Won't take long for someone to figure it out," Betty said. "What's your plan?"

Eleanor knew what her plan would be, but it wasn't really up to just her anymore. She almost missed the time when she was on her own, calling the shots, back before she'd found her mom. Now she had to sit and watch her mom and Dr. Powers just look at each other for a long moment before her mom said, "To be honest, we're not exactly sure what our plan is."

Betty turned to Luke.

"It's a complicated situation," he said.

"Well," Betty said, "you want my help, somebody better uncomplicate it." She turned away from them toward a door to Eleanor's right. "I'll put some coffee on."

"All right then," Luke said.

They followed Betty through the door into a much smaller room that seemed to be her entire living space, crammed with a sofa, a bed, a table, and a few chairs. Several crates lined the walls. The coffeemaker sat by a single-burner hot plate on a counter, next to a deep metal basin sink. Betty lifted the lid on a crate near the sink and pulled out a tin of ground coffee.

"So?" she said. "Somebody going to start talking or what?"

Eleanor wanted to speak up, but she knew the truth would be more believable if it came from the adults first, so she decided to keep silent for now.

"I think we should all have a seat," Dr. Powers said. Betty ushered them into chairs. Eleanor ended up on the sofa next to Luke, and as she sat down, she noticed the cushions and upholstery smelled of cedar. Betty sat on the sofa, too, on Luke's other side, as the coffeemaker sputtered to life.

"All right, so . . . this is going to sound unbelievable," Eleanor's mom said. "Let's just get that out of the way now."

"I believe a lot of unbelievable things," Betty said.

"Just wait," Luke said.

Eleanor's mom continued. "I recently discovered something underneath the ice sheet outside Barrow. An unusual energy signature. Massive. Dr. Powers came in to help me investigate, and we found a very large . . . device."

"A device," Betty said. "What kind of device?"

Eleanor remembered the towering Concentrator, a black metal tree with impossibly twisted branches, a visual maze that could trap the eye and confuse the mind.

"Are you familiar with the work of Johann von Albrecht?" Dr. Powers asked.

Betty raised an eyebrow and pulled her mouth into a one-sided frown. "Work? I suppose, if that's what you want to call it. Guy's a crackpot."

"But the telluric currents he writes about are real," Dr. Powers said. "And the device we found under the ice *concentrates* those currents into usable energy."

"How much energy are we talking about?" Betty asked.

"Enough to power a very large city?" Eleanor's mom said. "Ten very large cities? We don't actually know the upper limit. But as far as we can tell, the Concentrator then converts it into dark energy."

"What?" Betty asked. "How? Who developed it? The G.E.T.?"

This was the part Eleanor knew no one else wanted to say. The part they believed only because they had to. The part that made Eleanor feel alone, because only she could sense it. So it was now time for her to speak up, because the others wouldn't.

"It isn't G.E.T.," she said. "It's an . . . alien device."

"Alien," Betty said. "As in . . . ?"

Eleanor could smell the burned, nutty aroma of the coffee now, as the pot slowly filled. "As in extraterrestrial," she said.

Betty laughed, a warbly sound, but stopped abruptly when no one else laughed with her, and a deep scowl crept across her face, as if she suspected they were all party to some joke at her expense.

"My daughter is correct," Eleanor's mom said. "It is the only possible explanation that fits the data."

"That's right," Finn said. "And we met Amarok's tribe."

Betty's scowl remained embedded. "Amarok?"

Dr. Powers cleared his throat and shifted in his seat. "I don't know if we need to go into all that, son."

"Oh, no," Betty said, her hand beckoning like a crossing guard. "Let's keep going. We're already halfway down the rabbit hole. Who's this Amarok?"

"Well . . ." Dr. Powers leaned forward. "You see, uh, Ms. Cruz . . . the Concentrator's energy had a rather unbelievable localized effect. A rejuvenating effect. It created an ice cavern, and it . . . resurrected a village from the late Paleolithic that had been buried there. Amarok and his people were living in that cavern under the ice sheet, just as they had during the Stone Age. But the Concentrator had been there before them, which makes it older than the Pleistocene."

The coffeemaker finished filling the pot and gave a final, lingering hiss, but no one rose to pour a cup. Betty's right leg bounced up and down, but her expression was set. "I don't know what this is," she said. "But I think I'm going to regret letting you all in."

"Relax, Betty," Luke said.

She swiveled on the couch to face him. "What do you mean, relax? Are you in on this, Fournier?"

"Not in on anything," Luke said. "I believe it."

"You *believe*?" Betty stood up, took a step away from the couch, and faced them all with her hands on her hips. "Just what exactly is going on here?"

Eleanor knew how preposterous it all sounded. But the look on Betty's face in that moment was not so different from the looks on the others' faces when she'd told them about her connection to the Concentrator. The disbelief. The mistrust.

"We've uncovered a conspiracy," Eleanor's mom said. "The G.E.T. is involved. The UN too, we think."

"Oh, of course. A conspiracy." Betty threw her hands up to either side. "It *would* be a conspiracy, wouldn't it?"

"We're not crazy," Julian said, his voice emphatic, and loud, and sounding a little angry.

Betty rolled her eyes toward the ceiling. "Ever notice how people who believe in conspiracies always think they're the sane ones?"

"You think we're delusional, naturally," Dr. Powers said, sounding much more measured than his son.

"You're the one who brought up von Albrecht, aren't you?" Betty said. Then she glared at Luke. "And what about you, Fournier? You see any of this for yourself?"

Luke shrugged. "I didn't see any cavemen, if that's what you're asking. But I did see a crater a mile wide appear on the ice sheet outside Barrow, overnight. Looked like a meteor had hit. I saw the G.E.T. willing to do almost anything to find and protect that site. And I know . . ." He paused and turned to look at Eleanor. "I believe *her*."

Betty lifted her gaze from Luke and laid it on Eleanor, and under its weight, Eleanor felt her cheeks getting hot. Compared to her mom and the others, Luke had the least amount of actual evidence for any of it, and yet he'd believed her. That meant a lot.

"I need coffee," Betty said, and turned toward the pot. She poured a mug without offering one to anyone else. She sipped, and stared into the cup, then took another sip, then stared, then sipped. "I have no idea what to do with this," she finally said.

"There's more," said Eleanor. "There's a—"

A clanging sound echoed from the other room, in the direction of the front hatch.

"Someone's here," Betty said, setting down her mug.

Eleanor's mom straightened her back. "It's the middle of the night."

"Anyone else with you?" Betty asked.

CHAPTER
2

D R. POWERS TOOK A THREATENING STEP TOWARD BETTY. "Did you alert them?"

"Hey!" Luke said. "Easy now—"

"No," Betty said. "I didn't."

"What are we going to do?" Eleanor's mom asked.

"Wait here," Betty said. "I'll see if I can get rid of them."

She left the room and closed the door behind her; Eleanor could hear her footsteps as she crossed the workroom on the other side and the squeal of the hatch as she opened it. Next to reach them were voices, somewhat muffled by the distance and the masks. Everyone in the room with Eleanor held still, frozen as though they'd been caught unprotected on the ice sheet.

"Betty Cruz?" asked a man's voice.

"That's me," Betty said, sounding groggy, as though she'd just woken up.

"We're with the Global Energy Trust. Sorry to disturb you at this late hour."

"Then get to the point," Betty said.

"Are you aware of the Barrow terrorists? The ones who bombed Polaris Station?"

"I might have heard something about that, yes."

"A plane landed in Fairbanks in the last two hours," said a different male voice. "We have reason to believe the terrorists were on it."

Eleanor looked at Luke. It seemed they'd found *Consuelo*, and Eleanor had no idea what that would mean for their escape.

"What does this have to do with me?" Betty asked.

"You're familiar with the pilot. Lucius Fournier?"

Luke silently folded his arms and glowered.

"I know him," Betty said. "He brings my shipments on occasion."

"Have you seen Mr. Fournier tonight? Has he come here?"

"No," Betty said.

"Would you mind if we look around your workshop?"

Eleanor swept the tiny room with a panicked glance. They had nowhere to hide if the G.E.T. agents were to come through that door.

"As a matter of fact," Betty said, "I do mind."

"Why is that?" the first man asked. "Do you have something to hide?"

"Harboring terrorists is a serious crime," said the second.

"The work I do is sensitive," Betty said. "I don't think my clients would like the idea of a couple of G.E.T. suits snooping around. Some of them happen to be your competition. Besides, if these are terrorists, as you say, why is it *you* here looking for them, and not the feds? And just why exactly do you have those guns?"

A moment of silence followed that question.

"Whatever you're thinking about doing right now," Betty said, "I've got plenty of friends in town who owe me. Lots of people go missing up here."

"Are you threatening us?"

"No more than you're threatening me."

Another moment of silence.

"We can come back with law enforcement," the second voice said. "And a warrant. If that's what you want."

"You do that," Betty said.

"If you see Lucius Fournier," the first voice said, "call this number."

"Uh-huh," Betty said.

"We *will* be back, Ms. Cruz."

"Preferably during daylight hours," Betty said. "Good night, gentlemen."

A moment later, Eleanor heard the sound of the hatch shutting, and then Betty's stomping, coming toward them before she stormed back into the room, pointing a finger at Luke. "All right, you better tell me right now what happened to that research station."

"We didn't bomb it," Luke said.

"It was Skinner's fault," Eleanor said.

Betty's eyes widened. "Aaron Skinner?"

"Yes," Eleanor's mom said. "He came in to take control of the Concentrator. He placed Polaris Station directly over the site, to drill. When Eleanor shut the Concentrator down, the cavern collapsed, taking the station with it."

"Is that a fact?" Betty said, her tone not quite one of disbelief, but almost. She turned to Eleanor. "And what was this *more* you were going to tell me about before those G.E.T. goons showed up?"

Eleanor paused for a moment to consider how she might say it.

"Out with it," Betty said. "I can't see this getting any more far-fetched."

Okay, then. "There's a planet up there," Eleanor said, pointing up at the ceiling. "The Concentrator is feeding energy to it."

"A planet," Betty said, her voice flat. "A *planet* planet."

"Yes," Eleanor said.

"As in—Mars?"

"This planet is not from our solar system," Eleanor said. "It's a . . . It's come here to drain the earth."

"I was wrong," Betty said. "This is more far-fetched."

"But it's true," Eleanor said. "I swear."

"Do you?" Betty asked, and with a sarcastic chortle followed up with an equally sarcastic "Have you been there?"

Eleanor thought back to the vision, the way her mind had somehow connected with the Concentrator and then ridden on the back of a beam of converted dark energy to the impossible surface of the rogue world, which appeared every bit as contorted and unknowable as the Concentrator itself.

"Yes," Eleanor said. "I have. Sort of."

Betty looked sharply from Eleanor toward her mom, and Eleanor noticed her mom was gazing down at the floor. Dr. Powers wasn't looking up either, and

Finn and Julian were glancing sidelong at each other. This was the part none of them understood. But at least Luke gave Eleanor a gentle, if slightly worried, nod.

"Sort of?" Betty asked.

"Not physically," Eleanor said. "It was . . . a kind of dream. But it felt real."

"So this is all based on a dream you had?" Betty asked.

"No, there *is* a planet-sized object out there," Dr. Powers said. "A rogue world, one of countless drifting through the cold vacuum of space between solar systems. But this one has entered *our* solar system. It's why the earth's orbit has shifted, and why this new ice age has occurred. Why it's there . . . we're not entirely sure. But the invading planet's gravity is pulling us away from the sun. The mathematics prove it, without a doubt."

Despite what he said, Eleanor did know why it was there.

Next to their father, Finn and Julian kept mostly quiet but nodded along with him, appearing very accustomed to hearing him lecture, but also appearing more comfortable with this explanation than Eleanor's.

"Then why can't we *see* this planet?" Betty asked.

"It doesn't fully appear in the visible spectrum,"

Eleanor's mother said. "It may be that it's beyond our perception."

"Beyond our perception?" Betty asked. "What, like a dog whistle or something?"

"Something like that," Dr. Powers said. "Or infrared light. It seems we didn't evolve with the necessary biology to grasp the rogue planet."

"I see," Betty said. "And somehow you're the only ones who've figured this out."

"No," Eleanor's mom said. "The UN knows everything, the G.E.T. knows everything, and they're working very hard to hide it. That's the conspiracy."

"They *know* why the Freeze happened," Betty began, "and they're keeping it secret? Why the hell would they want to hide it?"

"We don't know the answer to that, but Skinner spoke of the Preservation Protocol."

"More conspiracy theory," Betty said. "And where is Skinner now?"

"He . . ." Eleanor took a breath and cringed as she continued. "He got trampled by a woolly mammoth."

"You know"—Betty tipped her head to one side— "considering everything you've been telling me, that sounds about right."

"He refused to see reason," Eleanor's mom said. "He was a brilliant man, but he got so much wrong. He thought we should use the Concentrator, tap its energy somehow. He didn't understand that it was connecting us to the rogue world. He believed he was doing what was best for the earth and the human race; it never occurred to him that we might not be able to control it."

"Hey," Julian said. "Now that he's gone, who's in charge of the G.E.T.?"

"That would be the chairman," Dr. Powers said. "Pierce Watkins."

"I've met him," Luke said. "That old lizard had the nerve to come on my plane."

"He's even more arrogant than Skinner," Eleanor's mom said. "And more ruthless."

Eleanor remembered Dr. Watkins, though from her stowaway hiding place, she hadn't seen him. She had only overheard the conversation in *Consuelo*'s cargo hold, back in Phoenix before she'd taken off for the Arctic in the first place. That seemed like a very, very long time ago.

"If what you're saying is true . . . ," Betty said, but didn't finish the thought.

"Come on, Cruz," Luke said. "You know me. I don't sign on for nothing unless it pays, and God knows there ain't any money in this. And I ain't a terrorist. So if I didn't do what they're saying I did, then why else would the G.E.T. be sending armed agents to your door to threaten you in the middle of the night?"

"Well," Betty said, "you must have done *something*." But she didn't sound convinced of it herself. "Speaking of which, those agents will be back, and probably with a warrant. They knew I was lying."

"Then we've gotta get out of here," Julian said.

"Agreed," Dr. Powers said.

"They're probably watching my place." Betty slumped down on the couch and leaned back into the cushions, arms folded, staring ahead as she pinched her lips a little with her thumb and index finger. "And they've got *Consuelo*. You're not going anywhere without a major distraction."

"Got any ideas?" Luke asked her.

"Maybe," Betty said.

"So you believe us?" Eleanor asked. "You'll help us?"

"I didn't say I believed you," Betty said. "At least, I don't know what to believe right now. But I know Luke, and if he vouches for the rest of you, then I believe him."

"So what's your idea?" Luke asked.

"Those two are probably the only G.E.T. agents left in town," Betty said. "If there were more, they would have brought them just now as a show of force. Most of the others got called up to Barrow several days ago, I guess for this Concentrator thing you found. That

23

means your plane won't be too heavily guarded."

"But won't they just pay some of the locals to help?" Eleanor's mom asked.

"Oh, definitely," Betty said. "That's why we need a *gush*."

"A what?" Eleanor asked.

Her mom, Luke, and Dr. Powers all nodded along with one another, obviously aware of something that eluded not only Eleanor but, it seemed, Finn and Julian as well.

"What's a gush?" Finn asked.

Betty rose from the sofa and left the room, and everyone else followed after her, ignoring Finn's question. In her workroom, Betty walked to a crate and pulled out a long, rolled-up piece of paper, which she brought to her desk and spread out beneath the light of the lamp. It was a map, as near as Eleanor could tell, with both concentric and crossing lines.

"Right here." Betty pointed to a spot that made no sense to Eleanor, because the map made no sense to her. "People have been poking around out here."

"They find anything?" Luke asked.

"Nah," Betty said. "There's nothing there. But it's believable, and it's pretty far out there." She reached into a drawer in her desk and pulled out a paper form, which she laid on top of the map and started filling in.

"What's a gush?" Finn asked again.

"Is it like a gold rush?" Eleanor asked. "For oil?"

"Yes," her mom whispered.

Luke leaned in closer to Betty. "Are you sure about this? It'll ruin you."

"It's the only way you're getting out of here," she said. "Besides, I was ruined the minute I let you all through that door. Even if you're gone when those G.E.T. agents come back, they'll make sure I'm black-listed. They might even try to have me arrested. Whatever's going on, they know I know something. I'm an accomplice now."

"I'm sorry," Luke said. "We shouldn't have come."

"No," Betty said. "I should've turned you away." And then they both chuckled. A moment later, Betty finished the form and held it up in front of her at arm's length. "There," she said. "This ought to get everyone's attention."

"What is it?" Julian asked.

"It's an analysis report," Betty said, "for a very rich oil deposit that doesn't exist."

"I see." Julian nodded. "So the goal is to make everyone think there's oil out there."

"Exactly," Dr. Powers said.

"There will be a huge rush to stake claims," Luke said. "No one'll want to be left behind. There won't be anyone left in town for the G.E.T. to hire, and in the chaos and confusion, we'll fly out of here."

"Wait," Eleanor said, looking at Betty. "Won't they all be mad at you when they find out there's no oil?"

"Oh, they'll be more than mad." Betty sighed. "There goes my reputation." Luke turned to Betty and stared hard at her. Her shrug in response had the appearance of someone trying not to care but failing. "But then, I'm finished in Fairbanks, either way."

"Well," Luke said, "you're welcome to come with us."

"Oh, Lucius, you adorable thing." Mockery lilted her voice, even as anger swelled beneath it. "I don't need your invitation. You owe me big-time."

Luke's shoulders fell to a sheepish angle, and he frowned. "Fair enough."

"In fact," Betty said, "I may just take your plane as payment." He opened his mouth to protest, but before he could say anything, she continued. "Now, you all stay put here while I go plant this."

"Where?" Eleanor's mom asked.

"There's a bar still open a few streets over," Betty said. "I'll accidentally leave it somewhere in plain sight. Shouldn't take long for word to spread after that. We just need to be ready to move in a few hours when all hell breaks loose."

"We'll be ready," Dr. Powers said.

Betty slipped into her polar gear, a nano-tech heated suit like those Eleanor and the others wore, and pulled on her mask. "Lock up behind me," she said, and left through the front hatch.

Luke locked the door, then turned back toward the others. "You didn't make it easy on her, did you? You couldn't have eased her into the part with the aliens?"

"Better she know it all now," Eleanor's mom said. "Better the whole world knows."

"The world won't believe us," Dr. Powers said. "Not without more evidence."

Julian yawned. "If it's going to be a few hours, can I go sleep?"

Finn turned to his older brother. "How can you possibly sleep?"

"How can you possibly stay awake?" Julian asked. "We've been up for . . . I don't know . . . forever."

"Go on," Dr. Powers said. "It's probably a good idea. Use the sofa in the other room. You too, Finn."

"Fine," Finn said, and he trudged after his brother.

A few moments later, Eleanor's mom said, "Why don't you go, too, sweetie?"

"I don't think I can sleep," Eleanor said. Not when she thought about the G.E.T. agents outside, probably watching this place. What if they tried to break in while Betty was gone?

"We'll be awake," her mom said. "Dr. Powers and Luke and I."

Luke cocked his head at the mention of his name. "What if I wanted to sleep, too?"

Eleanor's mom closed her eyes slowly. "Very well. Dr. Powers and I will be awake. We'll be right here, okay?"

"Are you sure?" Eleanor asked.

"I'm sure," her mom said. "Go now."

Eleanor nodded and returned to Betty's living space, where the scent of coffee still hung in the air. Julian had skipped the sofa and claimed the bed, and somehow he was already asleep. Finn, still awake, had taken one side of the couch with his head resting on the arm. Eleanor took the opposite end, so their legs stretched side by side but not touching. They lay there in silence for some time, long enough that Eleanor thought he might have fallen asleep, but then he murmured something.

"What?" Eleanor asked.

"I said, what're you thinking about?"

"Nothing," she said. "What're you thinking about?"

"My mom," he said.

Eleanor hadn't really expected a serious or sincere answer, so it took her a moment to find a response, even a lame one. "You miss her?"

"Of course," he said. "I've lived with her a lot more than I've lived with my dad."

"How come?"

"After the divorce, he just got busy with his work. Traveling and everything."

Eleanor didn't know what to say, because she didn't know Finn very well at all and knew his dad even less. So much had happened in the past several days, they didn't really feel like days at all. But it wasn't that they felt like weeks or months, either. They weren't longer; they were just weighed down by everything Eleanor had been through, so she could almost forget that she hadn't known Finn that long.

"What's she like?"

"Kind of a hippie," he said. "Frizzy red hair. Freckles. Nothing like my dad. They met in grad school." He was silent a moment. "I don't think Julian misses her like I do. Sometimes I think he'd rather live with my dad."

"I would've guessed it was the other way around," Eleanor said.

"Yeah," Finn said. "People think I'm more like my dad. Julian thinks so, too. But I don't."

"How come?"

Finn shrugged against the arm of the sofa. "I don't know."

He didn't say anything else, and Eleanor didn't ask him anything else, and a few moments later she was close to falling asleep. Her thoughts roamed freely in that way they do as they leave memory behind and approach the edge of a dream. She was back at home, heading to meet Jenna and Claire before school like she did every day, but just as she reached them, a blizzard hit with an unnatural suddenness and a ferocity that tore up the streets, and Eleanor realized she was imagining it, and woke herself back up. She did this a couple of times before she finally crossed the border into sleep, and it didn't feel as if any time had passed before her mom gave her shoulder a gentle nudge.

"It's time to go," she said. "It's early morning."

Eleanor sat up. Finn rubbed his eyes near her, while Dr. Powers struggled to shake Julian awake.

"What is it about teenagers?" he said. "He could sleep through a whiteout siren."

"I'll show you what works," Luke said, crossing to the bed. He leaned toward Julian and said, in a low and even voice, "Time for dinner, kid."

Julian opened his eyes. "What?"

"See?" Luke said, and walked away grinning.

Dr. Powers shook his head as Julian sat up. "It's time to go, son."

"Oh." Julian got to his feet. "Right."

Faint shouting and the sound of engines came from outside, and Eleanor turned to her mom. "The gush?"

"Yes," her mom said. "It's now or never."

⤙ CHAPTER ⤚
3

As Eleanor entered the workroom, Betty stood over her desk. While the others pulled on their masks and prepared to venture out into the frenzied town, she shoved papers and files and other things into a backpack. The pack bulged, and when it didn't seem it had room for anything else, Betty stopped, looked around her, and let out a long, pained sigh.

"Damn," she said. "Damn Global Energy Trust."

"I'm sorry," Luke said.

"Not as sorry as I am," Betty said, and shook her head. "Ten years of my life crammed in here."

"Long time," Luke said.

"Living is changing," Betty said.

Eleanor's mom stood near the hatch. "We'd better go now. If you're ready."

"I'm ready," Betty said.

"What is all that you took?" Dr. Powers asked.

Betty slung the pack up onto her back. "Call it insurance." Eleanor didn't know what she meant by that, but Betty pulled on her mask then, which seemed to say it was the only explanation they would get. Then she stepped toward the hatch. "Follow me close and try not to get separated. Stay to the side of the roads so you don't get hit."

"Hit?" Finn asked.

Betty opened the hatch, and they followed her through the air lock and out into the street just as a snowmobile shot past, engine whining, blowing gasoline exhaust, chewing white. Other vehicles charged up the street after it—more snowmobiles, and even enclosed, tanklike transports—all of them traveling in the same direction toward Betty's false oil find.

"You sure got 'em up and moving!" Luke shouted.

"Cashed in every last cent of reputation I'd saved!" Betty replied.

Eleanor's mask warmed the freezing air up before it could stab her lungs, and the sound of each breath through its subtle machinery echoed in her ears.

"Now!" Betty said. "This way!"

She dove across the street through a break in the traffic, then down the alleyway through which they'd come earlier that night. They all followed after her, and Eleanor felt relief that she hadn't seen the G.E.T. agents anywhere yet. Above them, the dawn sky was nearly as bright as the stars, but they could still be seen, less like diamonds and more like white lint on a pale-blue blanket.

Eleanor and the others crossed several more busy streets as the town emptied itself, until they reached the landing field and the hangar where Luke had left *Consuelo*. It was a very large building, a fortress, among several in a line of defense.

Betty pulled a small black pistol out of one of her coat pockets. "What's the play here?"

"Whoa!" Eleanor's mom said. "To begin with, we are not shooting anyone! They're calling us terrorists, and we are not going to prove them right."

"The G.E.T. agents in that hangar will have guns," Betty said.

"And Sam," Dr. Powers said, "don't forget Skinner was prepared to shoot *you*."

"I don't believe he actually would have," Eleanor's mom said. "And even if you're right, that doesn't mean—"

"What about Amarok?" Dr. Powers said. "His

people defended their village with—"

"You know I didn't agree with that, either!" Eleanor's mom said.

"However we do it," Luke said, "this is what has to happen. We have to get in there, and while I start up *Consuelo*, somebody's gotta get those hangar doors open. Then we have to get everyone on board, taxi to the runway, and take off. You think those agents are gonna just stand around and give us time to do that? We don't even know for sure how many are in there."

"I'll check," Finn said.

"No, son, don't—" Dr. Powers said, but Finn had already scurried away.

He made it across the street quickly and then down the side of the hangar to a small window. The echo of Eleanor's breathing ceased in her ears as she watched and waited. Finn had to stand up on his toes to peer into the hangar, and he lingered there for what seemed to Eleanor a dangerous amount of time before dropping to his heels and hurrying back to them.

"There are only two that I can see," he said.

"We could just try taking 'em without shooting them," Julian said. "There's two of them and seven of us."

"Still too risky," Dr. Powers said. "There're probably more agents nearby."

What they really needed was a way to get the agents out of the hangar for a little while. "What if we give them their own gush?" Eleanor said.

"What do you mean?" Luke asked.

"I mean, what if Betty goes in there and pretends to rat us out?" Eleanor said. "She can say we came to her and she let us stay at her place, and that's where we are. Right now. They'll have to leave to check it out, won't they?"

Silence greeted her plan as the adults looked at one another.

"That's actually not a bad idea," Luke said. "Can you pull it off, Betty?"

"I think I could manage it." Betty removed her backpack and handed it to Luke. "Be ready to move."

"We will," Eleanor's mom said.

Betty nodded once and marched toward the hangar's air lock. After she'd gone inside, Luke said, "Betty can sell it. She's an excellent liar."

Eleanor wasn't sure whether that was a compliment, but in this case, she hoped Luke was right. When several minutes passed without Betty's return, worry set in more deeply. They had no other plan if Betty somehow got caught.

"Something's not right," Dr. Powers finally said.

"Betty can sell it," Luke repeated, but he sounded unsure.

Another minute later, the hatch opened, and a G.E.T. agent came out into the street.

"Get down!" Eleanor's mom whispered, and they all ducked back into the shadows of the alley.

The agent looked up and down the street and went back inside.

"This isn't looking good," Julian said.

"Hang on," Luke said. "Just wait."

More time passed, and the agent came back outside, but this time, he trotted across the street and departed in the direction of Betty's place. No one else emerged from the hangar.

"Looks like they're not taking any chances," Dr. Powers said. "One goes to check it out while the other stays with Betty?"

"What now?" Finn asked.

"I'm going in there," Luke said.

Eleanor's mom shook her head. "But you—"

"She wouldn't be in this mess if it weren't for me. She might have a gun to her head in there."

"All the more reason to proceed with caution," said Dr. Powers.

"Betty's got thirty minutes until that agent gets

back." Luke checked something on his belt. "Less if he radios from Betty's place. What happens to her when they realize she was lying?"

No one answered him.

"Screw this," he said. "I'm going in." He left the alley and ran toward the air lock.

"Damn it," Eleanor's mom said. "Simon?"

"I'll go," Dr. Powers said, and he ran after Luke.

"Then I'm going, too," Julian said, and raced after his dad, followed by Finn, who left without a word.

"Wait!" Eleanor's mom called after them, but they ignored her, and she and Eleanor were left alone in the alley. It didn't take long for Eleanor to decide she'd rather stick with the others, and her mom seemed to come to the same conclusion. "Stay with me," she said with a huff.

They hurried across the street and into the air lock, where Eleanor found the others had stopped and gathered in front of the inner hatch.

"This isn't quite what I had in mind," Luke whispered.

"Then perhaps you shouldn't have charged ahead," Eleanor's mom whispered back.

"If I remember correctly," said Dr. Powers, "there was a stack of crates just inside the hatch."

"Right," Luke said. "So we slip inside and head for

cover there. Just me and Professor Powers here."

Dr. Powers nodded, and Luke grasped the handle to the hatch. He turned it slowly, gently, to avoid making noise, wincing in anticipation. When it gave a loud thunk, everyone in the air lock went rigid.

"That you, Fournier?" Eleanor heard Betty call from inside. "All clear. Get yourself in here."

Luke sighed and threw the hatch open. Eleanor and the others filed after him out of the air lock and into the hangar. They found Betty aiming her gun at the G.E.T. agent's back, while he knelt on the ground in front of her with his hands behind his head.

"Where've you been?" Betty asked. "I need you to restrain this gentleman's hands."

Luke rushed to her side. "You got it."

"He's got handcuffs on his belt you can use," Betty said. "Though I have no idea what a G.E.T. agent is doing with cuffs."

"I have an idea," Eleanor said. "But you'd call it a conspiracy theory."

Betty smirked. Eleanor noticed her mom looked furious, hands balled into fists at her side, staring straight ahead as Luke pulled the G.E.T. agent's arms down and bound them behind the man's back with the metallic zip of the handcuffs. Once the agent was safely restrained, Eleanor relaxed a bit, and it seemed the others did, too. Her mom, on the other hand, turned on Betty and shouted.

"What do you think you're doing? We decided no guns!"

"Relax—it's not even loaded," Betty said, tucking the weapon back into her coat, at which the G.E.T. agent looked up. "These goons didn't trust me, obviously, so when the other guy left, I had to improvise—"

"I don't care!" Eleanor's mom shifted her stance to put her weight on her other foot. "I still don't—"

"We don't have time for this." Luke pushed by her and headed for his plane. "Get those hangar doors open! Control panel's on the left."

"Right." Dr. Powers marched in the direction Luke had indicated, toward a terminal beside the entrance to the hangar.

"Simon!" Eleanor's mom said. "Are you going to allow—"

"Not now, Sam," Dr. Powers said without looking back. "We'll deal with it in the air."

Eleanor did not like seeing this tension between the adults, the ones who were supposed to have all the answers and know how to take care of her and Finn and Julian. The truth was that no one had the answers, and that unsettled her and reminded her of how alone she'd felt when her mom had first gone missing.

"You should turn yourselves in," the G.E.T. agent said. "This is only going to make things worse for you. Where do you think you can run? Dr. Watkins will—"

"Shut up," Betty said.

"You're terrorists," the agent said. "Everyone will be hunting you."

"Not when they find out what we discovered," Eleanor said.

"And what's that?" the agent asked.

"The Concentrator," said Eleanor. "The rogue planet."

The agent blinked and shook his head. "What?"

Eleanor folded her arms. "You know. The alien device under the ice."

He narrowed his eyes and frowned in what seemed to be genuine confusion.

Eleanor's mom inhaled and then said to her in a low and even tone, "Sweetie, let's get you and the boys on board. Finn, Julian?"

"Yes, ma'am," Julian said.

Her mom walked them around the battered plane toward the stairway. *Consuelo* was obviously not built for commercial travel. She was a cargo plane, and her gray metal skin bore the pockmarks of her many Arctic runs through scouring polar storms of ice and hail. Eleanor followed her mom up the stairs into the passenger cabin with its rows of seats, where she and Finn and Julian took places scattered from one another. Up the aisle, through a narrow hatch, Eleanor glimpsed Luke in the cockpit, swearing at the plane's controls. All the electronics looked dead and lightless.

"Is there a problem?" Eleanor's mom asked.

"They've done something to her," Luke said. He left the cockpit and stalked down the aisle toward the exit. "I'll find it."

Eleanor's mom watched him pass. "We don't have a lot of time, Luke. That other agent will be back in—"

"I know!" Luke shouted. "I said I'll find it!" He ducked out of the plane and stomped down the stairway.

Eleanor's mom bit one side of her lower lip for a moment. "You kids wait here," she said, and then she also left the plane.

When they were alone, Finn glanced at Julian and Eleanor. "Well, this doesn't look good."

"Luke will figure it out," Eleanor said.

"You sure about that?" Julian asked.

"Yes, I'm sure," Eleanor said, trying very hard to feel that way. Through the window near her seat, she saw Betty standing over the bound G.E.T. agent and Dr. Powers standing at the control panel. A moment later, a vertical seam opened in the middle of the hangar's side with a distant squeal of metal, admitting a rush of light and a few wind-borne vortices of snow along the ground. When the doors were completely open, Dr. Powers stepped away from the control panel and pulled his mask on. Betty did the same, and then she and Dr. Powers helped get the G.E.T. agent's mask over his head. Open to the elements, the hangar would be dangerously cold within moments. With the door open, the plane's cabin would, too.

"How long has it been since that other guy left?" Julian asked.

"Fifteen minutes?" Finn said. "Maybe longer?"

"So we've got ten minutes, tops," Julian said. He got up and pulled his mask out of a pocket in his polar suit. "I'm going to go see if I can help Luke."

Eleanor liked that idea better than sitting and doing nothing. "Me too."

Finn nodded and rose from his seat, and the three of them pulled on their masks before exiting the plane.

They found Luke and Eleanor's mom up by the nose. Luke stood on a stepladder beneath an open panel, reaching into *Consuelo* and fiddling with some wires.

"Can you fix it?" Eleanor's mom said.

"Just give me a minute." Luke grunted. "Fortunately for us, sabotage wasn't those agents' specialty."

Eleanor's mom turned toward Eleanor as she and

the others approached. "Sweetie, I told you to wait on the plane."

"We wanted to help," Eleanor said.

"Not much you can do," Luke said.

"Boys!" Dr. Powers called. "Get back on board!"

"We're fine, Dad!" Finn said.

"I know you're fine." Dr. Powers glanced down at the G.E.T. agent and then strode toward his sons, pointing toward the plane. "But I still want you back on board!"

"Dad, relax," Finn said. "We—"

"Hey!" Betty shouted.

Eleanor looked in her direction. The G.E.T. agent had seized the moment of distraction and now bolted headlong toward the open hangar doors, hands still cuffed behind his back.

Dr. Powers launched after him and shouted, "Stop!" while closing some of the distance quickly, but not all of it. As he neared the agent, Dr. Powers leaped forward, hands outstretched, to tackle him, but he only grazed the agent's ankles and landed in a hard roll on the ground. The agent passed through the doors and got away.

Finn and Julian ran to their father and helped him up. "Should—should I go after him?" Dr. Powers asked, rubbing his elbow as he returned to Eleanor, her mother, and Betty.

"Won't matter either way if we can't get this thing off the ground!" Luke shouted from the nose of the plane, where he continued to work.

"Right," Dr. Powers said.

"Just get everyone on the plane. I've almost got it."

They moved as a group toward the stairway and ascended in single file until they were all inside the passenger cabin. They took their seats, Eleanor and her mom next to each other in the front row, Betty across the aisle from them. Julian and Dr. Powers sat behind her, while Finn sat alone in the row behind Eleanor. A few moments later, Luke came in and slammed the door behind him, then moved quickly through the cabin toward the cockpit.

"Strap in," he said as he passed Eleanor. "We're not out of the blizzard yet."

Eleanor buckled herself in and leaned into the aisle to watch as Luke took his pilot's seat, removed his mask, and put on his headphones, almost wishing she were sitting up there with him as she'd done before. *Consuelo's* console lit up at his touch, more brightly than Eleanor remembered it, as if the plane were somehow eager to get away. Her engines rumbled to life.

"We're in business," Luke shouted over his shoulder. "Here we go."

Eleanor's mother took her hand and gave it a

squeeze. Eleanor squeezed hers back as *Consuelo* lurched forward. The whine of the engines pitched higher in the cabin, and the plane rolled forward, out of the hangar, into the spreading dawn. The sun wasn't up yet, but the stars had fully retreated.

"I'm not gonna radio the tower," Luke said. "They wouldn't give us permission, anyway. Let's just hope nobody's trying to land as we're trying to take off."

Fairbanks slid past the windows, even more quiet and empty now with the oil gush on, as the plane rolled into position on the runway. Betty leaned close to the glass, and Eleanor wondered what she must be thinking and feeling, leaving the only home she'd known all these years. It didn't seem likely she would ever be able to return after what she'd done to help them.

"Here we go," Luke said, and the plane heaved forward, pulling Eleanor deep into her seat.

They hadn't gone far when Luke shouted, "Blast! It's the other one!"

"What?" Eleanor's mom shouted back.

"The other G.E.T. agent!" Luke said. "He's on the runway!"

CHAPTER

4

ELEANOR LEANED INTO THE AISLE AGAIN AND COULD JUST see through the windows of the cockpit that out on the runway, in the distance, was a snowmobile.

"What do we do?" Dr. Powers asked.

"Can you lift off before we hit him?" Betty asked.

"Maybe," Luke said. "If not, this guy is about to lose this particular game of chicken in a pretty big way." The plane picked up speed, the engines at full roar. "There!" Luke said. "He's moving out of the way! He . . . Oh no . . . Everyone get down! He's got a gun!"

An explosive popping sounded above the plane's engines. Eleanor ducked forward, as low as she could, and felt her mom throw her weight over the top of her back. More popping, the sound of a hammer on metal, and then *Consuelo* lifted a little from the ground. A moment later, Eleanor sensed the loss of contact with the earth as the floor of the plane ceased trembling beneath her, and they were airborne. A few more pops followed them into the sky, but they soon stopped.

Eleanor felt her mom's frantic hands all over her, touching her back, her chest, her legs.

"Mom, I'm fine," Eleanor said.

"Oh, thank God," her mom said.

"Everyone okay back there?" Luke called.

"We're okay," Dr. Powers said, his hand on Julian's back.

"Rattled," Betty said. "But free of holes."

Eleanor remembered Finn was behind her and turned around to peer at him between the seats. "Are you okay?"

Finn nodded, but he was looking over at his father and brother. "Yup. Just fine."

"This old bird can take a beating!" Luke said. Eleanor saw him stroking the flight console as if he were smoothing it out. "Her skin is made to stop Arctic hailstones."

"He really shot at us," Betty said, her eyes wide.

"What did you expect when they showed up on your doorstep with guns?" Dr. Powers asked.

"I guess . . . I thought they were for show," Betty said. "Intimidation. But he *shot* at us."

"Those agents only know what they've been told," Eleanor's mom said. "And back at the hangar, with that one who got away, I don't think he knew anything about what the G.E.T. is really doing."

"Watkins can't possibly trust every employee," Dr. Powers said. "Probably only a select few know the whole truth. That might actually give us an advantage, if we can find allies within the company."

"No one will give us that chance if they believe we're terrorists," Finn said.

"Yeah," Julian said. "They'll just shoot at us again."

Eleanor wanted to agree with her mom that Skinner would not have actually killed them. But now that a G.E.T. agent had fired at their plane, that hope seemed to have been a bit naive. This secret was literally as big as the whole world, and everything was at stake. Skinner had made it clear, before he died, that anyone who learned of the threat to the earth had to agree to the Preservation Protocol, a secret UN plan designed to manage the slow and inevitable destruction of the world. It was the goal of the Protocol to preserve a small number of the most essential citizens, so that human life could go on, no matter what. But Skinner had failed to reveal what happened to those who refused to adopt the Protocol.

"What have you all gotten me into?" Betty sounded weak and defeated.

"We're sorry," Eleanor's mom said. "Truly sorry."

"But wouldn't you rather know the truth?" Dr. Powers asked, sounding a bit brusque.

"Actually," said Betty, "maybe not. Maybe I'd rather have just kept doing what I was doing. Blissfully unaware. Hoping a turn in the weather was just around the corner. What hope is there now?"

But Eleanor believed there was hope. "We might be able stop it," she said. "I shut down the Concentrator. If we can shut the others down—"

"Others?" Betty asked.

"We think there are several more Concentrators around the earth connected to the rogue planet. They're likely along the . . . Do you know what ley lines are?"

Betty nodded. "You're telling me they're real, too?"

"Yes," Eleanor said. "The ley lines of telluric current, the earth's energy, are where we'll find the Concentrators. We have a map. Von Albrecht's map."

"If we shut them down," Finn said, "we think that'll stop the rogue planet. Without any energy to feed off, it'll just . . . move on."

"How do you know that?" Betty asked.

"We *hope* it," Eleanor's mom said. "Which is all we've got right now."

"Okay then," Betty said. "But I have one more question, and I can already tell I'm not going to like the answer. Who, or what, put these Concentrators here?"

The cabin fell silent. No one wanted to say what they were all thinking, but Eleanor knew there was only one possible answer.

She wondered if Betty was believing any of it. She seemed to be. The actions of the G.E.T. agents might have been enough to convince her that some kind of cover-up was going on. Eleanor wasn't sure they'd convinced her of the rest of it, though, something for which she couldn't fault Betty. She was well aware of how absurd it all sounded, and there were the parts of Eleanor's experience her own mother seemed not to have fully accepted. But Eleanor couldn't blame her for that, either. She had no idea why her mind had joined with the Concentrator. Why it had chosen her, or what made her different. But it didn't seem to be good news that she could connect with a piece of ancient alien technology.

Except for the chance it offered them to stop it.

"So where is the closest Concentrator?" Betty asked.

"Bolivia," Finn said. "Near the Isla del Sol in Lake Titicaca."

"So I suppose that's where we should go," Betty said. "Right?"

They all looked at one another.

"I suppose that's right," Dr. Powers said.

"We need to make a stop first," Eleanor said.

"Where?" Finn asked.

"Phoenix," Eleanor said. "We have to pick up my uncle Jack."

"Uh, don't you think that's exactly what they'd expect you to do?" Julian asked. "You might as well just turn yourself in."

Eleanor's fear for Uncle Jack quickly turned to anger at Julian.

"I'm afraid he's right, sweetie," Eleanor's mom said.

Eleanor whipped a furious, disbelieving gaze toward her. "What?"

"It's too risky," her mom said.

Eleanor stammered, "I can't—I can't believe—Mom, it's *Uncle Jack*! You can't just abandon him—!"

"I am not abandoning him," her mom said, with a gentleness that seemed designed to counter Eleanor's anger, but that only made it worse.

"You *are* abandoning him!" Eleanor shouted.

"I'm keeping him safe," her mom said. "He doesn't know a thing about any of this. I'm certain the G.E.T. knows that. They've probably been watching him since you ran away to come find me. If we make contact with him, it'll be just like Betty—he'll be involved, a target, on the run with us. I can't let that happen to him. Is that what you want?"

That question made Eleanor pause. Uncle Jack was the best man she knew, and the closest thing to a father she'd ever had, or ever needed. When she thought about how she'd run away from him to go search for her mom, and how that must have scared him, and hurt him, the guilt ripped her up from her gut to her chest. She'd been waiting for the moment she could explain everything to him and say she was sorry, and that she loved him. But now she wouldn't have that chance, and she had no idea when she would, and she realized maybe that was what bothered her most about leaving him behind in Phoenix. Because she knew her mom was right.

"I miss him," Eleanor whispered.

Her mom's eyes turned glassy, and her voice came haltingly. "I know, sweetie. I miss him, too. But this is what's best for him."

"He doesn't know," Eleanor said. "He doesn't know I'm alive, and you're alive. Who knows what the G.E.T. has told him?"

"Uncle Jack is smart," her mom said. "Smarter than anyone has ever given him credit for. I would not be surprised at all if he's figured out for himself that things aren't what they seem. He's probably hoping even now that we'll come home soon, safe and sound. And you know what? We will. Won't we?"

"Yeah," Eleanor said, and even though she knew he wouldn't be able to feel it, she sent Uncle Jack a mental hug, and for a moment, it filled up every spare thought in her mind. "We will."

"So . . . ," Finn said after a moment. "Bolivia, then?"

"No," Luke said from the cockpit.

The passengers turned their attention to the front of the plane.

"Those G.E.T. goons messed with *Consuelo*," he said. "And I've been thinking. . . . We have to assume they put a tracking device somewhere."

"What do you propose?" Dr. Powers asked.

"I need help finding it," Luke said. "And I know just the folks to ask."

"Who?" Eleanor asked.

"Felipe's family."

"Who's Felipe again?" Julian asked.

"He's a mechanic in Barrow," Eleanor said. "Luke and I stayed with him. He's a nice guy."

"So where's his family?"

"Mexico City," Luke said.

* * *

The plane left Alaska behind, but not the ice. Below them, the endless white of the glacial sheet nullified the surface of the earth, rendering it blank. Away to the west, the highest peaks of the Rocky Mountains could occasionally be seen breaching the surface, but their upward reaching seemed a desperate act, as though the earth hoped someone or something would take its hand and raise it from the crushing depths of ice.

About six hours out from Fairbanks, they flew over the edge of the ice sheet, cresting like a mile-high wave of white over much of the state of Oregon, and then they reached the coastline of northern California. Luke had decided San Francisco would be as safe a place as any to land and refuel. The G.E.T. didn't have much of a presence there.

Eleanor's mom said the city was once one of the most beautiful places in the country to live. But not anymore. With the ice sheet only a few hundred miles away, and temperatures dropping, those with the means had gone farther south, to Los Angeles or San Diego, leaving those without means behind. From the air, Eleanor saw the Golden Gate Bridge, looking forlorn, almost out of place. According to her history classes, it had once been the pride of San Francisco, an engineering marvel spanning a wide bay. But as the

Arctic ice had taken up and trapped the ocean's water, coastlines had expanded, and the bay had largely emptied, leaving the bridge a towering monument to all the city had lost.

"Are you sure it's safe to land?" Finn asked.

"Safer than flying on an empty tank," Luke said. "We need to refuel or we won't make it much farther. Speaking of which, I've been using my own stash of money, but it won't last forever. Fuel is expensive. You should try to empty your bank accounts before the government seizes your money. Standard practice with those they've branded as terrorists."

"But that will alert them," Eleanor's mom said. "They'll know where we are."

"They'll know where we were," Luke said. "Hopefully we'll be long gone before they catch up to us. We'll just have to be fast about this."

He radioed the airport, falsifying their identity as he'd done in Fairbanks. Eleanor wasn't sure how long that charade would continue to work.

"How many aliases do you have?" Dr. Powers asked him.

"I've collected a few in my line of work. Let's hope they stay untraceable."

Even with his confidence, Eleanor found it impossible to relax once they'd touched down. Luke taxied the plane to where he could refuel, and Eleanor's mom got up to leave with Dr. Powers. Eleanor didn't like the idea of sitting there on the plane, restless and nervous, wondering what was happening.

"Can I come?" she asked.

"I suppose." Her mom turned to Dr. Powers. "What do you think, Simon?"

"It should be fine," he said. "Boys?"

Finn and Julian decided to stay, and so did Betty, which was probably best to avoid drawing attention, anyway. So Eleanor, her mom, and Dr. Powers left the plane. They didn't need to suit up, which was a relief; the San Francisco air was cold, but not so cold it could kill them. Out on the tarmac, they turned toward the airport terminal, where Eleanor's mom thought they would find an ATM, and after a short walk they reached it.

Inside, the terminal was largely empty, most gates dark and vacant, but there were some travelers here and there, waiting stoically for the few planes that still came and went. They sat watching the TVs suspended from the ceiling, or read books and newspapers. It struck Eleanor that people seemed so able to go on with life as they had known it, even as the Freeze dismantled the world around them. She could only attribute that to the powerful allure of denial.

"There's an ATM," her mom said, pointing down the wide passage between the gates.

Eleanor glanced up at the TV screens as she followed behind her mom and Dr. Powers. They were all tuned to the same news station, where a pretty anchor was interviewing a man the caption identified as Dr. Pierce Watkins. Luke had called him an old lizard, and now Eleanor saw why. He was bald, with small ears, a sharp nose, and a slight wattle of loose skin beneath his chin. As for being old, Eleanor wasn't actually sure she could call him that. He looked it, certainly, but he spoke with the animated vigor of a young man.

"Mom, look," Eleanor said. "It's Dr. Watkins."

The three of them stopped to listen.

"I'm not saying the situation isn't dire," he said to the anchor. "But I wish to spread a message of hope. I look around, and I do not see a world that is ending. I see a world that is finally coming together. Just look at the wonderful situation in Mexico City. Nations helping nations, neighbors helping neighbors, in the face of a profound challenge. I see people going on with their lives, with faith that there will be a tomorrow. That is what drives me. That is what inspires me."

Dr. Powers snorted. "That is what I call a great big pile of bull—"

"Shh," Eleanor's mom said.

"But how do you respond to your critics?" the anchor asked. "The ones who say you are using this crisis to, in their words, trample on our rights and freedoms? As in Egypt, for example."

"There will always be disagreement," Watkins said. "Personally, I think that's a wonderful thing. I welcome it. We need every idea on the table, so long as it is presented in a constructive way. But recent actions, like those of the criminals who destroyed our facility in Alaska, are not the answer. Those tactics will do nothing but speed our demise. And make no mistake. We at the G.E.T., with the full authority of the UN, will do everything in our power to find and stop such people."

Eleanor felt a chill as much from his words as from her memories of the Arctic. "Let's hurry," she whispered. "I want to get out of here."

"I agree," her mom said.

They walked the rest of the way to the ATM, and then Eleanor waited as her mom inserted her debit card into the machine, a slight tremble in her hands. She followed the prompts on the screen, and then she flinched.

"Oh no."

"What is it?" Dr. Powers asked.

"Look."

Eleanor peered at the screen with Dr. Powers, where a message flashed.

For security reasons, your card has
been suspended.
Please contact your bank's customer
service for more information.

Then the screen returned to the welcome message. The machine kept the card.

Eleanor's mom stared at it. "Luke was right. They've blocked my account."

"Let me try mine," Dr. Powers said, sliding in front of the ATM. But when he inserted his card, he received the same message. "This is bad," he said.

Eleanor looked up at the security camera mounted above the ATM and imagined in that moment people were watching them from somewhere, alarms blaring. "We need to get back to the plane," she said.

Her mom nodded. "Okay. Let's hurry."

They turned away from the ATM and set off through the terminal. Eleanor expected armed guards to come racing at them any second, and at one point, she heard footsteps and the static mumble of a radio around a corner. Dr. Powers hauled the two of them into the shadows of a closed and empty gate just as three TSA agents came trotting by, heading in the direction of the ATM.

From there, the three of them simply ran for it until they reached the exit to the tarmac outside, and then they sprinted for the plane.

"What if they won't let us take off?" Eleanor's mom asked.

"Luke will, anyway," Eleanor said.

When they boarded, they found the others relaxing in their seats, Luke back in the cockpit.

"We good to go?" he asked.

"Have you refueled?" Dr. Powers asked.

Luke nodded.

"Then I suggest we take off immediately," Dr. Powers said.

"They blocked our accounts." Eleanor's mom pushed Eleanor forward toward their seats. "And security was onto us."

"Right," Luke said.

The three of them buckled in along with everyone else, and Luke woke *Consuelo* and guided her toward the runway without radioing the tower. By now, Eleanor guessed the whole airport would be looking for them, and it wouldn't take long for security to figure out they were already back on the plane. She kept her eyes out on the tarmac, waiting for security vehicles to come barreling toward them with lights flashing. But none appeared, and Eleanor soon felt the pressure of their takeoff forcing her into her seat. Once they were back in the air, she tried to shake some of the tension out of her arms and shoulders.

"This is a blow," Luke said from the cockpit. "My cash won't last forever."

"Mine either," Betty said.

"We'll have to make it work," Dr. Powers said. "It may not be long before cash doesn't matter, anyway."

After that, they put twenty or thirty minutes behind them before anyone spoke again.

"Are you okay?" Eleanor's mom asked her.

"Not really. The world is ending."

"You know what I mean."

"I'm fine," Eleanor said.

"Are you hungry? Luke said he has some food."

"I'm hungry," Finn said behind them.

"Me too," Julian said from across the aisle.

Eleanor left her seat to raid Luke's stash in a bulkhead compartment. She grinned when she opened it, though, and glanced forward into the cockpit. "Peanuts?" she said. "Really?"

"What's wrong with peanuts?" Luke said. "There's some other stuff in there, too."

In addition to nuts, dried fruit, and trail mixes, there were chips, crackers, cans of beans, and a substance that passed for meat—but probably not if you asked Uncle Jack—candy bars, bottled water, and other snack foods.

"You've got a lot in here," Eleanor said.

"You don't fly into the Arctic unprepared," Luke said. "Ever."

"This could last us awhile," she continued, and then added, "if it had to."

"Yeah, well," Luke said, "help yourself."

Eleanor grabbed a candy bar, then tossed one to Finn and another to Julian. Eleanor's mom ate some trail mix, and Dr. Powers boldly chose a can of beans. After that, people started nodding off. Eleanor worried Luke might be getting tired, so she went to join him up in the cockpit, slipping into the pilot's chair next to him. The last time she'd sat there had been after Luke had discovered her as a stowaway on his way north.

He glanced at her and raised an eyebrow. "Déjà vu."

Eleanor brought her legs up and crossed them under her. "I know, right? Can you believe that was, like, a week ago?"

He shook his head. "Yeah, well, a lot's happened since then."

Eleanor frowned. "You do believe us, though, right? I mean, you didn't see the Concentrator. But you believe us."

He nodded.

Eleanor bit down on her lower lip with her upper teeth. "But do you think *I'm* crazy?"

"Why would I think that?"

"You know. With the whole alien thing. Even my mom seems weirded out by it."

"I don't know, kid," Luke said. "I mean, sure, it's strange. Makes you wonder why you, you know?"

Yes, it did make Eleanor wonder that.

"I know a guy," said Luke, "who thinks he can talk to llamas. And you know what? I really like that guy. So do lots of folks."

"Do the llamas talk back?" Eleanor asked.

"The point is," Luke continued, "right now, I think we ought to be looking for what we all have in common, and just let the rest go. We need to trust each other and stick together."

Eleanor liked that idea.

"Besides," Luke said, "you don't look nothing like an alien to me."

"And how would you know what an alien looks like?" Eleanor asked.

Luke shrugged. "That's a story I'll take to my grave.

And it may or may not involve an antique bedpan."

Eleanor laughed. "Thanks, Luke."

"Don't mention it, kid," he said. "You tired? Still another three or four hours until we hit Mexico City."

"I'm not tired," Eleanor said. "Are you?"

"A little," he said. "Not bad."

"Have you ever been to Mexico City?"

"Sure. A few times. It's . . . quite a place."

"That's what I've heard."

"It's got its World Trade Center. Some UN offices. The whole world in a city, taking in the poor and huddled masses."

"Are you worried about the G.E.T. finding us there?"

"No."

"Why not?"

"Wait until you see it. Then you'll know."

— CHAPTER —
5

For hours they flew over a landscape of segmented shades of green, a verdant geometry of sustenance, field after field, every spare piece of land given over to growing food for much of the Western Hemisphere. Small towns here and there interrupted the pattern with large processing facilities, while trucks plied the highway seams between the tracts of cropland, kicking up tiny wisps of dust.

The mountains they crossed were fairly low and restful, except for a brown, vague plateau on the horizon ahead of them that swelled high into the sky.

"What is that?" Eleanor asked Luke. "A mountain?"

"That's Mexico City," Luke said. "Or rather, the air

above it. That's pollution you're seeing."

Eleanor looked again, and as they descended and drew nearer, she saw that he was right. The plateau she'd glimpsed lost some of its substance and became an oppressive cloud that smothered the ground beneath it. Their plane entered into its miasma, which dimmed the sun, and then they reached the first tattered edges of the city. If it could be called that.

Miles and miles of brown tents massed below them in a haphazard grid and spread away almost as far as she could see. The landscape was choked with debris and smoke and people and a few lonely and desperate-looking trees, completely crowding the ground between their plane and the hazy city skyline that was still an impossible distance away. The tents must have numbered in the millions, along with other structures of scrap wood and corrugated sheet metal, each one giving shelter to who knew how many refugees. None of the news broadcasts she'd seen had shown this. This was the "wonderful situation" Watkins had mentioned?

"It's something, isn't it?" Luke said. "Poor folks."

Her mouth was open, but she was speechless, her words tripped up in terrible awe. "I . . . it's . . ." She swallowed, almost as though she could taste the ash and oil of the polluted air coating her mouth and throat. "I had no idea."

"Most people don't until they get here," Luke said. "In the beginning, Mexico was ready for it. The immigration. They invited it, even. But the ice kept coming, and so did the refugees, and now you have this—this place."

Eleanor pressed her fingers to her closed eyes and shook her head. "It's awful."

"Now you see why I wasn't worried about the G.E.T. finding us here," Luke said. "Six different airports and landing strips, not counting military. The chaos of the refugees. Finding us would be like finding a single hair in a human landfill."

As bad as it was for refugees in the government housing back in Phoenix, like Eleanor's friends Jenna and Claire, at least they lived in actual buildings. "It's so much worse than the Ice Castles," Eleanor said. "But Mexico is always sending aid to the US. I thought they had money."

"Oh, they do," Luke said. "You'll see soon enough."

They flew over a few more miles of tent city, and then Eleanor noted a boundary approaching them, a clear demarcation between the refugee squalor and something resembling a more normal city. When they reached this edge, she realized it was actually a wall, tall and towered and razor lined, crewed by uniformed soldiers carrying guns, with the desperate refugees on one side and a very different situation on the other, though the cloud lurked over both.

Here, the trees multiplied and gathered in lush canopies between and through neighborhoods of large houses with multiangled roofs, terraces, and even swimming pools, and more modest and orderly lanes of the kind of middle-class housing development where Eleanor was lucky enough to live. Soon, the suburbs gave way to larger offices and shopping centers, and then glass and metal-skinned skyscrapers that rose up into the smog.

"Mexico City is really two cities," Luke said. "The one you're lucky enough to live in depends on who you are." He nodded back over his shoulder. "We'll be landing soon. On the rich side. Why don't you head back and buckle in."

Eleanor nodded and climbed out of the pilot's chair, then ducked out of the cockpit back into the passenger cabin. Everyone was awake, blinking out the windows, but utterly silent, and Eleanor could guess they were all feeling something similar to what she had just experienced.

She took the seat next to her mom. "Have you ever been to Mexico City before?" she asked.

Her mother shook her head. "It's even worse than I've heard."

"With no relief in sight," Betty said from across the aisle.

"Unless Mexico alters its policies," Eleanor's mom said. "They could make things better for the refugees."

"They've already given us many times what the US ever gave to them," Dr. Powers said. "And it's hard to forget our own immigration stance just a few decades ago. A very different wall some wanted to build."

Eleanor's mom directed her gaze back out the window, while Luke could be heard on the radio with a flight tower, getting set to land *Consuelo*.

Behind her, Finn said, "Mexico isn't doing anything different from what we would do in their place."

Eleanor agreed with that. To her, this city was simply a smaller version of the world Skinner imagined, one with limited resources devoted to a select few, and the rest left on the outside to survive, for now, on what little was given to them or what they could scrounge for themselves.

The plane's landing gear groaned under Eleanor's feet, and the mounting pressure squeezed her ears until she plugged her nose and blinked hard and popped them. She wondered which of the six different airports and landing strips Luke had chosen as the plane descended sharply and her stomach jumped.

When they bellied hard into the ground, the view from Eleanor's window was of a busy commercial airport, with dozens of passenger airliners nosed up to a wide terminal like feeding animals.

"This appears to be the international airport," Dr. Powers said. "Won't this be more conspicuous? Risky?"

"Closest airport to Felipe's family," Luke said from the cockpit. "They're in the Tepito barrio, about three miles west of here."

Consuelo taxied to the side of the tarmac opposite the passenger terminal. It was just after five, and evening was approaching. After bringing them to rest and shutting down the plane, Luke emerged from the cockpit frowning.

"Listen up," he said. "Tepito used to be a pretty rough place. Barrio bravo, they called it. The fierce neighborhood. It's better now than it was, but it's still one of the largest black markets in the world."

"Should you be going by yourself?" Betty asked.

"Well, that's what we need to decide," Luke said. "I think the plane is safe here. For a little while."

"How can you be sure?" Dr. Powers asked.

"I doubt even the G.E.T. would go behind the back of the Mexican government. It'll take time to get clearance for an operation at their international airport. But just in case, I'd rather not leave anyone on board."

"You're suggesting we go with you?" Eleanor's mom asked. "To Tepito?"

"It should be safe enough if we all stick together," Luke said.

Her mom sat back farther in her seat. "That's not quite as reassuring as I'd like it to be."

"Let's just go," Julian said. "We've been on this plane for, like, twelve hours. I need to move."

"But should we split up?" Dr. Powers asked. "If we assume the G.E.T. put a tracking device on the plane, which is the whole reason we're here, then they know we're in Mexico City. Traveling as a group, matching their exact description of us, might not be wise."

"That's true," Eleanor said. "We should split up, and I want to go with Luke."

Her mom turned toward her.

"I met Felipe," Eleanor said. "He helped me out. I'd like to meet his family."

Her mom looked back at Luke, who shrugged. "I'll keep her safe," he said.

"*I'll* keep her safe," her mom said. "I'm coming with you."

"Me too," Betty said.

"I'll keep my boys with me," Dr. Powers said. "Meet back here in . . ."

"Before dark," Luke said. "Should give us enough

time to find Felipe's folks and sweep the plane. Assuming they're free to help."

Dr. Powers rose from his seat. "Two hours, then."

Julian rose with him, but Eleanor noticed Finn stayed in his seat, looking back and forth between Luke and his dad, but eventually he sighed and stood. They all took turns in the bathroom changing out of their polar gear, as Mexico City still had pleasant temperatures in the sixties this time of year. Luke grabbed a cell phone from what appeared to be a collection of them inside a compartment, then opened the plane's hatch just as an airport worker wearing big round headphones rolled a motorized stairway up to the plane. Luke met the man at the bottom and reviewed some forms, and Eleanor thought she glimpsed a palmful of money trading hands. Then they all descended the stairs and walked away, leaving *Consuelo* on the tarmac.

"They'll fill her up and tow her into a hangar," Luke said. "And hopefully I paid him enough to keep the plane registration off the books for a few hours."

"Where will you go?" Eleanor's mom asked Dr. Powers.

"We'll probably grab a bite to eat," he said. "Then see what we can see."

They walked between the airfield's hangars and administrative buildings, the light from the sun here unlike any Eleanor had ever felt, almost . . . *aggressively* warm, or at least warm with intent, until they reached a street and parted ways with Dr. Powers, Finn, and Julian.

"Don't take the red or green cabs," Luke warned Dr. Powers. "The VW bugs. The libre ones. They're not safe. Take the metro or the bus, or a hotel can call you a sitio cab."

"I know," Dr. Powers said.

Luke nodded and led Eleanor, her mother, and Betty down the street. The city was alive in a way Eleanor had never experienced. Phoenix was big, and crowded, but it also felt subdued, somehow. Resigned. Like someone with a distance to walk in grim weather, shoulders hunched and head down. Mexico City, on the other hand, flashed a smile and swaggered through the end of the world. It appeared there were actually tourists here, people wearing big sunglasses and wide-brimmed hats, walking with their cameras out.

At the level of the street, the smog hanging above the city smelled of car exhaust and oil. Horns blared and engines competed to be heard over one another, and at times the foot traffic swelled beyond the sidewalks. The city didn't feel dangerous to Eleanor at all, but they hadn't yet reached the Tepito barrio that Eleanor's mom worried about.

As soon as they arrived at a hotel, a narrow building sandwiched between offices and apartments, with potted flowers out front—flowers!—and iron grates curling into the street over the windows, Luke went inside and arranged for a taxi. In a matter of moments, a black, unmarked car squealed up to the curb, and Luke opened its rear passenger door.

"This is us," he said.

Inside, the vehicle smelled of leather and the driver's cologne. He was an older, round man, with thinning hair and several deep, craggy wrinkles on the back of his neck, in one of which nestled a thin gold chain. Eleanor sat shoulder to shoulder with Betty on one side and her mom on the other.

"Tepito," Luke said, climbing into the front seat.

The driver hesitated for a fraction of a moment, his eyes on Eleanor and her mom through his rearview mirror. "Sí, señor," he said, and pulled into the traffic.

Though their destination was only a few miles away, it took them some time to reach it through the congestion of cars, buses, and delivery vans. When they finally did arrive, Luke paid the driver, and as they got out of the car, the man leaned across the front seat toward them. "Be safe, señor."

Luke nodded, and then they all turned to face Tepito.

Eleanor had never quite understood what the word *teeming* meant until that moment. The streets of Tepito, which seemed an endless market maze, dove away from them in several directions beneath a multi-colored patchwork of bright tarps and canopies. People filled the space beneath it, *teeming*, clogging the thoroughfares and vendor stalls. From where she stood, Eleanor glimpsed a dizzying variety of merchandise for sale, from clothing to jewelry to electronics to music and movies. Things a lot of people she knew couldn't afford anymore. Things Eleanor now found it hard to care about, considering everything she'd learned. The music and movies blared obnoxiously from multiple TVs and stereos simultaneously, but the people selling their wares seemed able to make themselves heard above the noise.

"Stay close," Luke said. "I think it's this way. Try not to gawk."

Eleanor closed her mouth.

For the most part, people seemed to pay them no mind as they entered the barrio, but every so often someone would stare, and Eleanor's neck and shoulders would clench as her heart beat faster. The only way to relax again was to remind herself that Luke had said the Tepito was safe now. Though Eleanor could easily imagine it otherwise.

They left behind the watches and sneakers and entered an area of the market selling food. Vendors hawked fresh produce—and less-than-fresh produce—including fruits and vegetables Eleanor had never seen before, and herbs and spices she had never smelled. She wished Uncle Jack were there with her. He would probably know exactly what to do with all of it and could turn it into something delicious. Eleanor then smelled meat cooking on open charcoal, the smoke and char of beef, and chicken, and other meats more pungent and barnyardy, and felt truly hungry. Dogs and cats haunted the corners here, looking fearfully hopeful.

"Through here," Luke said, and turned them down a side street too narrow for any vehicle wider than a bicycle.

"Are you certain about this?" Eleanor's mom asked.

"Bit too late to ask," Betty said.

They reached a low, slim door, one that didn't seem any more remarkable than the dozens of other doors they'd passed.

"I think it's this one," Luke said, staring at it. But he didn't knock.

"Only one way to know, right?" Eleanor said.

Luke looked at her and then shrugged. "Right." He knocked on the door.

A moment of silence passed, and something stirred on the other side, the faint vibrations of footsteps, followed by the metallic catch of a lock being turned. The door opened.

A young man in a yellow soccer jersey, with a shaved head, scowled out at each of them in turn. Eleanor could see the resemblance to Felipe and felt relieved.

"Arturo?" Luke said.

The young man stared at Luke a moment, and then nodded as a smile gradually broke his severe expression. "Lucas? Yes? Lucas?"

"Right," Luke said. "Lucas. Felipe's amigo."

"Lucas," the young man said, still nodding, and then suddenly stepped aside and motioned for them to enter. "Please, come, come."

"Muchas gracias," Luke said, and with his American accent it sounded slow and blunt and awkward, but charming. He gestured for the rest of them to go first, so Betty led the way, followed by Eleanor, then her mom, and Luke behind them.

They entered a small, dim foyer at the base of a winding staircase. Arturo closed the front door and then squeezed around them. "This way," he said, and started up the stairs.

The echoes of their footsteps trampled all over one another as they climbed to the second floor, where Eleanor found a rather comfortable apartment. Clean carpet remnants, some still bearing their edges of plastic-coated mesh, overlapped on a cement floor painted white. The walls were white, too, hung with a few pieces of colorful landscape artwork, as well as a crucifix and a painting of a golden-haloed Virgin Mary. Decks of electronic equipment filled an entire wall, with blinking LED lights, a couple of computer monitors at the center, and banks of CD drives on either side. Through a doorway, Eleanor saw a brightly lit kitchen and smelled that something delicious and warm was simmering inside it.

"¡Mama!" Arturo called. "¿Te acuerdas el amigo de Felipe, Lucas?"

"¿Quien?" said a woman from in the kitchen, and then a moment later, a short piñon pine of a woman walked out, wiping her hands on a white apron embroidered with roses at the hem. When she saw Luke, she grinned and then gathered him into a genuine hug. "¡Ah, Lucas! ¡Es tan bueno verte de nuevo!"

"She say it is good to see you," Arturo translated.

"Tell her it's nice to see her, too," Luke said, smiling back at her. "And I want her recipe for that potion that keeps her looking so young."

Arturo translated, with a wink, and his mother swatted the air between her and Luke. "Eso costaría más de lo que puedes pagar."

"She say you can no afford it," Arturo said. "But you need it."

Luke nodded. "You're right about that."

Arturo's mother said something quickly and forcefully to her son, pointing toward the kitchen, and Eleanor would've thought it was a question, except the woman didn't wait for an answer before bustling away, and in the next moment, the clatter of dishes came from the kitchen.

"She feed you," Arturo said with a sigh. "You like migas?"

Luke let out a sigh of his own, but one, it seemed, of pleasure. "Oh, sí," he said, and then to Eleanor, her mom, and Betty, "You're in for a treat."

Arturo led them into the kitchen and sat them at a small table of gold-flecked formica, where his mother had already set out four mismatched bowls. On the stove, a large pot released an aroma so thick with spice and meat, Eleanor felt she could take a bite out of the air above it. Her mom, on the other hand, sat stiffly in her chair, and Eleanor knew this would not be easy for her. Whereas Eleanor enjoyed the excitement of trying new things, her mom did not; even Uncle Jack had a hard time coaxing her into eating some of his dishes.

Arturo's mother carried each of their bowls in turn

to the stove and ladled into them a hearty stew. When she set Eleanor's bowl back in front of her, Eleanor noted a thick bone jutting up beyond the rim, still full of marrow, tender stewed meat just barely clinging to it. When everyone was served, Arturo's mother said, "Please, eat." It made sense that those would be some of the few English words she knew.

"So, what is this?" Eleanor's mom asked with a wooden smile, her spoon poised above her bowl.

"Pork bones simmered with chilies," Luke said. "Thickened with stale bread. It's normally a breakfast food, but I'll take it."

"Me too," Betty said. "My aunt Celia cooked migas."

Eleanor dipped her own spoon into the soup, blew on it gently, and then tasted it. "Oh, that's good," she said. The broth was dark and rich and thick with chunks of bread, but it was quite spicy, too. Eleanor used the edge of her spoon to scrape a shred of tender meat from the bone, and it fell apart in her mouth. She almost couldn't believe how good it was, but then, she hadn't had a home-cooked meal since Phoenix. That thought made her miss Uncle Jack's cooking. He would've loved this stew.

Arturo's mother stood away from them, hands clasped at her waist, watching them eat with a look of expectant worry.

"You like it?" Arturo asked.

Luke nodded. "Heaven."

"Better than when my aunt made it," Betty said.

"Delicious," Eleanor said.

"Please thank her for us," Eleanor's mom said, going through the motions of eating without seeming to actually put any food in her mouth.

Arturo translated, and his mother beamed.

Eleanor felt a bit embarrassed by her own mom, and frustrated, too. Aside from basic manners, they needed help from these people, who seemed very kind. Couldn't her mom suck it up for once and just eat something different? But Arturo's mother didn't seem to notice. After she passed a few moments hanging back by the stove, she came around to the front of the table and stood there, still wringing her hands.

"Lucas?" she said. "¿Cómo está mi hijo?"

"What did she ask?" Eleanor said.

"She wants to know about Felipe," Luke said.

CHAPTER

6

L UKE REACHED INTO HIS POCKET AND PULLED OUT THE cell phone he had brought with him from the plane. Here at the table, Eleanor could see it was an older phone, one of the cheap burners you could buy at a grocery store. Luke checked his watch, nodded, and after punching in a number, held the phone to his ear.

A moment passed in which Arturo and his mother both stepped closer.

"It's me," Luke said into the phone. "Yeah, we made it. Uh-huh, they're right here." Pause. "No. Least I could do. Hang on a sec." Luke turned toward Arturo's mother and held out the phone toward her. "Felipe," he said.

Arturo's mother took the cell like a sacred offering, brought it to her ear, and whispered, "¿Hijo?" In the next moment her expression opened with a wide-eyed smile that quickly turned to laughter and tears. "Oh, hijo mío, es tan maravilloso escuchar tu voz!" A pause. "¿Qué?" She pressed the cell to her ear with both hands and left the kitchen.

Arturo gave Luke a slow, deliberate nod. "Thank you, amigo," he said before following after his mother. Their conversation could be heard in the next room, and though it was in a language Eleanor didn't understand, she could hear the joy and relief it contained.

"So what was that all about?" Eleanor's mom asked.

"You probably noticed the computer setup in the next room," Luke said. "You can buy anything in Tepito, much of it pirated or counterfeit. Felipe sold some, uh, merchandise that got him into trouble on all sides. So he had to leave, and landed in Alaska. I just wanted his family to know he was safe. Been carrying that burner phone for a while in case I ever had the chance to find them."

"That's good of you, Fournier," Betty said.

Luke shrugged and dove back into his soup. "Ain't hardly a thing. I'm about to ask a much bigger favor of them."

"Somehow, I don't think they'll mind," Eleanor

said, remembering how Felipe had helped her, and how glad she was to be a part of giving something back to his family. This was her vision of the world— one, she thought, that stood in opposition to Skinner's. A place where people took care of one another, and made sacrifices for one another, and no one was left behind.

They finished their stew, except for her mom, whose bowl looked entirely untouched for all her poking at it, and shortly after that, Arturo and his mother returned to the kitchen, both of them wiping their eyes. Arturo handed the phone back, and his mother grabbed Luke in a hug tight enough to squeeze a grunt out of him. He smiled and hugged her back.

"Dios te bendiga, Lucas," she said. "Muchas gracias."

"You're welcome," he said.

She let him go and began clearing their bowls away, appearing much happier than when they'd first met her, and Eleanor was pretty sure the amount of food left in their dishes was the last thing on the woman's mind.

"Felipe say you need help," Arturo said. "So I help you. What you need?"

"I think someone might be tracking my plane," Luke said. "I need to clean it."

Arturo nodded. "When?"

"Soon," Luke said. "Now."

"Okay." Arturo pulled out his own phone and staccatoed away at its screen with his thumbs for a moment. "Okay, sí," he said. "We meet you at your plane."

"Gracias," Luke said. "We're at the international airport. South hangars."

"Okay," Arturo said. "We will meet in thirty minutes. I take care of it."

Luke nodded and rose from the table. So did the rest of them, and Eleanor asked Arturo how to say *thank you for the soup* in Spanish.

He looked up from his phone and blinked. "Gracias por la sopa."

Eleanor nodded and tried her best to repeat that to Arturo's mother. The older woman smiled, said something back, and offered her a hug not quite as tight as the one she'd given Luke, but warm and more motherly than most of the hugs Eleanor had ever received from her own mom. Then Arturo showed them out, and they found their way back to the edge of the Tepito market through an evening sunlight that bronzed the canopies over their heads.

They summoned another black shadow of a cab that came and drove them back to the airfield. There they found their plane situated in a hangar near the runways, and it seemed Luke's bribe had worked for now, because no one else was around. Luke set about opening up panels he could reach from the ground and getting the plane ready for the sweep. Betty stayed by his side, helping, while Eleanor and her mom sat down on a couple of metal folding chairs they found near a mobile computer terminal.

"I guess Simon's not back," her mom said.

The way she said his name brought up a question that had been buzzing around her head for a while. "Simon?" she said, stretching his name into a tease.

"Oh, stop it," her mom said.

"He calls you Sam," Eleanor said. "No one calls you Sam."

"My friends do."

"So he's just a friend, then?"

Her mom hesitated. "He's a handsome man with a brilliant mind I admire. But given our present circum- stances, I have not given a lot of thought to romance. I'm sure you can understand that."

Eleanor smirked. "If you say so."

"We've become close," her mom said. "But nothing has happened, and I don't see anything happening." She crossed her legs, her ankle immediately bouncing in the air. "Maybe when this is all over."

"He is handsome," Eleanor said, smiling sideways.

Her mom gave her a gentle swat on the arm, and Eleanor felt the affection in it, but after watching Arturo's mother, she was left wanting . . . more.

Not long after that, Arturo came, and he brought with him a man and a woman. He introduced the man, a tall, gangly guy with curly hair, as Flaco, and the woman as Gabriela. She wore a battered leather jacket that could not possibly have looked as cool on anyone else as it did on her, and had her long, thick hair up in a chaotic knot. Flaco carried a couple of duffel bags with him, one in each hand.

"Is the G.E.T. after you?" Gabriela asked.

"What makes you say that?" Luke asked.

Eleanor didn't remember them saying anything about the G.E.T. to Arturo.

"They're outside the airport," Gabriela said. "Lots of them, just sitting in their cars like they're waiting for something."

"Waiting for clearance from the government," Eleanor's mom said.

Eleanor wondered what would happen if they decided not to wait. Not to mention the fact that Dr. Powers and Finn and Julian were still out there in the city.

"We need to hurry," Luke said.

Within minutes, Gabriela and Flaco were scurrying around and under and over the plane, wielding the different sensors and equipment they'd brought with them. It didn't take long for them to find the tracking device, or rather devices, since it turned out the G.E.T. had placed two of them in different parts of the plane. They resembled little metallic turtles.

"They really want to find you," Gabriela said.

"And now," Luke said, "thanks to you, they can't."

"I wouldn't say that," she said, and held up one of the tracking devices. "But they won't find you with these. We'll leave them running and plant them on another plane about to take off. Throw them off your scent and buy you some time."

"Much obliged," Luke said, and then Eleanor and the others each thanked them in turn. After Flaco and Gabriela left, Arturo and Luke stepped off to the side for a private conversation that lasted a couple of minutes. They concluded it with a quick embrace, and then Arturo left as well. "Let's get on board," Luke said. "Time to go."

"But Finn and Julian aren't back with Dr. Powers," Eleanor said.

"What?" Luke stopped and drilled his fingers through his shaggy hair, which had started to go lank.

Eleanor was sure she looked no better. They all needed baths. "I hadn't even noticed," Luke said. "Been so wrapped up in cleaning *Consuelo*."

"I'm sure they'll be back any moment," Eleanor's mom said.

"They should have been back by now," Luke said.

"What do we do?" Betty asked.

"Doc seemed to know what he was doing," Luke said. "Guess we wait."

The sun had been down for a couple of hours, and the city had changed its clothes and become its nighttime alter ego. Eleanor could hear the sounds of music, and see the lights, from where she stood in the hangar doorway, watching and waiting. Luke had gone aboard *Consuelo* to take the opportunity for some sleep. Eleanor's mom and Betty sat in the folding chairs, talking sparingly. Still, neither of them seemed to be as worried as Eleanor was.

She paced back and forth, rubbing her folded arms as the night air grew chilly. Still nowhere near as frigid as the Arctic, or even Phoenix, but cold enough that she felt goose bumps rising.

"Come sit down, sweetie," her mom called to her.

"The G.E.T. is out there!" Eleanor rooted herself. "Aren't you worried?"

"I am," her mom said. "But there's not much we can do right now. Worry about the things you can change. Dr. Powers is—"

"So he's back to being Dr. Powers?" Eleanor asked, feeling her anxiety denature into anger.

"You can keep reading into what I call him all you want," her mom said. "It's not going to change anything."

Betty had gone still next to Eleanor's mom, hands in her lap.

Eleanor rolled her eyes and turned away, facing the airfield, where planes roared up the runway and lifted off into the night, and the lights of the distant passenger terminal glowed in a row. The people in there were traveling for business, and possibly even for pleasure. Down here, farther away from the distant threat of the ice, the world just seemed to be getting on with things. But that was exactly what the ice wanted. Eleanor knew its methods well: its predatory patterns, the way the cold deceived, and circled, and waited, and then crept in to strike the almost gentle, final deathblow. It was only a matter of time before Mexico City became like Phoenix. And then like Fairbanks.

"Eleanor!" she heard Finn call as three shadows jogged around the edge of the hangar. They approached her, entering into the light of the hangar, and she could see they had all been running, dark rings of sweat under their armpits.

"We have to leave," Dr. Powers said, panting hard as he marched past her into the hangar. "The G.E.T. found us."

"They spotted us at a museum Dad wanted to see," Julian said, almost as an accusation. Eleanor could tell from his tone the suggestion of a museum hadn't been a welcome one.

"I wanted to go, too," Finn said.

Julian snorted. "I know you did—"

"Boys!" Dr. Powers said. "We're not doing this again!"

Finn and Julian fell silent.

Dr. Powers shook his head. "I'm not certain the agents knew who we were. But they were suspicious enough to follow us."

"But we didn't want to lead them back here," Finn said.

"We've been trying to shake them for hours," Julian said.

"It's too late," Eleanor said. "They're already here at the airport."

"We should take off immediately," Dr. Powers said. "Did Luke find the tracking device?"

"Yes, two of them," Betty said. "*Consuelo* is clean."

They boarded the plane and roused Luke from a nearly comatose sleep that required Dr. Powers to shake him by the shoulders. As the pilot staggered to his feet, yawning, Eleanor wondered if he was alert enough to fly. But he widened his red eyes and dragged his fingers down his cheeks as they explained the situation, and he seemed to be mostly himself by the time they finished.

"Let's get this bird in the sky," he said, and shambled up into the cockpit, where he switched on *Consuelo*'s controls and then hurried a bit more sure-footedly down toward the airplane's main hatch.

Eleanor and the others all took their seats, the same ones they'd had before, and soon Luke was back in the cockpit, and the engines spoke up, and the plane inched ahead. They crept out of the hangar into the night, the lights on the tips of *Consuelo*'s wings blinking as Luke radioed the tower, asking permission to take off.

"Let's hope we don't get shot at this time," Betty said, cinching her seat belt tighter.

"The tower's asking us to sit tight," Luke said.

The cabin went quiet.

Did that mean they were onto them? Were they holding their plane there until the G.E.T. could arrive, or the police? Gabriela had taken the tracking devices to plant on another plane, but what if she hadn't succeeded in that?

"It's probably nothing," Luke said. "Bottleneck on the runway."

But still no one spoke, and the plane's engines bored into the silence. Eleanor listened for sirens and watched the airfield for approaching vehicles. The only thing she saw was a luggage truck ambling by, beams of light from its headlights bouncing gently on the tarmac. Each minute that managed to somehow pass did so shouting threats. After several of those, Eleanor's mouth had gone dry beyond swallowing.

"Affirmative," Luke finally said into his headset. "Roger that." Then he said over his shoulder toward the cabin, "We're clear to line up."

"So we're not taking off yet?" Eleanor's mom asked.

"Not yet," Luke said. "But in a few minutes, it will be our turn."

Consuelo rolled along in that slow and awkward manner planes have, like a duck walking, clearly moving in a way far beneath its design. Eleanor noticed other planes rolling toward them, all merging together into a single column.

"There's four planes ahead of us," Luke said, and Eleanor let out a sigh that could easily have passed as a groan.

Minutes. Minutes. Minutes.

Then Luke spoke into his headset again and announced, "We're up."

Consuelo moved with purpose then, gathering speed in her charge down the length of the runway, until her nose lifted up, and then her feet lifted up, and they were airborne once again. No bullets followed them into the sky. Only the fading light of the city behind and beneath them as its smoggy exhalations choked off its glow.

"We're twelve hours out from Juliaca, Peru," Luke said. "That's the nearest airport to Lake Titicaca I dare land at. You all might as well settle in."

Eleanor sighed again, but this time in relief. They had managed to escape from the G.E.T. twice now, which gave her hope that perhaps it wasn't crazy after all to think that they could do this. She turned a smile toward her mom, an unspoken attempt to make up with her for getting angry before. But her mom didn't smile back.

"What's wrong?" Eleanor asked. "We made it."

Her mom's gesture was part shaking her head and part shrug.

"What is it?" Eleanor asked.

"It's just—" She paused and lowered her voice. "It's the Concentrators. We know so little."

Eleanor dropped her voice too. "We're figuring it out."

"But we still don't really understand what they are. How they work. How they do what they do."

"Well, we know how to shut them down," Eleanor said. "If they're all like the last one, then I can . . ." But she trailed off when she saw the expression on her mother's face—the wrinkled brow, the frown, the worried eyes. That look of mistrust, and confusion, and perhaps even fear.

"Sweetie," her mom said, "at some point we're going to have to really talk about that."

"About what?" Eleanor asked.

"What you did."

Eleanor's defenses rose as quickly as her anger. "And what did I do?"

"I don't like—" Her mom looked up at the cabin ceiling. "I don't like to think of you . . . *connecting* with the Concentrator. It feels like I'm letting you put yourself at risk when we don't—"

"I'm not at risk."

"You say that, but—"

"I'm not," Eleanor said. "It worked just fine, didn't it? I'm fine."

Her mom said nothing.

"I'm *fine*," Eleanor repeated.

"It seems so, yes."

"Seems so?" Eleanor unbuckled so she could spin sideways in her seat and lean away from her mom. "And what is that supposed to mean?"

Her mom held up her hands in front of her, empty palms upward. "Nothing, sweetie. I didn't mean anything—"

"Why don't you just say it?" They were still speaking in hushed voices, and while Eleanor didn't think the others could hear them, she almost didn't care. "You think there's something wrong with me. You think I'm some kind of freak."

"No, I do not, and I've never thought that."

"Then why do you look at me like that?" Eleanor said. "Why do you treat me like one?" She faced forward again, slamming her back hard into the seat, and shook her head. "You know," she said, as if to herself, when she wanted her mom to hear every single word. "I know we haven't always gotten along, but things were going good. I went into the Arctic. I saved your life. We were good. Better than we've been in a long time. But then I saved the day again by shutting down a big alien tree, and the truth comes out. My mom thinks I'm a freak. My mom—"

"Would you stop saying that? I do not think you're a freak."

"Then what is it?"

"Eleanor, you said you *talked* to that thing."

Eleanor nodded defiantly. "That's what I did. I talked to it."

"But that's the thing, sweetie."

"What is?"

"Communication is a two-way street. When you talk to someone . . ." Her mom's voice grew quiet. Serious. "Usually they talk back."

— CHAPTER —
7

THERE WEREN'T MANY PLACES ON A CARGO PLANE ELEA-nor could go to find privacy, except for the cargo hold itself. So that was where she went. It was noisy, and chilly, and dark except for the weak glow of an angry little red lightbulb. It reminded her of the last time she'd been in there, when she'd stowed away on Luke's plane back in Phoenix. That was before she knew anything about the Concentrators, or the rogue planet. Back when she worried she could lose her mom forever to the ice.

Eleanor sat down on the cold metal floor, the cargo bay's empty mesh cages running down from the ceiling around her.

The thing was, she knew her mom was partly right. The Concentrator *had* talked back. Eleanor had felt it in her mind, and that sensation had not been a pleasant one. But she had kept it in check, and then taken control, mentally stomping on the squirming, alien intelligence within the device.

No one else had seemed capable of doing that. No one else had the connection. Eleanor didn't know why that was, but she believed that meant it was up to her to stop all the Concentrators and save the earth. Did that make Eleanor a freak?

Maybe.

Probably.

But she had always felt a bit like a freak. The way her mom and everyone looked at her now wasn't really so different from the way Jenna and Claire had looked at her when she'd almost gone sledding off the third story of their school. If Eleanor was honest with herself, that look had always hurt. She never let it stop her, but it hurt.

The hatch opened behind her, and Eleanor turned to see Finn come through from the cabin.

"You okay?" he asked.

Eleanor turned away. "Fine."

He shut the hatch and came to sit down beside her. "I heard what you were saying to your mom."

Their argument must have been louder than Eleanor had thought. But she wasn't sure she wanted to talk about any of that with Finn.

"I know how you feel," he said. "Well, I think I do. I mean, I've never talked to an alien tree or anything. But I know how you feel."

Eleanor turned to look at him. "How?" she asked, not really expecting an answer that would satisfy her, but curious about what he'd say.

"Lots of ways, actually." He leaned back and spread his arms a little. "I mean, my dad is black and my mom is white. My mom's side of the family, they all look like her. Red hair and freckles. People would look at Julian and me, and they'd assume we're refugees, kids that my mom just adopted, since we were never with my dad. And that's another thing. I know there are lots of kids with divorced parents, but it's still hard. It still makes you feel different."

"I don't even know who my dad *is*," Eleanor said.

Finn looked at her but didn't ask the question that was obviously on his mind.

"My mom went to a clinic," Eleanor said, answering it. "My dad was an 'anonymous donor.'" She used air quotes.

Finn was silent a moment. "Have you ever wanted to find him?"

"No," Eleanor said, and she truly hadn't. Maybe if she'd ever felt like there was something missing in her life, she would have. But Uncle Jack had made sure she never felt that way.

Finn nodded and looked down at his boots. "I think that's why Julian wants to go live with my dad. Or part of the reason. My mom's family doesn't exactly like my dad, since he wasn't really there for my mom, and sometimes I think they just see him when they look at us." He sat back suddenly. "They're not racist or anything. It's just . . . I don't know."

"I get it," Eleanor said, realizing that of course she wasn't the only one who knew how it felt to be different. To be an outsider. "What about you? You don't want to live with your dad?"

"I don't know where I want to be," he said. "My dad and me don't really get along."

"How come?" Eleanor asked. Finn and Dr. Powers certainly seemed more alike than Dr. Powers and Julian did.

Finn shrugged. "I think he just likes Julian more. It's like an oldest-son thing."

"I'm sure he loves you both," Eleanor said, and cringed at how she sounded.

"Yeah, sure," Finn said. "But that's different from liking."

Eleanor nodded. She knew her mom loved her, too, but there had definitely been times when she wasn't sure if her mom liked her very much.

"It's cold out here," Finn said, looking around. "Are you okay?"

"I'm okay," Eleanor said.

"Okay," he said, and got to his feet. "I think I'm going to go back inside."

"Okay," Eleanor said. "I'll come too, in a minute."

Finn nodded and returned to the passenger cabin through the hatch. Eleanor sat for a moment longer on the hard floor, alone, thinking about all the ways she was different from her mom. Her mom was so cautious and worried all the time. Her mom didn't have a sense of humor about anything. If Eleanor ever wanted to do anything exciting, or have any fun, or got a cool new idea, her mom would be there to find the one problem with it and point it out with a big red marker, which was exactly what she was doing now.

Eleanor didn't want to hear about the problems. Maybe it was risky for her to connect with the Concentrators, but wasn't saving the earth worth it? They were on their way to Peru, and they would find the Concentrator, and then Eleanor would shut it down. She could do that, and that was the plan, even if her mom wasn't convinced.

Eleanor decided to let it go for now. She was tired and her butt hurt from sitting on the cargo bay floor. So she rose to her feet, brushed herself off, and returned to the passenger cabin. But instead of going back to her seat next to her mom, she went to the empty third row behind Finn, flipped up the armrests, and stretched out across all three seats to sleep.

"Hey," a voice said.

Eleanor opened her eyes. Finn was leaning over the seats in front of her.

"We're landing," he said. "You might want to buckle in." Then he turned back around and sat down in his seat.

Eleanor sat up and rubbed her eyes. They'd flown through the night, and somehow, she'd slept the entire flight. But she realized it was the first chance she'd had for a good, long sleep since everything had happened with Skinner. That already felt like ages ago, even though it had only been a few days.

She thought about buckling in where she was but found the sleep had improved her mood considerably, so she got up and went up to the front row, where she sat in her old seat, next to her mom.

"You were out cold," her mom said.

"Yeah," Eleanor said. "Did you sleep?"

Her mom nodded. "But not as long as you." Then she leaned in to whisper, "Or Betty."

Eleanor glanced casually across the aisle, where Betty slept upright in her seat, her head craned backward, mouth gaping open, breathing not quite heavy enough to be considered a snore. Eleanor looked at her mom, who smiled, and then they leaned together over a shared, suppressed laugh.

From the window, Eleanor could see the landscape below them, a wide green plain turned over to crops in the same way the land outside Mexico City had been, though not quite as large, with a few gentle hills rising up as if billowed from below, an unhurried river curling back and forth, and a wide ribbon of dark blue laid along the horizon.

"Before the Freeze," Dr. Powers said, "this part of the Altiplano was basically a desert, if you can believe it."

"Is that Lake Titicaca up there?" Eleanor asked.

"I believe so," her mom said. "It's still twenty or thirty miles from here."

"Do you think the G.E.T. are here?" Finn asked.

"Based on what we've seen," Dr. Powers said, "we should probably assume they are."

Consuelo dipped suddenly, startling Betty awake with a snort, and their descent became more rapid, the ground rushing up to them. Eleanor felt light in her seat and leaned back against the headrest until their wheels touched the runway and the plane gave a subtle bounce before settling into its heavy landing.

"That could have been smoother," Julian muttered.

"I heard that!" Luke said from the cockpit. "I can show you rough next time if you want it, kid."

"No, thank you," Finn said.

They taxied to the airport terminal, which appeared new, and still under construction in places. There wasn't an available hangar, so Luke had to park *Consuelo* out in the open at the edge of the airfield, next to a couple of other planes. They packed up a few supplies, some food, and the Sync communication device, with all its data and files on the Concentrator and the ley lines. As they left the plane and crossed the tarmac under a rather sharp sun, Eleanor was surprised to find herself very quickly out of breath.

"It's the elevation," Dr. Powers said. "The air is thinner, so your body isn't getting as much oxygen as it's used to. Some people even get altitude sickness."

"What's that?" Betty asked, panting.

"A condition with some potentially dangerous neurological effects," Dr. Powers said. "Especially if you don't get to a lower elevation quickly."

It seemed they had more than the G.E.T. to worry about.

From the airport, they split up into two taxis and headed into town. Juliaca was a curious mix of new and old architecture, of people with money who had come recently to find a refuge from the Freeze and those who had lived there before and had no money at all. Many of the poorer houses were built of nothing more than bricks and mud, their brown walls crowned with shards of broken glass bottles. The newer buildings gleamed in white stucco, villas with colorful roofs and trim around their windows and doors. Their taxis passed banks, office buildings, and street markets with tented storefronts stacked with enormous bags of chilies, spices, and a rainbow of produce Eleanor had never seen before. She stopped counting the numerous churches they passed and instead focused on spotting any signs of the G.E.T.

"What's with the guinea pigs?" Julian asked.

Eleanor had seen them, too, caged in front of some of the stores and running around people's yards. Big furry loaves, larger than any guinea pigs she'd ever seen.

"They are for eating," their cabdriver said. He was a slight man, wearing a knit cap that covered his ears and a coarsely woven blue sweater. "Delicious!" he said, and kissed his fingertips like a cartoon chef.

"Oh, my goodness," Eleanor's mom said, covering her mouth.

"What?" Julian said. "I'd try it."

Eleanor figured she would, too, if it were put in front of her, but it would probably take a little effort to get her mentally from *pet* to *food*.

"I think they're reserved for special occasions," Dr. Powers said from the front seat. "So we likely won't have the opportunity."

"Yes, special," the driver said, nodding enthusiastically.

Since they needed a boat, Dr. Powers asked to be taken to a tour guide office, and the cabs dropped them at a square near the middle of town. It boasted the most impressive church Eleanor had seen thus far, with a high bell tower and an arched entry carved with saints. There were a couple of nice-looking hotels, a central fountain, and trees surrounded by knee-high wrought iron fences. A building labeled *Turismo* occupied a prominent place on the square's far side.

"I'm not sure how to go about this," Dr. Powers said.

"Not exactly the man with a plan, are you, doc?" Luke said. Eleanor suspected he sounded gruff because, unlike the rest of them, he hadn't just slept for most of the flight.

"You're free to charge right in there," Dr. Powers said. "We'll all wait here and listen for the police sirens."

Luke chewed on a mouthful of air.

"We don't know how widely the G.E.T. has circulated our descriptions," Dr. Powers said. "With the UN involved, we might be wanted by Interpol, at this point. We also don't know if the G.E.T. is aware of the Concentrator presumably located somewhere near here. We *do* know they tracked us as far as Mexico City. As I said before, we need to assume they might have inferred where we would be heading next."

His logic made Eleanor want to look over her shoulder.

"Let me go in, then," Betty said. "I wasn't listed on that first terrorist bulletin. The G.E.T. has probably figured out by now I've joined up with you, but maybe word hasn't made it this far south yet."

"She's right," Eleanor's mom said. "That seems our best chance."

"Could we just try to explore on our own?" Eleanor asked.

"I think that would only draw more attention to us," Eleanor's mom said. "We don't know the area. Our best chance is to try to blend in like tourists."

"Tourists." Julian snorted. "Can you believe there are still tourists?"

"All right," said Dr. Powers. "Betty, go in and see if you can hire a boat to take us around Lake Titicaca, specifically the area around the Isla del Sol."

That was the location marked on Johann von Albrecht's map, the nexus of several ley lines, which they all hoped meant the presence of another Concentrator.

"But if anything feels off," Luke said, "get out of there."

"Will do," Betty said, and gave a casual salute before turning away from them and striding confidently across the square. Eleanor watched her with both admiration and nervousness, and they all milled around and waited.

The men and women in the square walked by in business suits, some of the men in plain white button-down shirts with no ties and dark slacks. A few of the women wore what seemed to be more traditional clothing: long woolen skirts, blouses, and sweaters, with colorful shawls around their shoulders, knotted in front at their necks, and little round bowler hats, their dark hair in braids. Some of the locals took note of Eleanor and the others, staring as they passed them by, but with nothing beyond mild curiosity, it seemed.

Several minutes passed, the wind up here cold with an almost Arctic aggression. Eleanor was already listening for the wail of approaching sirens, imagining the rapid convergence of multiple police cars from all directions on the turismo office, so that when she heard the sound of a real siren, she broke out in an instant sweat and felt her entire body go cold. But it turned out to be an ambulance, and it barreled by the square without slowing.

Shortly after that, Betty returned.

"No problems," she said, slicing the air in front of her horizontally with her hand. "They made some calls and set something up with a guy named Amaru. He's got a boat, and he'll meet us in Puno."

"That's the next big town," Luke said. "Right on the lake."

"They said we could hire a cab to take us there," Betty said.

Dr. Powers clapped his hands. "Let's get going. The less time we spend in one place drawing attention, the better."

They flagged two more taxis and headed out of town. Eleanor and her mom ended up in a cab with Betty and Finn, while Luke, Dr. Powers, and Julian ended up in the other. They rolled through Juliaca and passed a stadium of some kind off to their left, and after that what appeared to be a small university. When they reached the edge of town, the road collapsed from four lanes to two, and they entered a wide, flat plain. Tall grass and crop fields spread away from them on both sides, tossed by the wind in waves as unremitting as the ocean.

The highway shot along a straight course for several miles, the sky overhead a rich blue punctuated with frenetic, ever-changing clouds, the road lined with billboards in Spanish that Eleanor couldn't read. But she could understand the G.E.T. billboards, which bore images of happy and prosperous Peruvians.

But that was a lie. Skinner's plan held prosperity for only a few. For those in poverty, things would only get worse.

"Looks like the G.E.T. are making inroads here," Betty said, apparently having noticed the billboards, too.

"It's what they do everywhere," Eleanor's mom said. "They come in promising jobs and economic relief. But it usually doesn't quite work out that way."

Eventually, the road veered to the left to skirt some low, rounded hills that had risen up, and away on her left Eleanor caught another short glimpse of the dark lake. From there, the highway inclined upward, gently winding them over and through some of the hills, their folds and valleys sprouting with tall trees.

A few miles later, they crested the hump of the highest hill, passed under a sign that read *Bienvenidos a Puno*, and entered a town that resembled Juliaca, with its brown and red brick construction, and the same juxtaposition of old against new. They followed a sudden bend in the road, and as they made the turn, a wide vista opened up below them.

The city rolled away from their vantage, thick and congested, filling a hilly valley bowl to the brim and leading right down to the shores of the lake. Titicaca was enormous, its contours reaching inward and outward around distant mountains to a point on the far horizon, its water a rich shade of blue that would no doubt confound anyone trying to replicate it.

They followed the road as it curved around and down the valley sides to its floor, and there the cab turned left and took them into a nice part of the city, clearly its center of tourism. Here the streets had tree-lined islands in the middle, and the old colonial architecture had been restored. There were more churches, hotels with balconies and ornate details, and restaurants with painted murals.

"We're supposed to meet this Amaru fella in the Plaza de Armas," Betty said. "In front of the Puno Cathedral."

"We almost there," the cabdriver said.

— CHAPTER —
8

THE PUNO CATHEDRAL WAS AN IMPRESSIVE EDIFICE, MADE
of gray stone, with two solid, square bell tow-
ers on either side of its arched entry. Eleanor and the
others waited at its feet by a set of wide stone stairs
that led up to the church. The square around them
bustled with business and tourism, and the air carried
the scent of woodsmoke and grilling meat.

"That is making me hungry," Luke said.

"Me too," Eleanor said. It smelled like chicken,
and she realized it was lunchtime now, and she hadn't
eaten anything that day. "How long do we have to wait
for this Amaru guy?"

"I don't know," Betty said. "At the tourism office,

they made it sound like he knew we were on our way."

"Perhaps we should eat something," Eleanor's mom said.

"Perhaps?" Luke said, and took a step away from the group, both hands in the pockets of his jeans. "Who's with me?"

"I'll go," Eleanor said.

"Me too," Julian said.

"Don't go far," Eleanor's mom said. "We still don't know if the G.E.T. are anywhere nearby. There's probably something right here on the square you could find."

"The rest of us will stay here," Dr. Powers said, "and wait for Amaru."

Eleanor gave a little salute, like Betty had back in Juliaca. "We'll bring you back something."

They stepped out into the square and through a series of stone-encircled beds of manicured shrubs and trees. Luke seemed to be literally following his nose, walking with it high in the air, as Julian and Eleanor followed behind him.

"So what were you and Finn talking about?" Julian asked her.

"When?"

"Back on the plane. In the cargo hold."

"Oh, nothing," she said. "He was just trying to

make me feel better about that fight I had with my mom. I'm sure you heard it, too."

He nodded.

"Why do you ask?" Eleanor said.

"Just curious," he said. "I wondered if he said anything about me."

"Like what?"

"Oh, I don't know," he said. "I don't get along with my mom, either. I think I might want to live with my dad. When this is all over. That kinda pisses Finn off."

"Why?" Eleanor asked.

"He's jealous. Little-brother stuff. But I don't know why. Everybody says *he's* the one just like my dad."

Having heard Finn talk about it, Eleanor didn't think it was quite that simple. But she was still trying to figure out her own mom, let alone somebody else's dad, so she kept quiet, and Julian didn't say anything more about it.

"There," Luke said suddenly and with such intensity, Eleanor wondered if he'd heard anything she and Julian had been saying right over his shoulder. He pointed off to the right and walked that way with increased vigor. "That's what I'm smelling."

Eleanor noticed the food cart on the side of the street, billowing fragrant, meaty smoke. A young woman worked the grill, wearing the same kind of clothing as the women back in Juliaca—a long skirt and bowler hat. But her shawl held an infant wrapped up against her back. The baby was a little girl, perhaps a year old, in a knit cap that came down almost over her eyes, and she rested against her mother's shoulder quietly.

"Hola," Luke said, approaching the woman.

Her broad smile was missing a tooth, and she bowed her head without saying anything, waiting.

"Mmm," Luke said, surveying the food. "¿Qué es?"

"Anticuchos," she said.

The grill bore various kinds of skewered meat, sizzling over white coals that burned red where they gathered close together. Eleanor didn't know what kind of meats they were, or whether some of it might be guinea pig, but it all smelled incredible. Luke picked out a variety, a dozen skewers all together, which the woman wrapped up in a blanket of tinfoil.

Eleanor took the hot bundle from her, and then Luke asked, "¿Pollo?" He held his hands out in front of him like he was holding an invisible basketball between them, so Eleanor didn't think he was talking about the skewers.

The woman smiled and nodded, and went to a metal door in her food cart. Steam rushed out as she opened it, and then she reached into it with a pair of tongs and pulled out a whole roasted chicken, which she set on the grill. Its blackened skin soon began to crackle, and after a couple of minutes over the heat, she wrapped it in foil and handed it over as well.

"Gracias," Luke said with audible sincerity.

The woman showed the gap in her teeth again and nodded.

They left her and returned to the cathedral, where the others still waited, and together they all dove into the food. The skewered meat was good, some of it a little chewy, the flavoring full of garlic. The chicken was spicy enough to bring tears to Eleanor's eyes, but it was delicious enough to endure the heat. Luke devoured nearly half the bird by himself, though Dr. Powers and Betty seemed to enjoy it, too. Eleanor's mom nibbled on some of the meats but stayed away from the skewers Luke guessed to be beef heart.

It would have been unthinkable to find food like this sold on the street back in Phoenix, at least not at a price most people could afford. And Eleanor was pretty sure no one in the refugee camp around Mexico City would turn it down the way her mom was doing, beef heart or not. This mission they were on might have been about the Concentrators, but it was also showing Eleanor a great imbalance that existed in the world, which would only get worse if the G.E.T. got its way.

They were all still sitting there on the steps of the cathedral, finishing up their meal and licking their fingers, when a handsome young Peruvian man approached them. He wore jeans, white sneakers, and a soccer jersey, his jet hair cropped short.

"Excuse me," he said. "Are you waiting for Amaru?"

"We are," Dr. Powers said.

"Then you have found him," the man said, touching his chest. "I am Amaru."

Everyone got to their feet, and Dr. Powers extended his hand for a shake. "Very nice to meet you," he said.

"We would offer you some food," Betty said, holding a wad of crumpled tinfoil. "But I'm afraid it's all gone."

"Please, do not trouble yourselves," he said. "Besides, if that was Nina's chicken"—he nodded in the direction of the food cart with a grin—"it is much too spicy for me. Are you all ready?"

"Yes, please," Eleanor's mom said.

Amaru clasped his hands together in front of him. "Then please, come with me. I have a car."

He turned away, and as they followed him through the square and down a colorful side street, it occurred to Eleanor that they were putting a great deal of trust in a man they didn't know. She was sure tourists did that every day, and if Eleanor had been a tourist, she probably would not have worried. Amaru seemed like a very nice man. But she was not a real tourist, and trusting the wrong person could be very, very dangerous.

Eventually, they reached Amaru's vehicle, a long, tall, boxy white van. He opened the door for them and helped them all climb in, and Eleanor found that the van had three rows and was big enough to fit them all comfortably. It was also very nice inside, with leather upholstery and a clean scent of citrus. Once they were all in, Amaru walked around the front of the vehicle to the driver's side and got behind the wheel.

"How long have you been in Peru?" he asked as he turned the key and started the engine.

"A week," Dr. Powers said. "We were visiting Lima."

Eleanor wondered if the lie was necessary but decided it was better not to take unnecessary chances.

"Ah," Amaru said. "I see. Do you have luggage?"

No one answered at first. Everything they had was back on the plane.

"We left it at our hotel," Eleanor's mom said. "It'll be safe there."

Amaru nodded and pulled the van into the road, taking the streets of Puno at a leisurely speed. "So, you want to see Lake Titicaca," he said. Eleanor could see his eyes in the rearview mirror as he looked back at them.

"Yes, a boat tour," Eleanor's mom said.

Amaru nodded, his left hand draped over the steering wheel. "It is a very large lake. Are there any areas you would like to see in particular? The tourism office mentioned the Isla del Sol?"

"People have recommended it," Dr. Powers said.

"That's a popular destination," Amaru said. "I think you'll like it."

"Do you still get many tourists?" Eleanor asked.

"Oh, yes," he said. "But there are fewer every year. I worry for my business."

"Is there time to go to the island today?" Eleanor's mom asked.

"Yes, but it's sixty miles to the southeast," Amaru said. "We will reach it before evening, but I suggest you stay the night in Copacabana, which is close to the island, and then we can do more sightseeing tomorrow, if you wish. Will that work?"

"That sounds like a good plan," Dr. Powers said.

"Sixty miles?" Julian said. "How big is this lake?"

"It's about a hundred miles long, and fifty miles wide," Amaru said. "About half the size that Lake Erie used to be."

"You're familiar with the Great Lakes?" Luke asked.

Eleanor had learned about them in school, of course,

but they were entirely covered by the glacial ice sheet now.

"My grandparents immigrated to New Jersey before the Freeze," Amaru said. "When the ice reached Montreal, my parents moved to Florida. That's where I was born. When the ice reached New York, my family came home to the Altiplano. Now I am married with a son of my own. South America is now the land of opportunity."

Eleanor wondered how long that would be the case. There were glaciers clawing their way up from Antarctica, too. They already covered the southern half of Argentina, and much of Chile, and could eventually reach Peru. How long would the rich keep coming to Lake Titicaca? How much longer would there be tourists anywhere? And what would Amaru do then to support his family?

He drove them through town until they reached the city's pier, where numerous tour boats were either lined up along the docks or moving about on the water. The part of the lake around Puno appeared to be more of a lagoon, with shallow waters and island-like patches of reeds, and long-legged birds with curved beaks flying about.

There were also a couple of policemen wearing dark-blue uniforms, patrolling the pier in a way that seemed designed to appear casual but that only looked suspicious. As Eleanor and the others left Amaru's van and walked toward his boat, she worried that, together as they were, they would likely match any description that had made it to the Peruvian authorities. But as the officers passed them, they gave Amaru a plain-faced nod and walked on without taking any note of the rest of them.

Eleanor's mom exhaled and shared a look with Dr. Powers. It seemed they had been nervous, too. But should they have been?

If the cops didn't know anything, perhaps Eleanor was being paranoid to worry that the G.E.T. had as much influence here. Perhaps the conspiracy was not as far-reaching as Skinner had made it seem, and Betty's skepticism was deserved. Could they be safe here?

"This is mine," Amaru said as they thumped along the wooden pier. He gestured toward a long, wide pontoon boat. "The *Consuelo*."

"You're kidding," Luke said, before he could stop himself.

But he wasn't. The name was right there, painted in blue against white on the side of the boat.

"That's kind of reassuring, isn't it?" Betty said.

"Why?" Amaru asked.

"We've seen a craft with that name before," Luke said, and left it at that.

Amaru opened a little door on the side of the boat, and everyone stepped aboard. A blue canopy arched over the vinyl seats that ran the length of the boat on either side. A captain's chair perched near the steering console at the front and right—Eleanor could never remember if that was starboard or port. Everyone found a place to sit, and Eleanor ended up between Finn and Luke, facing her mom, Dr. Powers, and Julian on the opposite side. Betty took a seat at the rear of the boat, in the sun, facing forward.

"I get seasick if I'm not looking straight ahead," she said.

Amaru untied the boat from its moorings and heaved it away from the pier before hopping aboard. The sound of water sloshing and slapping the pontoons echoed beneath Eleanor's feet, and the boat gently bobbed on the lake's small waves.

"Here we go," Amaru said, jumping into the captain's chair. He turned a key on the console, and the boat's engine chugged awake and sputtered them along until they were a safe distance from the dock. "To the Isla del Sol," Amaru said, and pushed on the throttle. The engine grew louder, and the boat leaped over the water.

With the wind whipping at them, and the lake spray against her face, Eleanor felt cold pretty quickly. Amaru sped them across the lagoon, around and through some of the patches of reeds. As they entered a deeper channel, he pointed at some islands off to the left and shouted above the motor and the wind.

"Those are man-made!" he said.

Eleanor looked more closely and saw that what she had thought were flat, natural islands resembled floating mats and bore houses made of straw, and people, and even cattle.

"Those people are the Uros," Amaru said. "They make those islands out of reeds, and they live on them."

"That boat looks like a dragon," Finn said.

Eleanor looked, and in the distance, two men paddled a swollen-looking boat made of bundled reeds, with an animal head snarling from the end of its high, curved prow.

"It's not a dragon," Amaru said. "It's a puma. Some people translate Titicaca to mean 'rock puma.'"

"Cool," Finn said.

Some distance later, they left the lagoon and emerged into a wide expanse of the lake, where the waves came at them higher and stronger, tossing the boat more up and down and sometimes slamming into them in a way that jarred Eleanor's back. The constant sounds of the motor, and the wind, and the tearing of a seam in the water by their boat, soon became background noise, at least until she or one of the others had to shout over it to be heard. So none of them really tried talking.

They traveled through those waters for twenty minutes or so, and as the far side of the lake drew nearer, Eleanor realized they were merely crossing a smaller bay and had yet to enter the real body of the lake. Another fifteen minutes later, once they rounded a large, mountainous spit of land, Eleanor saw just how big Titicaca really was, and it felt like the ocean. What she'd thought was the opposite shore turned out to be nothing more than an island, and not the Isla del Sol. The true far shore of the lake was too far away to even be seen, as was their destination.

Amaru checked a compass and turned his boat a little to the right in a sweeping arc. "Isla del Sol is a little over forty miles ahead!" he said. "Less than two hours!"

Eleanor realized now why he had suggested they stay the night in Copacabana. It would be late afternoon before they reached the island. Eleanor settled a bit lower in her seat and closed her eyes. The motion of the boat and the sounds of their lake crossing in her ears lulled her into a kind of daze, broken only by the occasional jolt of a larger wave, and the time passed neither especially slowly nor quickly, but it passed.

Then Amaru said, "There it is!"

Eleanor opened her eyes and looked ahead of the boat toward a large island of grassy slopes and terraced rocky ledges. Several smaller islands emerged from the waves around it like pieces splintered from the whole, and a few birds soared in wide orbits overhead.

Eleanor's mom pulled the Sync out of the pack Dr. Powers had been carrying and woke up the screen. She tapped and swiped, opening the file with von Albrecht's ley-line map of telluric currents.

"We're close," she said, as quietly as she could to be heard over the engine. They hadn't yet discussed how they would search for the Concentrator with Amaru around. She looked up, then glanced back down at the screen, and then up again. "If we swing around the head of the island, there, we'll be right on top of it."

"What's that?" Amaru asked over his shoulder, his eyes on the water. "Where do you want to go?"

"Uh, what's around that point?" Dr. Powers asked, indicating the right side of the island.

Amaru eased up on the throttle and brought the boat to a gentle drift, quieting the engine to a purr, and swiveled in his captain's chair. "There is a bay over there," he said, "and above that on the hill, you find the Chinkana."

"What is that?" Eleanor's mom asked.

"It means labyrinth," Amaru said. "It is a large Inca ruin. And above that, at the top of the mountain, is the Titikala."

"The what?" Eleanor asked.

"The sacred stone of the Inca," he said. "The legends say Manco Cápac came out of a cave in that rock. He was the first man. The son of Inti, the sun god."

Eleanor and her mom looked at each other and then passed glances among everyone in their group. The mythical birth of a legendary child of a sun god, and an alien device that produced massive amounts of energy, both at the same location? It did not seem likely to be a coincidence.

She felt a wave of excitement, though it was threaded with a vein of fear. The Concentrator was close. It had to be.

"Tourists enjoy it," Amaru said. "Do you want to go there?"

"Yes," Eleanor said. "I think we do."

CHAPTER 9

THERE WAS A SINGLE, LONG DOCK JUTTING FROM THE beach of the small bay. Amaru was able to pull his pontoon boat up alongside it, and then he leaped out, eased his craft into place, and secured it to the moorings. Then he opened the door on the side of the boat, and they all stepped out onto the pier.

"Allow me to take you up there," Amaru said.

"I think we can manage," Eleanor's mom said.

"Oh. Okay, then. I'll wait here." He checked his phone. "Come back in two hours? We should go to Copacabana before dark. I will call a good hotel for you."

"Two hours." Luke looked at the watch on his wrist. "Got it."

"Thank you," Eleanor's mom said.

"Okay." Amaru stepped aside, allowing them all to pass. "You see that road? It will take you up to the ruins."

Eleanor saw the path he referred to, but she would not have called it a road. It was about four feet wide, smooth and lined with rocks on either side. She and the others formed a column and began the trek up the hill, but slowly, for the altitude made it arduous after only a few steps. The trail switched back and forth up the slope, buttressed in places by stone walls that looked very, very old.

The higher they climbed, the more Eleanor felt the wind's anger, and the more the thin, stubborn air refused to do for her what air was supposed to do, leaving her feeling a bit light-headed. It took them some time to reach the ruins, but eventually the steep path brought the Chinkana into view.

The ruins spread out across several hundred feet of the hillside and rose up in terraces to an imposing vertical wall of deep alcoves just below the mountain's peak. Even from below it, Eleanor could see why it was called a labyrinth. Multiple arches and doorways opened up in the tightly fitted stones, each passage leading off in a different direction. Whatever roofs the walls and chambers had once supported were gone, leaving an interconnected maze of rock open to the air and sun.

"Should we split up to explore?" Dr. Powers asked, sounding out of breath.

"Before we do that," Betty said, her tone reminding Eleanor that she hadn't yet accepted the full reality of their mission, "I need a better idea of just what it is we're looking for."

The rest of the group turned toward Eleanor. As the freak who could talk to Concentrators, she was evidently expected to have the answer to that question.

"The Concentrator is large," Eleanor said, thinking something that conspicuous could not have gone unnoticed all this time out in the open, in a place so overrun by tourists. "It's probably buried or hidden somehow. Where does the map show it, Mom?"

"The chart isn't that precise," Eleanor's mom said. "But it's in this area."

"If only we had some of our equipment," Dr. Powers said. "Telluric scanners or sensors could find the Concentrator, just like they found the first one."

"Let's just go look around," Julian said. "This place isn't that big."

"The legend mentioned that Inca guy coming out of a rock," Eleanor said. "Maybe we should start with that? Maybe there's a cave or something."

"Amaru said that rock's above the labyrinth," Finn said.

"Then let's go up and check it out," Eleanor's mom said, and she took the first step into the ruins.

They all followed after her, the narrowness of the passageways in places forcing them into single file. There were many sharp turns, and many doorways that opened into small chambers, and as Eleanor climbed higher into the labyrinth, she was able to look back down the hill, over the descending terraces, toward the ocean below.

There were a few wrong turns and dead ends before they reached the upper wall of the Chinkana, having explored for nearly an hour, but from there they continued along a second, upper path that brought them onto a plateau at the top of the island and continued along its length. The view of the lake from up here revealed a panorama of deep-blue water and hilly green shores.

"What's that up ahead?" Finn asked, squinting.

They followed the path and arrived at an ancient altar, which was made of a solid slab of stone longer than Eleanor was tall, and about two feet thick, surrounded by a circle of twelve square, hewn boulders, each a few feet tall.

"It's like a small Stonehenge or something," Julian said.

"It does have a cermonial quality," Dr. Powers said.

Eleanor's mom pointed at a large rock formation nearby, the only other prominent feature on the hilltop. "That must be the sacred rock Amaru was talking about. The Titikala."

There didn't seem to be anything particularly singular about it to Eleanor. It was about the height and size of a modest house, made of rough brown rock with yellowish streaks. She supposed if she really used her imagination, it resembled a crouching cougar, with folds and crevices that suggested a body with legs tucked under it. But she would have probably walked right by without noticing it had Amaru not mentioned it to them. But *something* had made the Inca worship this place. Something had made them center that myth here.

Eleanor walked toward the Titikala, studying its contours, searching for openings. There was a prominent overhang that created a shadow beneath it, but this hid nothing but an alcove that led nowhere. The rest of the group joined Eleanor in circling the stone, but no one found anything. No cave or tunnel or fissure through which a man could ever have emerged. Dr. Powers pointed out that caves weren't even common to that kind of rock and geology.

"What did you expect?" Luke asked. "This place

has been overrun by tourists for decades. Don't you think they would have found something by now?"

Eleanor argued inside herself against a mounting disappointment. No one else said anything, but they all glared at the ground, and Eleanor could sense their frustration. It was hard for her not to feel some of that directed at her.

"What now?" Betty asked.

"Now," Dr. Powers said, "it's been over an hour. We should head back to meet Amaru soon."

But Eleanor didn't want to leave. They had come all this way, and she'd been so sure they would find a Concentrator here. She realized now that had been stupid and naive. In fact, she wondered if it was possible that von Albrecht had been wrong about the lines. . . .

"We'll just have to come back tomorrow," Eleanor's mom said. "Make a thorough survey of the area."

"What for?" Betty asked. "Look around. You really think there's a big alien tree just hiding somewhere?"

"I think we haven't really searched yet," Eleanor's mom said. "And I'm not giving up."

"I never thought it would be that easy," Luke said.

"Me neither," Eleanor said. "The Concentrator is here. Somewhere."

"Regardless," Dr. Powers said, "we should return

to the boat. Unless we want to spend the night on this island."

Eleanor reluctantly agreed, and moments later they turned down the hill the way they had come, back through the Chinkana, the slanted orange light of the setting sun casting shadows and creating false tunnels and portals in the maze. It seemed a place that could shift and change, depending on the time of day one visited it, and it took them some time to navigate through it.

The descent was certainly easier on the lungs than climbing up had been, and they made it back down to the dock more quickly than they had left it.

Amaru was waiting on the pier for them next to his boat and waved to them as they approached. "Did you enjoy the ruins?"

"Very much," Eleanor's mom said. "I think we'd like to come back tomorrow."

"There are others places I could take you to," Amaru said. "On the southern part of the island."

"Thank you, but I don't think we're done with this side," her mom said, smiling.

"It's up to you." Amaru smiled back.

They boarded the boat, and their guide pulled away from the dock and turned them in the same direction they had been traveling before, continuing along the length of the island for a short distance, and then pulling farther out into the body of the lake.

Several miles of waves rolled beneath them as they made their way toward the distant, mountainous shore. The sun dipped lower and lower to the right of the boat, and before long they reached the end of the Isla del Sol on their left, where it stretched toward a mainland peninsula, forming a narrow strait. From there, Amaru aimed them toward a little hill that seemed to jut up from the lake in front of the range that lined the shore. But as they approached the hill, Eleanor realized it was connected to the shore by a low flatland, and as they circled around, she saw the lights of Copacabana situated there, bright in the dusk light.

"I called a hotel for you," Amaru said. "A good place. They will feed you, too."

"Thank you," said Eleanor's mom.

They reached the town's many piers, and Amaru chose a dock lit by strings of bulbs running overhead from post to post. He then guided them from the boat through the streets of Copacabana, which were even more festive than Puno's had been, although the town seemed much smaller. Vendors sold foods that smelled very similar to what they'd already eaten that day, and bands performed music with guitars, drums, and large pan flutes. As twilight turned to dusk, the air quickly grew quite cold, and Eleanor shivered.

"The hotel is just up this way," Amaru said before rounding a corner.

Dr. Powers was close behind him but stopped immediately and retreated, arms outstretched to back everyone else up with him.

"Simon, what is it?" Eleanor's mom asked.

"G.E.T.," Dr. Powers whispered. "They have a van on the street. Up ahead."

"What?" her mom said.

Luke crept forward and peered around the building. "How can you tell? It's not marked."

"I can tell," Dr. Powers said. "It's the same model of vehicle they used in Venezuela, back when I was doing some work there."

Amaru returned then, clearly looking for them, eyebrows low and close together. "Is everything okay?"

"Fine," Dr. Powers said.

"Good," Amaru said. "Then shall we continue?"

No one moved.

"Is there a problem?" Amaru asked.

"I noticed, um, a van," Dr. Powers said. "I believe it belongs to the G.E.T."

Amaru looked over his shoulder and up the street. "Ah, yes. I see it."

"The thing is," Dr. Powers said, "I used to work for them, and . . . we didn't part on the best terms. Bad memories, to be honest."

"I see," Amaru said. "And you want to avoid them?"

"It's a bit embarrassing," Dr. Powers said.

"Not at all," Amaru said. "We'll go around." And he led them across the road and down a different street. After taking a right turn, and walking a few more blocks, and then taking another couple of turns, they arrived at the Hotel Imperial.

The building was brightly lit and inviting, painted the color of daffodils in photos Eleanor had seen. Amaru walked them in through the front door, where they were greeted in the lobby by a tall, elegant woman wearing an outfit that had clearly been inspired by the traditional clothing Eleanor had already seen other women wearing: a long flowing skirt, a very nice sweater, and a silken shawl.

"Hola, hola," she said. "Amaru tell me you were coming. I am Isabela, and I welcome you to my hotel." She bowed her head.

"Thank you," Dr. Powers said.

"You have a nice day on the lake, sí?" she said. "You go to the Isla del Sol?"

"Yes," Eleanor's mom said. "A lovely day." But there

138

was a weary impatience to her voice, and Eleanor knew she was still thinking about the G.E.T. van. Eleanor was, too.

"I took them to the Chinkana," Amaru said.

"Bueno," Isabela said. "But I see you are tired. Three rooms, sí? Come, I will show you."

"I'll leave you now," Amaru said. "What time in the morning?"

"Early," Dr. Powers said. "Seven?"

Julian groaned.

"Very good," Amaru said, and with a nod and a smile he departed.

"He is a nice man," Isabela said after he had left. "His wife is very beautiful. And his hijo, oh!" She clapped her hands together at her chest. "Muy lindo. Come, we go to your rooms."

They followed her and crossed a floor of red tiles, the walls around them stuccoed and painted white, framed by exposed timbers of rich, dark wood, the corners filled with plants in terra-cotta pots. Isabela led them up a flight of flagstone steps to the second floor, and there she opened up the first door on the right in a long hallway of doors.

"Who want this room?"

Eleanor and her mom peered through the doorway. The room appeared comfortable, if a bit small. A thick woven rug covered a smooth and polished hardwood floor. The cream-colored bedding looked clean and fluffy, and even though the leather sofa was old, it seemed ready to welcome Eleanor like a broken-in baseball glove.

"Eleanor and I can share a room," her mom said. "And I assume you'll have your boys with you, Simon. . . ." She looked at Betty.

"Not to worry," Betty said. "Luke and I can share. His charms have long since worn off."

"So you keep saying," Luke said. "But I'm fine with the couch."

Eleanor's mom turned back to Isabela. "My daughter and I will take this one."

"Good, good," Isabela said. "The others are down here."

Eleanor stood in the doorway of her room and watched to see where the others ended up. Isabela gave the next room down on the left to Dr. Powers, Finn, and Julian, while Luke and Betty ended up three doors beyond them to the right.

"Will you come down for dinner soon?" Isabela asked as she returned to the stairway.

"Yes, thank you," Eleanor's mom said.

Isabela nodded, and after she'd gone, Dr. Powers came to Eleanor's room with his sons, and so did Luke and Betty. They all crowded in, and Eleanor's mom shut the door.

"Is the G.E.T. here for us or for the Concentrator?" she asked.

"Maybe both," Finn said.

"Could they have tracked us?" Dr. Powers asked, and turned to Luke. "Are you sure your plane was clean?"

"Positive," Luke said.

"Maybe it's just for the Concentrator," Eleanor said. If Skinner and the G.E.T. were aware of von Albrecht's work, they might have sent agents here looking for it.

"Or maybe," Betty said, "*just* maybe they're here because the G.E.T. is an international energy company, and they've got business to conduct. Customers. Projects. Why does it have to be this conspiracy of yours? Who says they know a thing about us?"

Eleanor certainly hoped that was the case but didn't think it wise to take chances and assume they were safe. "I still think we should be careful, and not go anywhere near them."

"I agree," Dr. Powers said.

"I'm hungry," Julian said. "Can we talk about this over dinner?"

Dr. Powers frowned but nodded. "Fine."

They left the room and went back down the stairs

to the lobby. At the far end, a doorway led to a restaurant and bar, crowded and dimly lit by candle lanterns ensconced in the walls. Once they were inside, a server ushered them to a table.

"I want some more of that chicken," Luke said, scanning the menu.

"What's ceviche?" Finn asked, reading his.

"Seafood marinated in lime or lemon juice," Betty said. "It's good."

Eleanor looked at her mom, who she knew hated seafood, but her mom seemed not to have heard Betty. Her eyes were fixed over Eleanor's shoulder, and when Eleanor glanced behind her, she saw why.

At a table just a few yards away, four men sat eating dinner, all of them wearing similar clothing: dark slacks, polo shirts, and jackets. They looked quite out of place in that restaurant, and not like tourists at all.

They had to be G.E.T.

ELEANOR WHIPPED BACK AROUND AND STARED AT HER menu, though she wasn't really reading it and certainly wasn't about to order anything now. Slowly, an awareness of the G.E.T. agents spread around their table, and everyone went quiet. The waitress came then and asked if they wanted something to drink.

No one answered her with anything but a blank stare.

After a moment she said, "You like Inca Kola?"

"Yes, fine," Dr. Powers said.

The waitress frowned a little and moved away.

Once she was gone, Luke leaned into the middle of the table and whispered, "Now what?"

"We stay calm," Eleanor's mom said. "They're just eating. If we don't draw attention to ourselves, maybe they won't even notice us."

"I'd still like to know what they're doing here," Dr. Powers said.

"We could ask them," Betty said.

"What?" Dr. Powers said.

"Just walk up and announce yourself?" Eleanor's mom said.

Eleanor didn't think that would be a good idea. Even assuming the best-case scenario, that the G.E.T. here knew nothing about them, that might not last if they drew attention to themselves in some way.

"I wouldn't say who I am," Betty said. "I could just say I'm a geologist and ask if they know of any work."

The waitress returned then with a tray of bottles, the beverage inside them the color of gold, and placed one before each of them at the table. Then she was gone, and Julian went straight for his bottle.

"Mm," he said. "That's good. Tastes like . . . cream soda? Bubble gum?"

Finn glared at him, mouth half open. "Seriously?"

"What?" Julian asked.

Finn's eyes went wide. "What do you mean what?" he whispered.

"Those guys aren't even looking over here," Julian said.

"So?" Finn said. "They might—"

"Boys," Dr. Powers said. "Now is not the time."

Luke took a swig from his own bottle. "Bubble gum," he said.

"What are we going to do?" Eleanor asked.

"What's wrong with my idea?" Betty asked. "You all go back up to the rooms before they've noticed us. Then I'll talk to them alone. See what I can find out. Either way, it's not helping our chances, sitting here in a group that probably resembles the latest G.E.T. all-points bulletin about us."

Eleanor's mom and Dr. Powers looked at each other as Luke drank more of his soda. Eleanor didn't like the idea of Betty going anywhere near the G.E.T. agents, but the woman had proven herself both capable and smart. If she were alone, perhaps she could learn something about what the agents were doing there. But it wasn't as if the G.E.T. would just tell her they were there for a piece of planet-sucking alien technology.

"You think they'll just tell you about the Concentrator?" Eleanor asked.

"Of course not," Betty said. "But I'll know if whatever story they *do* tell me is the truth, or if they're lying to me for some reason."

"She will," Luke said. "Trust me, she always knows."

"I suppose if we don't do something about it," Eleanor's mom said, "we'll spend the rest of our time here wondering and looking over our shoulders."

Eleanor knew she would be doing that anyway. But Dr. Powers nodded. "All right. The rest of us will go. Betty, you'll pay for the drinks?"

"Sure," Betty said.

"Wait, we're not eating?" Julian asked.

No one answered him.

They rose quietly from the table and filed out of the restaurant, back through the lobby, and up the stairs to Eleanor's room, where they all waited for Betty to come up.

Eleanor threw herself into the baseball-glove sofa and sat there chewing on her thumbnail. She was not convinced this wasn't an incredibly stupid idea. The only reason Betty had been so eager was probably that she didn't believe there was a conspiracy. Maybe this was her attempt to prove that to everyone, or maybe just to herself.

Luke lounged next to Eleanor on the sofa, while her mom sat on the bed, hugging her knees. Julian leaned into a corner, sulking, and Finn eyed him angrily from the other side of the room. Eleanor still didn't understand what was going on there. A tangled knot of sibling rivalry and envy, with both of them feeling like outsiders in different ways. Dr. Powers sat on the bed, staring at a blank wall, and Eleanor wondered if he was oblivious to what was going on between his sons, or if he chose to ignore it.

It often seemed that Eleanor's mom ignored her, or pretended not to notice the things she didn't want to deal with. There were so many things they used to argue about: Eleanor's grades, her reckless stunts, her lack of concern for what other people thought. Sometimes, Eleanor even wondered if her mom was glad to be away from home so much for work, in spite of what she said about it breaking her heart to leave Eleanor with Uncle Jack, because it meant she didn't have to deal with her daughter. Was it like that with Dr. Powers? Was it a parent thing? Or just hers?

"What happens if we can't find this Concentrator?" Dr. Powers asked.

Everyone dialed toward him.

"If we can't find it," he said, "what do we do next? That would effectively end this whole enterprise, would it not?"

If they couldn't find the Concentrator here, did that mean there weren't Concentrators anywhere else? Eleanor had no idea. She only knew she had seen one of them, and they were the only way she could think to stop the rogue planet. She also knew the rogue was still up there, connected to the earth. She could still feel the weight of its shadow.

"I believe that would necessitate a change in our strategy," Dr. Powers said. "From offense to defense. Settle in for a long winter's nap."

"The Preservation Protocol, Simon?" Eleanor's mom said. "You'd sign on with the G.E.T.? After what they did?"

Dr. Powers shook his head. "I didn't say that. But if we have absolutely no way to avert what's happening, to stop whatever it is the rogue planet is doing, we'll need another plan. And they might have the right idea, even if they're going about it in the wrong way."

Eleanor didn't even want to consider that possibility. She couldn't accept that kind of world, one where some were saved and others left to freeze, a world without hope, existing only by grim resignation. That was giving up. And Eleanor refused to surrender.

"Let's just . . . ," Eleanor's mom started. "Let's not go there until we have to."

Luke crossed his legs and folded his arms. "Sounds like some of us are already there."

"What about the humming?" Finn asked.

"What's that, son?" Dr. Powers asked.

Finn looked at Eleanor. "You heard a humming

148

before, right? Or felt it, or whatever? With the other Concentrator."

That was true. The closer she'd gotten to it, the louder it had seemed, like standing under a charged, crackling power line. "Right," she said, and then knew where he was going. She felt stupid for not thinking of it herself.

"Did you feel that back on the island?" Finn asked.

"I didn't," she said, and didn't like what that meant. "But that doesn't mean it's not there. Maybe just that we weren't close enough."

"So then we—what?" Dr. Powers asked. "Walk around and hope you 'feel something'? Like some kind of human voltmeter?"

"Simon!" Eleanor's mom said.

"No offense intended, Sam," Dr. Powers said. "I'm simply uncomfortable with how much of all this is . . . let's call it metaphysical."

It was hard for Eleanor not to think that meant he was uncomfortable with *her*.

"Be that as it may," Eleanor's mom said, "I won't tolerate another demeaning comment toward my daughter. I might not understand what's happening with her any more than you do, but I know she does not lie. And I also know that the only reason we were able to shut down the Concentrator in Alaska was because of her."

149

Eleanor felt less alone hearing her mom defend her that way, and it removed some of the sting from their argument back on the plane.

Dr. Powers tipped his head. "My apologies, Eleanor. I truly meant nothing by it."

"That's okay," Eleanor said, because that was what she was supposed to say. But she wasn't sure that she meant it. "Tomorrow, when we go back to the island, I'll try to focus on feeling that humming."

Dr. Powers seemed to be struggling with how to reply to that and ended up on a simple "Okay."

The door opened, and everyone looked up as Betty walked into the room.

"Well," she said, "they're staying at the hotel just down the street. The Copacabana Royal. And there is definitely something going on. They claim they're here exploring the area to possibly build a hydroelectric plant."

"And you don't believe them?" Luke asked in mock surprise.

"Not a word," Betty said. "They're hiding something. And it sounds like they're looking for something, too."

That confirmed Eleanor's fears. "How do you know?" she asked.

"Because they're *diving*," Betty said. "They say it's

for measuring water currents. But I don't buy it."

"Diving?" Dr. Powers said. "Does that mean . . . could the Concentrator be underwater? Not connected with that Inca site at all?"

That gave Eleanor an idea. "Mom, can I see your Sync for a minute?"

Her mom handed it to her, and Eleanor opened a browser window, running a search for Lake Titicaca's geologic history. She found that its water levels had fluctuated greatly over the last few thousand years. Archaeologists had found several submerged temples and artifacts at the bottom of the lake, and there were even legends of a lost underwater city. It seemed possible that whenever the Concentrator had been planted, the lake had not been what it was now. That would also explain why Eleanor hadn't felt the humming when they were walking around the island. She shared all of this with the others.

"Of course," her mom said. "I just assumed, what with von Albrecht's map, and then that legend . . ."

"I did as well," Dr. Powers said. "But like you said, the chart isn't precise, and the island is relatively small. The Concentrator could be located offshore."

Eleanor shut down the Sync. "I think we need to do what the G.E.T. agents are doing. I think we need to dive."

"I can't see how *that* could possibly go wrong," Luke said.

"You have any better ideas, Fournier?" Betty said.

"No, but— Wait, hold on," Luke said. "Somehow we got turned around here. I'm supposed to be the believer, and you're the skeptic. You saying you believe them now?"

"I believe the G.E.T. is hiding something," she said. "Something they've already shot at us over. And I want to know what it is."

"Good," Eleanor said. "Then it's settled. Amaru's company runs dive tours, right? Tomorrow, we'll just ask for one."

"Diving is dangerous business," Luke said.

"And besides, what then?" Julian looked at Eleanor. "Can you shut that thing down underwater?"

"I don't know." Eleanor hadn't thought that far ahead.

"The first order of business is to find it," her mom said. "Then we can figure out our next step."

Everyone agreed with that plan, and the others returned to their rooms while Eleanor and her mom settled in for the night. The bed was large enough for them to lie next to each other without crossing the invisible line into each other's space. They both lay on their sides, Eleanor staring at her mom's back, moonlight falling through the window in an icy stripe across the middle of the bedspread.

"Good night, sweetie," her mom whispered.

"Good night," Eleanor said.

When she closed her eyes, her thoughts wandered back over the water to the island and up its slope to the Titikala and the Chinkana, with its maze of corridors and chambers. It did not take long for the image of the Concentrator to invade her mind, though, tangling her thoughts up in its confounding branches, a bramble her eyes could not comprehend because they were not built to. She felt herself being lifted up in those branches and turned around, squeezed, stretched, sundered, and scattered until all that remained of her was her awareness that she had been changed.

It was the same vision she had experienced under the ice, and she wanted to stop it but couldn't.

The Concentrator shot her up into the sky, through the void of space, until she reached the rogue world, which appeared to her as something she could not say was truly there, but that nevertheless filled her perception to its farthest reaches. The surface of the immense being had the twisted and impossible quality of its seedling Concentrator, an oil slick that sent the eye skimming off it.

This was Eleanor's destination. This was where the earth's energy was sent, and where she was now sent, against the only thing left to her, which was her will. If she had still possessed a mouth, and a throat, she would have screamed.

The planet drew nearer, a void with teeth that whispered a stream of incomprehensible language, and she prepared to be devoured, unable to close the eyes she no longer had.

"Eleanor!"

She woke up.

Her mom leaned over her, her face worried and horrified in the darkness of the hotel room. "My God," she whispered. "Eleanor."

"What?" Eleanor said.

"You were . . ." Her mom rolled onto her back and covered her face. "No, it wasn't talking in your sleep. It was . . . I don't know what it was."

"What was I saying?" Eleanor asked.

"It was just noise." Her mom shook her head, still covering her face, still, apparently, unable to look at her daughter. "Terrible, terrible noise."

Eleanor inhaled deeply and slowly, afraid to explain but determined to do it anyway. "I was dreaming about the rogue planet."

Her mom brought her hands down. "I . . . that's

what I thought. What I was afraid of back on the plane."

"You mean about the Concentrator talking to me?" she said. "It was just a dream, Mom. I can handle it."

"I know you believe so. But think about it. When was the last time you had this dream?"

Eleanor wondered where her mom was going with that. "In the Arctic. Next to the Concentrator."

"Exactly."

"Exactly what? Maybe that just means there's one close by. Maybe that means we can find it."

"Or maybe it's reaching out to you. Just like you're trying to reach out to it. Maybe it's— Oh, for God's sake, Eleanor, you sounded . . . I don't want to say it."

"No." Eleanor sat up in bed, and the blankets fell away from her, raising instant goose bumps. "Say it. Whatever it is, just say it."

"All right. You sounded possessed."

Eleanor said nothing. Her body started to shake, in fear and from the cold, so she dove back under the covers and turned her back on her mom. She wasn't *possessed*. Possessed people weren't in control. There was something else inside them calling the shots, some demonic presence. Eleanor felt in control of herself, mostly, except for the vision, the only thing that came to her unbidden. Whatever was happening to her, one thing was certain: her connection to the Concentrator was a good thing, because for all her mom's fears, it meant that Eleanor could find it, and stop it.

"Good night," Eleanor said.

"Sweetie," her mom said. "Ell Bell—"

"Don't call me that," Eleanor said, "That's not—" and her voice broke over the memory of Uncle Jack. That was what *he* called her.

"Okay," her mom said. "I won't."

"I'm done talking about this," Eleanor said. "All of it."

Her mom was quiet for a while, just watching her; Eleanor could feel it, until Mom also rolled over, and they both went back to sleep.

CHAPTER
11

Eleanor woke before her mom did. She eased out of bed and tiptoed across the cold floor to the tiny bathroom, and then stepped into its narrow coffin of a shower. The water never really got hot, but it was warm enough that she wasn't miserable. As she rinsed off, she thought about the dream from the previous night, and the confrontation with her mom, and planned what she might say if her mom tried to bring it up again. When she came out of the bathroom, drying her hair, her mom was already awake, standing at the window, looking outside.

"Morning," her mom said.

"Morning."

"It's a neat little town, isn't it?"

"Uh-huh," said Eleanor. She was happy to pretend the previous night hadn't happened if that was her mom's plan.

"I guess I'll shower, too." Her mom moved past her, into the bathroom.

Eleanor sighed and sat down on the sofa to wait. Before her mom came back out, someone knocked at their door.

"Who is it?" Eleanor asked.

"It's Julian. My dad says to tell you Amaru is already here. We'll be down in the lobby." He sounded grumpy, but maybe that was because he hadn't eaten dinner the night before.

When her mom came out of the shower and dressed, they went down together and found that Isabela had apparently heard that they had all skipped dinner the previous night, and insisted that they eat some breakfast in the restaurant. The others were already seated at a table when Eleanor and her mom walked in.

"She says it's on the house," Luke said. "She seems convinced we'll starve to death out on the water without it."

"I told Amaru we wanted to try diving today," Dr. Powers said. "He said he'd get the equipment and he'll come back for us shortly."

"Very well," her mom said, taking a seat. "How did everyone sleep?"

"Fine," Dr. Powers said. "The boys, too."

"As comfortable a couch as I've ever tossed and turned on," Luke said.

"The bed wasn't bad either," Betty said. "What about you and Eleanor?"

"Good," Eleanor said, waiting to see what her mom would add, if she would bring up the dream, and Eleanor speaking in alien, with the others at the table. She really didn't need them thinking she was even more of a freak than they did already.

"I woke once or twice," her mom said. "But it was okay." She gave Eleanor a look but said nothing more.

Isabela brought out their plates, all laden with the same thing: rice stir-fried with beans and sausage, with a fried egg on top, and hot chocolate to drink.

"We call this calentado," their hostess said. "Enjoy."

They did. Every plate at the table was empty in a matter of minutes, and then they all went to wait in the lobby for Amaru. When he returned, they walked together out into the bright morning sun and a city that seemed a bit bleary somehow. Many vendors hadn't yet set up their stalls or opened their storefronts, and those who had did not appear alert or happy about it. It was cold, too.

Eleanor strolled up alongside Amaru. "So how old is your son?"

"He is two years and four months old," Amaru said, and the smile that appeared on his face was spontaneous and genuine. "His name is Lucio, and I think he might be a devil."

Eleanor laughed. "I think they're supposed to be at that age, right?"

"Very true," he said. "And if he were not also an angel, I don't know what I would do with myself. Or with him. He breaks my heart and puts it back together in the same day." He closed his mouth and looked down at the ground suddenly.

"What is it?" Eleanor asked.

"It's . . . I wonder what kind of world he will have when he grows up. Your mother probably has the same thought when she looks at you."

"You don't want to know what my mom thinks when she looks at me."

"No?"

"We haven't exactly been . . . getting along."

"But I'm sure she still loves you and would do anything for you. As I would do for Lucio."

Eleanor knew he was right, even if she didn't always agree with her mom.

Amaru led them through town, back down to the

pier. Aboard his pontoon boat, Eleanor saw just four diving tanks, with suits and masks and flippers.

"That was all I could get," he said. "The city has suspended diving tours."

"Suspended?" Dr. Powers asked.

"Yes," he said. "The Global Energy Trust is working on something in Titicaca, and they asked us to cease our tours."

"What about us?" Eleanor asked.

Amaru winked. "We'll be careful."

The boat pulled away from the dock and back onto the lake, its water a fluid and faceted gem in the morning sun. The return trip to Isla del Sol seemed to take longer than the trip to Copabanana had the previous night. Perhaps that was because Eleanor felt both anxious and eager. Rather than sit along the side of the boat, under its canopy, she stood at its bow, hands on the front rail, trying to sense the humming of the Concentrator. She felt nothing yet, but it was difficult with the engines roaring behind her, and the rush of the waves and water against the boat.

Twenty minutes out from the dock, they reached the island's first spit of land and continued along its length, past a few ruins both smaller than the Chinkana and not as old in appearance, the central mountain ridge rising up behind them in grassy terraces.

Eventually, they swung around a rocky, jagged point and pulled into the same bay as the day before, the one beneath the Titikala rock. Amaru steered the boat back to the docks and tied them off. No sign of the G.E.T., and they seemed to be the only ones on this part of the lake and island.

"Okay," he said. "Who will dive first?"

"I will," Eleanor said.

"As will I," her mother said.

"So we can take one more," Amaru said, looking around.

"I'd rather not," Betty said.

"I'll go," Julian said, just a breath before Finn, who seemed about to say the same thing.

"Neither of you are going without me," Dr. Powers said. "Your mother would kill me."

"You're going to worry about that now?" Finn said.

Eleanor laughed at that, as did her mom and Betty.

Then Luke stepped forward. "I'll go."

"Good," Amaru said. "We will start with a quick lesson in the shallow water, and then we go down deeper to a submerged temple. Many tourists enjoy seeing it."

Eleanor wondered if that meant they were as unlikely to find anything there as they had been up on the island.

"Is this really safe?" Betty asked.

"Yes," Amaru said. "Some people say you need scuba certification, but for this dive . . ." He shook his head. "We won't go too deep."

They helped him take all the diving equipment off the boat, along the pier, to the lake's shore where the waves slapped the rocks. Eleanor had never been particularly frightened of water but also hadn't had many opportunities to go swimming. Here, staring at the impenetrable surface of the cold lake, her breathing sharpened, her heartbeat kicked up, and the altitude magnified the effects of her fear on her body.

"Let's put on your suits," Amaru said.

Eleanor swallowed and turned away from the lake toward their guide.

He explained that the suits he had for them were dry suits. "Wet suits are not warm enough. The deep lake water is below fifty degrees at all times."

Then he gave them each a thermal undersuit, which they took turns changing into using the privacy of the boat, before helping them each get into their outer suits. Eleanor took the smallest, which Amaru said would work even though it was a bit large on her. Its shell was made of blue rubber and smelled like it, with tight seals at the ankles, wrists, and neck. It was cumbersome to wear, particularly at her elbows and knees, where it was harder to bend, but she felt instantly warm inside it. After that, they pulled on neoprene gloves, boots, and hoods, then strapped their flippers to their feet.

"Here is a flashlight for each of you," Amaru said. "Now, your diving tanks."

He helped each of them put on the backpacks that carried their diving cylinders, held to their bodies by a complicated set of straps that went over their shoulders and around their waists and legs.

"It's heavy," Eleanor said, shifting the weight, her rubber suit squeaking.

"About as heavy as you were riding on my back at three years old," her mom said.

Next, Amaru helped them put on their face masks and the breathing apparatus he called a regulator. It went into Eleanor's mouth, stretching her lips.

Amaru then turned on the air in their tanks. "Breathe," he said. "Through your mouth, not your nose."

Eleanor's mask covered her nose, so she couldn't breathe out of it, and she quickly got used to the stale-tasting air coming out of the hose into her mouth.

"Take full breaths," Amaru said. "That is very important, especially at this altitude." As they grew accustomed to the regulators, he put on his own equipment, and when he was finished, he watched them for a moment longer. His mask was different from theirs and covered his whole face. "Good," he said, his voice now coming through an earpiece in Eleanor's mask, sounding like a radio in the next room. "Are we ready to go into the water?"

With the regulator in her mouth, Eleanor couldn't say a word, but she gave a thumbs-up, and they all waddled forward, clumsy as penguins, lifting their knees and their flippered feet high. When Eleanor reached the water, she hesitated a moment and then took her first step into it.

She couldn't feel the water's coldness, but she could sense its pressure against her suit, like hands climbing up her legs, and then her waist, with each step ahead.

"Stop there," Amaru said. "Now, lower yourself into the water. Go slow. I want you to put your head under the surface. But try to keep your breathing normal."

Eleanor bent at her knees and waist, letting the water's hands climb up the rest of her, surrounding her up to her neck. Then she dunked her head under. And stopped breathing. She couldn't help it. Through her mask, she could see the ground clearly beneath them, her mom next to her, bubbles rising up from around her face. But it was hard for Eleanor to override the instinct to not, under any circumstances, take a breath underwater. Moments went by. She felt a light-headedness setting in, and a burning urge in her lungs to gasp, which she finally did, involuntarily. But that seemed to get her over the threshold, and afterward, she found she could breathe normally. The hiss of the air through her regulator sounded loud in her ears, but over it she could still hear Amaru.

"Very good," he said. "Let's stay here for a few minutes. Try moving around. Swim."

Now that Eleanor's body had accepted that she could breathe underwater, she felt ready to *go*. She kicked her flippers and swam forward, into deeper water, and dove downward to the rocky, weedy bottom, where she pirouetted using her arms and looked back up at her mom. Both she and Luke were slowly stretching and kicking, moving about like whales.

Eleanor pushed off toward them, slowed by the drag of her suit, but found the sensation thrilling. She was weightless. She was flying. Up, down, left, right, any direction she chose.

"Good," Amaru said. "You are all doing very well. Give me an okay sign if you feel ready to go down to the temple."

Eleanor formed a circle with her thumb and index finger and looked right through it at him. Her mom and Luke gave the same sign.

"Okay," Amaru said. "I will go slowly. Stay with me."

He spun in the water and kicked his flippers, swimming with his arms trailing at his sides. Eleanor adopted the same posture and worked to make the scissors movement of her legs smooth and even. Her mom swam up alongside her, and they shared a smile with their eyes and a thumbs-up.

A short distance on, the bottom of the lake plunged away from them into darker water, and Amaru switched on his flashlight and guided them down into it. The fear Eleanor had first experienced at the lakeshore returned, an irrational and insistent dread that felt the same as a fear of snakes, or of spiders. Some deep warning painted on the walls in the caveman part of her brain.

Movement at the edge of her eye caused her to flinch, but she realized it was only a brownish fish, and not a very large one. She kept her eyes on Amaru and the blade of his flashlight and made sure her mom stayed in her peripheral vision, which was limited by the edges of the diving mask. Before long, the tunnel of her vision and the narrow reach of her own flashlight tightened her claustrophobia, even as the pressure on her ears mounted.

"We're over sixty feet deep now," Amaru said. "The temple is close."

Eleanor strained to see ahead into the murk. Then she tried to shift her awareness and listen for the hum of the Concentrator, wondering if at any moment she would see its dark outline loom out of the depths like black coral. She even stopped breathing for a couple of moments to find a space of silence in which to focus.

"You okay, Eleanor?" Amaru asked, looking back toward her.

She nodded and inhaled.

"Try to keep your breathing even," he said. "Very important at this altitude."

She gave him a thumbs-up.

They resumed their dive, and a moment later, among the chaotic contours of rock and grasses along the bottom, Eleanor spotted a straight line, part of a large stone wall carved at right angles, taller than Uncle Luke, and half again as wide, stretching off into the depths.

"You see that?" Amaru asked. "It goes on for two thousand feet."

Eleanor marveled at it as they swam along it, and soon they reached a wide flight of stone steps cutting through it. Amaru turned them upward, and at the top of the stairway they reached a flat terrace of paving stones.

"This is the temple platform," Amaru said, planting

his feet on the ground as if standing on dry land. "It is six hundred and fifty feet long, and it is much older than the Inca. They don't know who made it. There is a statue ahead. Come."

They followed him along the terrace, its even surface broken only by the occasional lake weed sprouting from the cracks between the stones. Eleanor wished she could see the whole of it, instead of just the small span their flashlights could illuminate. As they swam on, deeper into the complex, Eleanor thought perhaps she could feel something, down in her stomach. The hum. But then a face leaped at her out of the dark water, and she recoiled, thrashing in the water.

"It is only a statue," Amaru said. "Try to be calm."

Eleanor settled herself and saw that it *was* a statue, a face jutting out of a second wall made of stones cut with astonishing precision. The face was highly stylized, with bulging eyes, a prominent brow, and a long nose, and Eleanor felt foolish for reacting to it the way she had. It was actually one of many faces carved in the wall, each one unique.

Amaru led them up a second stairway to an even higher terrace, and here they found the monolithic figure of a man twice as tall as Eleanor. His features were square, his arms and legs mere lines carved from a thick column of stone.

"We do not know the name of this god," Amaru said.

The statue stared off into the lake with blank eyes, lifeless and forgotten, in that way more like bone than stone. As Eleanor studied it, she tried to imagine the people who had once worshipped here at this temple. How long ago had that been? Eleanor's mind cast back through time, trying to imagine that place, now immersed, above the surface of the lake. This temple was buried, just as Amarok's village had been buried, silent in their graves. That is, until the Concentrator had awoken them . . .

Eleanor slowed her breathing, quieting the hiss of air in her ears, and closed her eyes, searching, listening, reaching.

There it was.

She felt the hum again, stronger than it had been at the base of the temple. She could sense its direction.

"Are we ready to return to the surface?" Amaru asked.

Eleanor shook her head. She had no way of speaking to the others, so she tapped her mom's shoulder to get her attention. Then she stretched her arms up like tree branches and pointed in the direction from which she felt the hum. Her mom and Luke both nodded, having apparently understood what the gestures meant. But Amaru did not.

When Eleanor kicked forward, past the statue, in the direction of the Concentrator, he said, "Wait, stop, where are you going?"

They could not answer, of course, and the three of them simply kept swimming.

"Please," he said. "Stay with me. It is dangerous."

But Eleanor ignored him. This was what she had come for, and she wasn't turning back.

CHAPTER
12

THE UNDENIABLE AND FAMILIAR HUM GREW STRONGER AS Eleanor let herself be drawn toward it. Her legs were tired from kicking her flippers, and she wished her flashlight could reach farther. The temple complex through which she swam had begun to feel haunted, the faces and statues its ghosts. Her mom and Luke stayed by her side, while an anxious-sounding Amaru swam slightly ahead, looking back at them, holding his hands out like a crossing guard.

"Please!" he said. "Stop! We must go up."

Eleanor felt bad for him, but there wasn't any way to explain the situation. She could only press on, and there wasn't really anything he could do about it.

The hum of the Concentrator shook her by the bones. She felt it in her teeth. She could almost see it rippling the water, and even distorting and bending the light from her flashlight. She followed it to the edge of the temple terrace, where the carved stones met a slope of rock. She guessed they stood at the roots of the Isla del Sol some distance away and above them. The humming called her upward, so she swam up the rocky incline.

"Yes," Amaru said. "This is good. Let's go up."

But Eleanor wasn't going all the way to the surface. Instead, the hum led her toward a large, anvil-shaped boulder that jutted out from the mountain just above them. Beneath it lay a shadow her flashlight could not fully scatter, a dark opening into the ground. She pointed at it, and her mom and Luke nodded.

It was a cave, and she knew they needed to enter it.

Amaru apparently guessed what they were doing. "No! You are not trained to dive in a cave! That is very dangerous!"

Eleanor knew he was telling the truth. But she could barely hear him anymore, the hum consuming all her senses. The Concentrator was in there, and she had no choice.

She moved toward the entrance, which was about four feet across, and shone her flashlight down the cave's throat. The illumination did not go far, for the tunnel twisted and turned out of sight, constricting to a very narrow passage. Now, the thought of going in there raised a deafening alarm in Eleanor's head. The panic rising in her chest chilled her, even within her insulated dry suit. Her breathing was a windy storm in her ears, and her heartbeat thundered away beneath it. She had never been particularly claustrophobic, and she'd been stuck in a tunnel before, back at Polaris Station in the Arctic. But this was different.

The hum, meanwhile, continued to radiate from the cave. Eleanor could sense the Concentrator within, draining away the earth's energy, sucking it dry.

She felt a hand on her arm and turned toward her mom. A part of Eleanor hoped she would pull her away, take her back to the surface, and tell her they would find another way. But that wasn't what her mom did. She nodded. So did Luke.

Eleanor didn't know if the trembling in her limbs was visible through the layers she wore, but she tried to still herself, slow her breathing, and make herself do what she needed to do.

"Please," Amaru said with plaintive finality as Eleanor ducked down and pulled herself into the cave.

Her unsteady flashlight threw chaotic shadows about her. She bumped into the sides of the narrowing cave, felt the sharp rocks through her suit, and her tank clanged against the ceiling.

"You must be careful!" Amaru said. "If you damage your tank, you will suffocate. If you rip your suit, it will fill with water and you will freeze."

The ways Eleanor could die were not what she wanted to be told in that moment. She heard the sandpaper sound of the rubber shell of her suit rubbing against the rock, and the panic she had only begun to suppress returned. If she could have turned around, she would have. But the passage was too narrow for that now. All she could do was press forward. The cave angled downward and around a bend, squeezing inward, and Eleanor had to become a snake, twisting and rolling her body around the edges and turns.

"Your mother is now behind you in the cave," Amaru said. "Luke will go next, and then I will follow him." He seemed to have accepted that they were doing this over his objections.

Eleanor felt her head getting fuzzy and realized her breathing had become very quick and shallow, just what Amaru had warned her against. She focused on taking deeper breaths, but this took her concentration away from the cave, and her tank banged into the wall again. Her progress became measured in careful inches, and in the times she had to close her eyes and throw all the weight of her resolve against the fear.

Every so often, her mother touched her foot or her flipper, gently, reassuringly. Eleanor needed that contact as the cave tightened to a mere crack she could barely fit through. She then had the chilling thought that perhaps this cave didn't go anywhere, or perhaps it would eventually grow too narrow to move forward. They would have leave the way they had come, only backward, and Eleanor didn't know if she could.

That would take so long.

She could run out of air.

She had to get out. Now. She had to stretch and kick, but she could do neither, nearly pinned by the rock as she was.

Forward.

That was the only way.

A few more feet in, and she felt her mother tug on her flipper, but not in the gentle way. She shook it. Vigorously. Something was wrong.

"Eleanor," Amaru said. "Luke's tank isn't working."

A sudden fear for Luke flooded and drowned Eleanor's fear for herself.

"He isn't getting enough oxygen," Amaru said. "He is blacking out. We need to find an opening."

Eleanor shone her flashlight ahead. She still could not see an end to the tunnel, but they had to keep going. There had to be something up there. The humming had only grown stronger. Her movement lost its hesitancy. She propelled herself forward as fast as she could, wincing at each collision with the cave wall.

"Yes," Amaru said. "Keep going. Look above you for air pockets."

The course of the fissure seemed like that of a crack in a cement sidewalk, a winding zigzag path.

Hold on, Luke, Eleanor thought, wishing she could say it to him aloud. *Stay with us. Keep moving.*

Shortly after that, the glow of her flashlight vanished up ahead. The tunnel simply sucked it up, returning little of it to her in reflection, which could only mean an opening of some kind lay ahead of them.

Eleanor scrambled the last few feet and burst from the tunnel into a chamber. She gave no thought to it yet, but turned back and helped pull her mom through the last stretch, and then Luke, who came out of the passage a bit listless and limp. But bubbles still rose from around his head. When Amaru reached the chamber, he hooked an arm under Luke's shoulder and immediately swam upward.

"Come with me," he said.

Eleanor and her mother followed him, and the combined light of their flashlights illuminated the chamber around them. It was the size of a classroom at her school, but with a bowl-shaped floor and a ceiling with only three corners. The fourth was a seam of shadow that Eleanor now recognized as another tunnel.

"He has lost consciousness," Amaru said. "Help me."

Eleanor's mom kicked up to Luke's side and took his other shoulder. The four of them moved ahead into the darkness, until their flashlights seemed to strike an iridescent mirror.

"There is air ahead," Amaru said.

Hope and relief proved to be better fuel for driving Eleanor forward than fear had been, and she raced toward the wavering mirror until her face broke the water's surface. They were on a kind of rocky shore, but still underground. The regulator fell from her mouth, and she breathed earthy air as she helped Amaru and her mom drag Luke from the water.

"I know CPR," Eleanor's mom said, and she started in on the chest compressions, alternating with mouth-to-mouth breathing. This continued for a few moments, and then Luke's chest heaved slightly on its own.

"He's coming around," Amaru said.

Luke's eyelids fluttered open, and he coughed, and breathed, and then he swore.

"Oh, thank heavens!" Eleanor's mom said.

"Luke," Eleanor said.

He turned his head toward her and coughed again. "Kid. You're as brave as they come."

"And as reckless," her mom added.

Eleanor bent down to hug him, feeling the scratch of his beard against her cheek. "I'm just glad you're all right."

"I'm fine," he said. "Now does somebody want to tell me just where the heck we are?"

Eleanor sat upright. Their flashlights danced around the chamber, crisscrossing one another's beams.

"I think we are under the Isla del Sol," Amaru said.

The chamber was larger than the one they had just swum through, with formations along the ceiling and floor, stalactites and stalagmites, and curtains and ribbons of mineral deposits draped along the walls. They were sitting at one end of it, while the opposite end exceeded the reach of their light.

"Can you walk?" Eleanor asked Luke.

"I think so," he said, laboring to his feet. "If I can lose this tank."

Armaru helped him unstrap it and shrug it off. The metal cylinder fell to the ground with the hollow toll of a bell, and the cave rang with the echo. Amaru inspected the tank and kneaded his forehead. "The pillar valve is damaged. I don't know how we'll get you out of here."

Luke stared at the tank. "Well. We'll deal with that later, I guess." Then he turned to Eleanor. "You want to lead the way?"

He was referring to her ability to sense the Concentrator, but Eleanor couldn't think about that now. She was too worried about him. It would be impossible for Luke to swim back without a dive tank.

"Is it here?" Luke asked. "Can you feel it?"

"Luke, I—"

"Can you feel it?" he asked.

Eleanor stopped and tuned her mind to the hum. "Yes."

"Which way?" he asked.

Eleanor pointed into the darkness at the opposite end of the chamber. "It's that way."

"Then let's do this thing," he said.

"What are you speaking about?" Amaru asked.

Eleanor looked at her mom. There really wasn't any way to keep Amaru from finding out. It wasn't like they could just ditch him down here. But she figured it might be better to just let him see it for himself than try to explain, and deal with the aftermath of that later.

"You'll know soon enough." Eleanor unbuckled the dive tank from her back and lowered it to the ground, and so did her mom and Amaru. The cavern felt quite cool, so Eleanor left her suit on, and together they picked their way slowly across the uneven floor. Their flashlights turned the dripping stone formations into glossy, melted wax.

"This is beautiful," her mom said. "I've never really studied caves like this one, but I can see the appeal."

Eleanor felt the hum passing through her, reaching the point where she could almost feel it on her skin. They were very close now.

"What the hell?" Luke said, aiming his flashlight at another tunnel ahead of them. This one, unlike the other, had obviously been carved. Its opening was a square rectangle, slightly taller than Luke, and its floor had been smoothed.

The three of them stared at it for a few moments, trying to make sense of it.

"Maybe it was the same people who built the temple," Eleanor said.

"There are legends about this," Amaru said. "They say the Inca had miles and miles of tunnels where they hid their gold, connecting their whole empire."

"Let's see where this one goes," Luke said.

Eleanor led the way forward through a corridor much more comfortable than the one she had just passed through. A slight draft blew by her cheeks, the air cool and humid. The tunnel was not uniformly square and in some places opened wider with the natural, rough cave walls, but it never became narrower than its size at the entrance. It curved and turned, and at times it seemed to be ascending, and other times descending. When the corridor intersected with another tunnel, Eleanor had to use the direction of the hum to guide them down the right path.

"I wonder how many tunnels are down here," Luke said. "You could get lost."

"Let's hope not," Eleanor's mom said.

"The Concentrator is close," Eleanor said. The hum felt and sounded as though it were right in her ear, setting her jaw throbbing.

Another few turns, and then the tunnel opened into a room that had been similarly shaped by ancient hands. The carved walls bore more of the same faces from the underwater temple, and several monolithic statues stood in a circle, facing an object at their center.

The Concentrator.

The alien device rose to the height and size of a large tree. Halfway up its length the black metallic trunk divided into the chaotic branches that so defied human perception. Eleanor could feel them working, could sense the Concentrator's roots reaching deep into the earth's crust, gathering up telluric energy, which it folded and twisted into the dark energy the rogue planet needed.

"I always believed you," Luke said. "But I had no idea." He twisted the top off his flashlight and set it on the ground, like a lantern.

"It's monstrous," Eleanor's mom said. "I wish I had my instruments."

"No time for that," said Eleanor. "I'm going to shut it down."

"No, sweetie—" Her mom reached out as if to grab her, but caught herself and pulled back. Eleanor could see the conflict going on inside her, beneath the surface, the skin around her eyes tight and quivering. She didn't want Eleanor connecting with the Concentrator, but she also knew that was the entire reason they had come.

"Mom, it's okay." Eleanor smiled and stepped toward the device, searching its trunk for the same interface console she had used to stop the other one in the Arctic. Before she'd stepped between the ring of statues around it, she heard a click behind her.

"Please," Amaru said. "Stop."

Eleanor turned toward him. He held a pistol. Pointed at her.

"Amaru!" Eleanor's mom said. "What are you doing—?"

"Stay back," Amaru said. "Or I will shoot her."

"What the—" Luke began.

"Believe me, I don't want to hurt any of you," he said. "And I won't, if you do what I say."

This was the second time someone had pointed a gun at Eleanor. The third if she counted the G.E.T. agent on the runway. But she felt curiously calm about it this time, and yet she knew how strange it was that she wasn't scared.

Amaru pulled out another device, a small silver disk, and pressed a button on it. A green LED light blinked on, and kept blinking. Amaru watched it for a moment before slipping the disc back inside his suit.

"What was that?" Luke asked.

"A locator," Amaru said.

"For whom?" Eleanor's mom asked.

"The Global Energy Trust."

Luke took a step toward him, and Amaru swung the barrel of the pistol toward him. "Stay back. And please keep your hands where I can see them."

"You're with *them*?" Eleanor's mom asked.

"Course not," Luke said. "He's just working *for* them. A mercenary for hire."

"I am *not* a mercenary," Amaru said.

That much was obvious to Eleanor. She wanted to know something else. "Why are you doing this?" she asked. Amaru had apparently been spying on them the entire time, and now that they had found the Concentrator, he'd used the locator in his pocket to send the coordinates right to the G.E.T.

"Dr. Watkins, the head of the Global Energy Trust . . . he promised he'll take care of my family," Amaru said. "I watched the ice take everything my parents had. I won't let that happen to my wife. My son."

"It won't," Eleanor said. "I can stop it. I can shut it down." She turned her back on him and took another step toward the device.

"No, sweetie," her mom said. "Don't—"

The gunshot was deafening in the stone chamber. Eleanor froze, her shoulders tensed, her ears ringing. She slowly pivoted back to face Amaru.

"That was a warning," he said. "If you go near the Tree of Life, I will kill you. I don't want to. But I will."

"TREE OF LIFE?" ELEANOR SAID.

"That is what Dr. Watkins called it," Amaru said. "He's been looking for this for a long time. But now you found it. Just like he said you would."

"Do you know what this does?" Eleanor asked.

"It provides energy we will need to survive the Freeze," he said.

"That's what Dr. Watkins told you," said Eleanor's mom.

"Yes," he said. "He also told me you destroyed another one, in the Arctic, and might be coming here to destroy this one." He shook his head. "Why would you do that?"

Eleanor had thought they were escaping the G.E.T., but it seemed that Watkins had suspected where they were heading all along, and he had let them go. He had used Eleanor to find the Concentrator, and she had led Amaru right to it. But something else confused her. Skinner hadn't known about the Arctic Concentrator before he saw it, which meant that Watkins had been behind this from the start and had kept secrets even from the company's CEO. Eleanor had thought Skinner was in charge of the G.E.T., but it seemed he had only been its public face. Watkins was the real authority. And it seemed he knew everything.

"Amaru, this isn't what you think," Eleanor said. "This . . . this Tree of Life isn't giving us energy. It's taking it."

"Dr. Watkins told me you'd say that—"

"Dr. Watkins is wrong," Eleanor said.

"And the kid is right," Luke said.

"Look at it, Amaru." Eleanor pointed at the Concentrator, stuck in the ground like a harpoon. "That thing should not be here. You can see it's all wrong. I know you can. It's *hurting* the earth."

Amaru swallowed.

"The G.E.T. didn't put that here," Eleanor said. "No person did."

"What are you saying?" Amaru asked.

Eleanor's mother spoke slowly and calmly. "Think about it. Who built that tunnel we just came through? And that temple out there on the bottom of a lake? How long ago? How long has this Tree of Life been here?"

"That is . . ." Amaru readjusted his grip on the pistol.

"Look at that thing, bub," Luke said. "That look especially human to you?"

Amaru squinted at the Concentrator for a few moments. "Are you . . . are you saying *aliens*?"

"Yes," Eleanor said. "And Watkins knows it. He thinks he can control it. But he can't. That thing is what's causing the Earth to freeze. And it's going to keep doing it unless we shut it down."

She could see the doubts racing through Amaru's mind, the confusion weakening his resolve, and she decided to risk another step toward the Concentrator. "I can stop it," she said. "If you let me."

Amaru raised the weapon. "I told you to stay away from it."

Eleanor stopped moving.

"Please, Amaru," her mom said. "If we can shut these things down, we can set the earth right again. Things can go back to the way they were. No more Freeze. No more refugees. The best thing you can do—for your wife and son—is let us do what we came here to do."

"I will not listen to terrorists telling me what is best for my family," Amaru said.

"We're not terrorists," Eleanor said. "We can help you. We can save your family."

"Can you?" Amaru said. "And what if you're wrong? What if the Freeze doesn't stop? Can you promise me that my family will survive when the ice comes? Can you guarantee we will have food and warmth, as Dr. Watkins has? Can you?"

Eleanor wanted to say yes, but she could not bring herself to make him such a promise when she still had doubts of her own. The truth was that she didn't know what would happen after the Concentrators were shut down. The rogue planet would still be up there, pulling the earth away from the sun. Without the earth's energy streaming to it, what would it do? Would it move on? Eleanor thought so, but she didn't know. And she didn't think she could lie about it.

"That's what I thought," Amaru said. "Dr. Watkins promised me that my family will be saved, if I help him."

"I think you'll find his promises aren't worth much," Luke said.

"He is an honorable man," Amaru said. "He has

treated me with kindness and respect."

"He is using you," Eleanor's mom said. "That's all."

But Eleanor could see now they wouldn't be able to convince him. Amaru was driven by fear for those he loved, and he was doing what he thought was best for them, choosing to believe the side that offered him survival, if not hope. Eleanor found it difficult to be angry at him for that. But it didn't seem that he would let her get anywhere near the Concentrator, and the G.E.T. now knew where it was. She had to do something before it was too late.

She sat down on the ground and closed her eyes.

"What are you doing?" Amaru asked.

Eleanor ignored him. She focused on the Concentrator's hum, its reach into the earth, the way it strummed the ley lines of energy. She listened, and she tried to follow those lines, reaching back toward the Concentrator with her mind. She remembered the sensation of touching the Arctic Concentrator, the way it'd felt as if something moved and convulsed beneath its skin, the consciousness she'd found waiting inside it. She remembered the way she had connected with it and tried to do so now with this Concentrator, even without touching it.

"What is she doing?" she heard Amaru ask.

"I don't know," Eleanor's mom said.

"Well, make her stand up."

Eleanor's mom chuckled. "You give me far too much credit. I've never been able to *make* my daughter do anything."

Eleanor could hear Amaru's footsteps come closer to her and then sensed him standing over her, but she kept her eyes closed.

"Whatever you are doing," he said, "you will stop. Right now."

Eleanor said nothing. She ignored him, even as he kept talking, warning her, threatening her. It felt as if her mind were getting closer to something, tracing the Concentrator's roots beneath her, following the lines of telluric energy pulsing toward it like blood through veins. She didn't need to touch the console. She could connect with it from here, because it seemed to be responding to her. The awareness inside was waking up.

The ground rumbled, and the Concentrator emitted a kind of metallic groan.

"What was that?" Amaru asked loudly, in audible panic. "Are you doing something to it? Is she doing something to the Tree?"

No one answered him.

"Listen to me," Amaru said, his voice quivering. "Dr. Watkins said no one must be allowed to interfere.

It is a matter of life and death. If you attempt to do anything to the Tree, I am supposed to shoot you. Do you understand me?"

At that moment, the Concentrator's awareness was like some wild thing looking out from the bushes at her, suspicious, and Eleanor was coaxing it, trying to draw it nearer to her.

She felt something hard and cold against the side of her head.

"Amaru, no!" her mom screamed.

It was the gun. Eleanor could not ignore that, and as she gave the weapon her attention, the awareness in the Concentrator vanished into the shadows, retreating into itself.

"Stop what you are doing," Amaru said. "Please."

"You son of a—!" Luke shouted. "You'd kill a kid?"

Eleanor opened her eyes and looked up. Amaru was shaking. He was sweating. He looked terrified. This wasn't something he wanted. "I stopped," she said.

He sighed. "Thank you," he said, and pulled the gun barrel away from her head. "What were you doing? That was—"

Luke came out of nowhere. He slammed into Amaru with his shoulder, and they both tumbled to the ground, grappling and rolling, fighting for control of the gun. Eleanor scrambled clear of them toward her mom, eyes wide and fearful.

"Luke!" she shouted. "Be careful, don't—"

Somebody was going to get hurt. Somebody was going to—

The explosion of a gunshot filled the cavern. The two men went still for a moment, and then Luke pulled away from Amaru, holding the weapon. Amaru lay partly on his side, curling up a little, looking at his abdomen. A small amount of blood came out of a hole in his dry suit.

"No," Eleanor whispered, and rushed past Luke to Amaru's side.

"Please," he said, "leave the Tree alone. Let Dr. Watkins—" He grimaced and convulsed in sudden pain, breathing hard through gritted teeth. "He . . . he told me what it can do."

Eleanor's mom dropped to Amaru's side. "We need to get him out of this suit. Quickly."

She and Luke unzipped the dry suit enough to open it away from the wound. Once they did, all Eleanor saw was blood. It was pouring out of him, soaking into his thermal suit inside the rubber shell.

"No!" her mom shouted, and put both hands over the wound, pressing hard, blood pooling between her fingers. She had the basic medical training of anyone working in the Arctic, but Eleanor knew this wound was beyond her skill. Amaru was bleeding to death right in front of them, and he groaned beneath her hands.

"Promise me," he whispered.

Tears blurred Eleanor's vision. "We will save the earth, Amaru," she said. "I will promise you that."

"No." He shook his head, eyes clenched tight. "Please, I—" Then his eyes popped back open, almost as if in surprise. "Mi hijo . . . ," he whispered. Then his body went limp, and he slowly rolled onto his back, eyes staring up into the shadows.

None of them spoke for several moments.

Luke's voice came out hoarse. "I didn't mean— He had a gun to her head."

"He left you no choice," Eleanor's mom said, looking at her blood-covered hands. "And you saved my daughter."

Eleanor wiped her eyes. "It wasn't your fault, Luke," she said, but that didn't mean it was Amaru's. She still found it hard to blame him for doing only what he thought he had to for his family. If anyone was to blame for his death, it was Watkins, and Eleanor's grief for Amaru very quickly turned into rage. She got to her feet and turned toward the Concentrator.

"Sweetie, be careful," her mom said.

"I will," Eleanor said.

She walked toward the alien device, stepping through the ring of statues, and circled the trunk until she located the console. Its porous metal looked a bit like the surface of the lake, with waves of bumps and divots. Her mom had followed her and stood to her left, while Luke stood to her right.

"I don't even want to think of the hands those controls were meant for," he said, staring at the console. "Or tentacles, I guess. Or . . . whatever the heck they have."

Eleanor's mom shuddered.

"You're a scientist, Mom," Eleanor said. "Aren't you interested in this?"

"I probably would be if my daughter wasn't about to let this thing into her mind."

"You sure about this, kid?" Luke asked.

"Got a better idea?" Eleanor asked him.

His mustache twitched. "Can't say I do. So how does this work?"

"Like this." Eleanor closed her eyes again and laid her palm against the console. Even though she had done this once before and knew what to expect, she recoiled violently when she felt the larva-like consciousness squirm within the Concentrator's fibers and machinery. But she forced herself to leave her hand in place as the alien awareness seized the nerves in her arm and made its way up to her mind. She let it in, but not far. Only enough that she was able to connect with it, and then take control.

It was almost like she was part of the Concentrator, or like the Concentrator was part of her. She was able to manipulate its roots, shifting them out of alignment with the telluric currents, thus cutting off its supply of energy. Then she found the wiggling consciousness, the intelligence that she could not say was artificial or natural, but that governed the Concentrator, and she killed it, like stepping on a worm.

The ever-present hum ceased, but the silence that followed seemed to take something vital out of Eleanor. She felt weakened and out of breath, but not from the altitude or from everything that had just happened. The drain on her ran deeper than that, deeper even than her bones. But she managed to open her eyes.

"It's done," she said.

"I'll be damned," Luke said. "It's like it just went quiet."

"You can tell?" Eleanor asked.

"Yeah, I can tell," he said. "Can't say how, though."

"I think we should save this discussion for later," Eleanor's mom said, still eyeing the branches of the Concentrator overhead. "The G.E.T. are probably mobilizing right now. Coming this way."

"Right," Luke said. "Then let's figure out how we can get out of here."

"But . . . ," Eleanor said. They couldn't go back the way they had come. "Your air tank is broken."

"You could use . . . ," her mom said, but didn't finish. They all went quiet as they looked at Amaru's lifeless body.

"I don't know if we can use *any* of the tanks," Luke finally said. "I don't know how to work 'em. Hell, I don't even know how to tell if they have air left in 'em." He looked at Eleanor's mom. "Do you?"

She shook her head. "I didn't pay close enough attention."

"Seems awful risky trying to dive that tunnel again," Luke said. "I barely made it the first time."

Eleanor shone her flashlight around the chamber, sending the shadows of the statues chasing each other along the walls. "Maybe there's another way out," she said. "But should we do something about Amaru? I hate to just . . . leave him here."

"I feel the same," her mom said. "But we can't carry him out, and we can't bury him."

"I'm sorry, kid," Luke said.

He screwed the top back on his own flashlight, and the three of them searched the chamber for openings.

197

Before long, in a far corner, they found a second corridor like the one that had brought them there: carved out of the stone by something other than nature. Eleanor's mom was about to lead the way into it when Luke stopped her.

"Hang on," he said, and jogged back toward the Concentrator.

"What's he doing?" Eleanor's mom asked.

Eleanor shrugged, and a minute or two later Luke returned, jangling some keys in his hand. "We need a way off this island," he said. "Amaru's boat won't start without these."

"Good thinking," Eleanor's mom said, and then she entered the tunnel.

They had not walked far before the corridor curved to the right and slightly upward. It continued along that course, around and around, up and up. That seemed like a good sign to Eleanor. If the Concentrator was located under the island, as it seemed to have been, then they were now climbing up through it.

The air grew warmer as they went, and Eleanor thought about removing at least the outer rubber shell of her dry suit. But her mom said to leave it on, because they might still need it. The physical exertion of the climb sapped Eleanor's air, her gasping made worse by the weakness left by the Concentrator's silence, and she wondered how long it would take for them to reach the end of wherever this tunnel was leading them.

A short distance on, Eleanor's mom stopped, bringing their climb to a halt. "Turn off your flashlights," she said, switching off her own. Eleanor and Luke did the same, plunging them all into a moment of total darkness, but then Eleanor's eyes began to adjust, and she saw there was a very faint glow spilling down the walls and floor toward them.

"I think we're almost at the top," her mom said.

They switched their flashlights back on and hurried up the remaining turns of the tunnel until they reached its end, where they met with a stone wall. Eleanor felt an initial flutter of panic.

"I don't understand," her mom said. "Why go to all this work carving a path to the surface, and then leave it blocked?"

"Maybe it's not," Eleanor said. "Turn off your flashlights again."

They did, and Eleanor saw a thin thread of light outlining the edges of a door in the rock.

"I guess we push?" said Luke.

All three of them leaned against the stone, straining, over and over again, but no matter which direction they tried, it wouldn't budge. Eleanor used her flashlight to study the door and realized the stone sat in a kind of channel, or track, that had been carved in the rock. On one side, down in the bottom corner of the door, she noticed a smaller rock lodged in a little notch.

"Stand back," she said, and after her mom and Luke had backed up a couple of steps, she pulled the little rock out.

The door rolled slowly and ponderously along the track with a grating sound that raised chills along Eleanor's back. A spreading crack of light appeared, which grew wider and brighter by inches, until the opening was a few feet wide. Eleanor shielded her eyes against the blinding brightness until the view settled, and she looked out of the doorway toward the stone altar that they'd seen at the top of the island the day before.

"It's . . . the Titikala," she said. "We're inside it!"

"Makes sense," Luke said. "I suppose."

They stepped through the opening, out into the sunlight, and Eleanor took a long, deep breath. Then she turned around and regarded the entrance. It was there under the outcropping she had seen the day before, but hidden. She smiled to herself, proud that her first hunch had proven correct.

"Fascinating," her mom said. "Apparently, the

people who lived here incorporated the Concentrator into their religion." Now that she and Eleanor and Luke were out of danger, it seemed her scientific mind had returned. "Perhaps they worshipped it. Maybe they even used it somehow. Von Albrecht has speculated that some ancient people may have made use of telluric energy."

"Who is this von Albrecht you keep talking about?" Luke asked.

"A fringe scientist," her mom said, "who until now was not taken seriously."

"Bet he'd like to get a look at this. Have the last laugh. Where's he at now?"

"I have no idea. It's been years since anyone in the academic community has heard from him."

"That's all very interesting," Eleanor said. "But I think we should go find the others and get the heck out of here."

After a last lingering glance at the Titikala, her mom nodded. "I agree."

They crossed the plateau at the top of the hill and took the path down to the Chinkana, where they tried to retrace their steps through it as they had done before. At one point, a vista opened up through an archway, and Eleanor looked down over the terraces

— CHAPTER —
14

"They're already here," she whispered.

Luke and Eleanor's mom followed her gaze down through the archway.

"That's not good," Luke said.

"Where's Simon?" Eleanor's mom asked. "And the boys?"

"And Betty?" Luke said.

They were too far away to discern the identities of the people moving around on the dock and the shore. They could've been G.E.T. agents, or Finn and Julian, or even Watkins. But even at this distance Eleanor could see that some of them were getting into diving suits, and several of them were wading into the lake.

203

There wasn't any way Eleanor and the others could get to Amaru's boat now.

"What do we do?" she asked.

"We stay here in the labyrinth," Eleanor's mom said. "We wait and we watch."

"Let's find someplace more hidden, though," Luke said. "They could spot us here with binoculars."

They ducked down and moved deeper into the Chinkana, off the main path into the smaller chambers, but no hiding place they considered seemed secret or safe enough. If the G.E.T. decided to make a thorough search of the ruin, the agents would eventually find them. The G.E.T. had tracked them this far, after all, and Watkins knew they were somewhere on the island. Amaru's locator had made sure of that, and it seemed likely that Amaru had also been reporting back since meeting up with Eleanor and the others in Puno. The agents down on the shore knew this. It was only a matter of time.

"Psst," someone said behind them.

Eleanor spun around. So did her mom, and Luke had his fists up, like a boxer.

It was Betty. "You're alive," she whispered. "I was afraid you all had drowned."

"Almost did," Luke said.

"What happened?" Eleanor's mom asked. "Where—"

"Not here," Betty whispered. "Come on."

She led them back through the labyrinth toward one of its far corners. When they reached it, they found an alcove in the wall of an upper chamber that was much deeper than it first appeared, most of its length choked with shadow. Betty ushered them all in, and they found Finn crouching at the back end of it.

"Eleanor!" he whispered.

"Finn!" Eleanor's mom said. "Where's your father?"

"They have him!" Finn said. He was scared; Finn was never scared. "They caught Julian, too. They— Is that blood on your hands?"

"The G.E.T. has them, you mean?" Eleanor's mom asked, ignoring Finn's question.

"We managed to make it here," Betty said. "Best spot I could find for us to hide. Doesn't look like much until you get close. We can see out, but they can't see in, unless they're right on us."

Eleanor turned outward and saw she was right. The alcove afforded a view of most of the labyrinth, the docks, and a good length of the shoreline, but she realized the shadows would keep them obscured inside it. For now.

"Tell me what happened," Eleanor's mom said.

"I don't know." Betty sat down on a rock that jutted out from the wall a little farther from the rest. "After you all went underwater, we waited on the dock. You were gone a long time, and we started to worry. Then Julian spotted some boats, heading right for us. Finn's dad said we should scatter and hide, to make it harder to catch us all. So he gave me the pack and I headed up here."

"I went with Betty," Finn said, "and Julian stayed with my dad." Eleanor didn't know how to interpret the flat tone in his voice.

"The G.E.T. caught them pretty quick," Betty continued. "They tried to hide in the rocks down below. We came up here, and we've been holed up since then." She smiled at Eleanor. "It's good to see you, though. Where's Amaru?"

Eleanor looked down at the ground, where the gray funnel of a spiderweb made a dark hole in the cracks between the rocks. At the mention of Amaru's name, her ears filled with the sound of his groans, and her eyes with the fountain of blood from his chest. Tears were there, right behind those memories, but she didn't let them out.

Eleanor's mom looked at her hands. "He was working for Watkins."

"It was an accident," Luke said. "I was trying to get the gun away from him."

"A gun?" Finn said. "So . . . he's dead? You shot him?"

"Yes," Eleanor's mom said. "He betrayed us and

held a gun to Eleanor's head. We had no choice."

"Watkins promised him protection if he helped the G.E.T.," Eleanor said. "He was just trying to take care of his family, the only way he thought he could."

The alcove fell silent after that, save the wind whistling past its opening. As Eleanor considered what Amaru had said, the world she thought she knew became confusing and disordered, as if its borders were changing on her. Amaru would have done anything for his wife and son. Skinner had sincerely believed he was serving a greater good, too, preserving some semblance of human life on the planet, even if he had to let billions of people die in order to do it. Eleanor was sure Watkins had his own reasons, and he probably felt equally justified in his actions. This wasn't about good versus evil, this was about survival, about the best way to do the most good for the most people. It wasn't a simple black-and-white question anymore. Perhaps it never had been.

"Did you find what you were looking for, at least?" Betty asked.

Eleanor nodded. "There was a Concentrator. I shut it down."

Betty turned to Luke with a raised eyebrow.

"Yes," he said. "I saw it this time. It's all true, every word."

"Well, I'll be darned," Betty said with a finality that seemed to have settled something for her.

"So, how're we going to rescue my dad?" Finn asked.

Eleanor's mom peered outside, down toward the docks. "Do we know where they are?"

"I think they've got them on one of the boats," Betty said.

Eleanor had no idea how they could possibly free Julian and Dr. Powers. G.E.T. agents swarmed the beach and the dock, and though it was hard to count from here, there had to be at least thirty of them. At the moment, their activity centered on the divers in the water, and while that kept Eleanor and the others safe in the labyrinth, it made any plan to get Dr. Powers and Julian off the boat nearly impossible.

"What are we going to do, Mom?" she asked.

"Finn, I . . . ," her mom started to say. Eleanor could hear the change in her voice and in that moment realized what she was thinking. But it was Luke who said it aloud.

"I don't think we can get 'em out."

"What?" Finn said.

"It's too much of a risk," Betty added.

"I'm sorry, Finn," Eleanor's mom said.

"What are you saying?" Finn asked. Tears had

begun to flood his voice. "We're, what, just going to leave them with the G.E.T.? How can you do this?"

No one replied to him. Eleanor knew what the adults were thinking. They had only two options. The first was to try to free Dr. Powers and Julian, in which case they would all be caught and their mission would fail. The second was to escape and leave Dr. Powers and Julian behind.

"Kid, believe me," Luke said. "If there was anything we could do to help them, I'd be the first to do it. But I know one thing. If we got you caught trying to jailbreak your dad, letting them get their hands on you and killing the mission, he'd be angry as a bear. With *us*."

"He's right," Eleanor's mom said. She was keeping her expression calm, but Eleanor could tell she was barely holding it together. "I know your dad, and he suspected something like this might happen. That's why he split you up to begin with when he saw those boats."

"But we can't just leave them behind! Tell them, Eleanor!"

"Finn," Eleanor began, "I . . ." She glanced down at her feet and then at the faces of the adults. The truth was that nearly every part of her wanted to disagree with them. But then she thought about how far they'd come. They'd shut down two Concentrators already. They had a chance to finish this thing, to sever the connection and save the planet. She was certain of it.

But only if they didn't get caught.

Finn must have seen the change in her, and he fixed her with a glare that was in some ways as frightening as the gun Amaru had pointed at her. "You flew up to the freaking *Arctic* to find your mom." Then he started toward the alcove entrance, as if he meant to leave and walk down to the boats. Luke reached for him, but Finn threw him off. "Don't touch me," he said. "I can't believe you. Any of you. We're here because the G.E.T. doesn't care about losing most of the people on earth to this rogue planet, and we didn't want to accept that. But I guess everyone's got something they're willing to sacrifice for the mission."

His words cut into Eleanor and left her speechless. She couldn't hold his gaze. It was Betty who walked over to Finn and put a hand on his arm, and he let her. "Before we take any big risks," she said, "I think we should sit tight and wait to see what the G.E.T. does down there. All right?"

Everyone agreed that seemed best for the time being, and even Finn nodded. Eleanor doubted this was over, but she guessed that Finn knew it was pointless to argue anymore.

They settled down in the alcove and kept watch on the activity below. A few hours went by in that way, with little said between them. Divers came up and went down. One of the boats pulled away from the dock and around the bay in wide, lazy circles. They knew where Amaru's locator was, but they didn't know how to get down to it. It might be a long while before they found the entrance to the underwater cave. Meanwhile, the sun was descending toward the horizon.

"It's hard to know what we're up against," Eleanor's mom finally said.

"What do you mean?" Betty asked.

"I'm just putting all the pieces together." She stood and paced. "Skinner knew nothing about the Concentrator before he saw it. But it seems that Watkins has known about them for some time. He just didn't tell Skinner. But Watkins did tell Amaru about this one. He called it a Tree of Life."

"I think Barrow changed the game," Luke said. "Watkins was able to keep a lid on everything until you went and blew it open. Seems like he's gone on the offense now."

"Maybe you're right," Eleanor's mom said. "But how many Concentrators does Watkins know about?"

"How many do *we* know about?" Betty asked.

"The Sync is here in the pack," Eleanor's mom said. "It has the map."

But Eleanor remembered the image. "Two more, I think. One in Egypt, and one in the Himalayas."

"We have to assume Watkins is searching for them too," her mom said.

"Or maybe he's found them," Luke said. "He's got the resources of the entire G.E.T. at his disposal. He could be searching for them all at the same time."

If that was true, it would make shutting them down much more difficult.

Luke snapped his fingers. "We've got movement down there."

Eleanor looked and saw the G.E.T. agents loading up their gear. The divers were leaving the water. White patches bloomed behind the boats as they started their motors.

"Are they leaving?" Betty asked.

"That's what it looks like," Luke said.

A few moments later, with the shoreline cleared of equipment and agents, a single figure walked along the dock from one of the boats. He held something up before his face, and the squeal of a megaphone reached all the way up to the alcove.

"My name is Pierce Watkins!" the figure said, his voice amplified, echoing up through the Chinkana. "I am acting CEO of the Global Energy Trust!"

"The old lizard himself," Luke whispered.

"I don't know if you can hear me," Watkins continued. "But if you can, I want to make two things very clear to you. The first is that you will shortly be marooned on this island. Tomorrow, we will return with sufficient numbers to find you, wherever you are hiding. I can assure you I am very good at finding things. The second is that I mean you no harm. We have not mistreated Dr. Powers or his son in any way."

Eleanor sensed Finn tense up next to her.

"If you turn yourselves in," Watkins continued, "I promise you will be dealt with fairly."

"Dealt with?" Luke whispered. "Wonder what he means by that."

"Now!" Watkins said. "I will wait sixty seconds for you to show yourselves and come down to the boats. If you do not, you have a cold night ahead of you, I'm afraid, and you will only be prolonging the inevitable."

He lowered the megaphone and stood there, waiting.

Eleanor felt so nervous she lost track of the time. No one in the alcove breathed, it seemed, for what had to be much longer than a minute. After that endless interval had passed, Watkins spun on his heel without another word and boarded one of the boats. Then each G.E.T. craft pulled away from the dock in succession, the last one towing Amaru's pontoon boat behind it, and together they plowed away across the lake toward Copacabana.

"He's right about one thing," Betty said. "It's going to be a cold night."

"We should have turned ourselves in," Finn said.

"You don't believe that," Eleanor said. "You could have shouted and given us away. But you didn't. You know this is the right decision. And you know it's what your dad would want."

Finn said nothing.

"Well, we are truly good and marooned here," Luke said. "They took Amaru's boat. And last time I checked, none of us can walk on water."

But that gave Eleanor an idea. It was risky, and possibly even stupid, but she spoke up anyway. "Not *on* the water. But maybe under it."

"What are you thinking, kid?" Luke asked.

"The tunnels," Eleanor said. "We passed some down there after we came out of the water. Amaru mentioned they go for miles and miles."

"Are you suggesting we go back?" Eleanor's mom asked.

"Maybe?" Eleanor said, still a bit unsure of the idea, but growing more confident with each moment that she considered it.

"That seems almost as dangerous as turning ourselves in," Luke said. "We don't know where those tunnels go. Or if they go anywhere. What if we get trapped? Or lost?"

"If we stay here," Eleanor said, "we're iced. They'll find us tomorrow for sure. This is our one chance."

"So what are these tunnels you're talking about?" Betty asked.

"They supposedly ran beneath the entire Inca empire," Eleanor said. "Amaru said they were a legend. But we saw them. They're real."

"You *think* you saw them," Luke said. "All we really saw were the openings to a couple of tunnels that might be twenty-foot dead ends."

"I've read about the Inca roads," Finn said, sounding sullen. "They're pretty famous. The Inca king could eat fish that was only two days old, if he wanted. He lived in Cuzco, and the coast was three hundred miles away."

"That's a hundred and fifty miles a day," Betty said. "How is that possible?"

"Relay runners," Finn said. "Lots of relay runners. But I haven't read about any tunnels."

"They're down there," Eleanor said, and turned to her mom. "You saw them, too."

Her mom laid her hooked index finger across her

lips. "Yes, I saw the entrances to some tunnels," she said. "I agree with Luke that we don't know where they lead. But I also don't think we have any other options. If we're going to just wait here for Watkins to catch us, we might as well have surrendered and saved ourselves a cold and uncomfortable night."

"So you agree with Eleanor?" Betty asked.

"Unless someone has another suggestion, I agree it's worth a shot," her mom said.

Eleanor was grateful to have her mom's support, mostly because it felt good to agree with her about something. Finn looked pale and scared, but Eleanor understood why. She didn't know what she would do if someone told her she had to leave her mom behind. And it was true that she'd hopped a plane for the Arctic to go find her. But this was different. The situation and the stakes were different now, and she hoped that under the same circumstances, she would have the courage to do what needed to be done.

Luke scratched his head. "If we're going to do this, we better move quick."

"Will I get to see the Concentrator?" Betty asked.

"Yes," Eleanor said. "And then you'll understand why we're doing all this."

Eleanor, her mom, and Luke decided to remove the outer rubber shells of their dry suits and proceed wearing the thermal suits underneath. Betty removed three pairs of shoes from the pack and handed them to Luke, Eleanor, and her mom, for which they were grateful. Then they all left the safety of the alcove and made their way back up to the Titikala and its secret stone door. Eleanor turned on her flashlight, as did the others, and they entered the tunnel. Once everyone was inside, Eleanor turned to see if there was any way to close the door behind them. If there wasn't, Watkins would find the opening when he searched the island the next day, and that would take him directly down to the Concentrator. Eleanor didn't want to make it easy for him, but she couldn't see any mechanism for rolling the giant stone back into place.

"All the more reason to hurry," her mom said.

They descended the spiraling pathway down through the mountain. The corridor was familiar to Eleanor, and she moved quickly, but Betty and Finn took it more slowly, unsure of their footing.

When they reached the bottom and entered the Concentrator chamber, Betty stopped and stared in an almost comical way, complete with the gaping mouth. Finn had seen the Arctic Concentrator, so he merely nodded in recognition as he came in and trudged off to look at the ring of statues.

"Believe it now?" Luke asked Betty.

"I do," she said.

"And what do you think?" he asked.

"I . . . all I can think is what my aunt Celia would say."

"And what's that?" Eleanor asked.

"I feel like a cat in a room full of rocking chairs." Then Betty shook a little, as if a chill had just taken her by the shoulders. "Is that thing safe?"

"I turned it off," Eleanor said.

"That doesn't answer my question," Betty said. "On or off, that thing doesn't look very safe to me. And it makes me want to get as far away from this place as I can."

"Then let's not waste any more time," Eleanor's mom said.

They crossed the chamber, and Betty hugged the wall, maintaining the maximum possible distance from the Concentrator. When they reached the far side, with the corridor that led to the sea, Eleanor called to Finn, who was still studying the statues.

"What were you doing?" Eleanor asked as he caught up to them.

"Just curious," he said, head bowed. "I was trying to decide if those statues were supposed to be the aliens."

"Maybe they helped build this place." Luke grunt-laughed. "Maybe the pyramids, too?"

"No," Finn said. "Not like that. We know the Concentrators predated Amarok's people, so that puts them on earth long before the pyramids were constructed. But if some early human ancestors saw the aliens, maybe that got passed on in legends and myths."

That was same idea that had led Eleanor to study the Titikala. She didn't think the Inca actually knew about the aliens, but rather, perhaps they simply knew that this site was somehow connected to some mysterious power.

"That's an interesting idea, Finn," Eleanor's mom said. "But we'd best keep moving."

They entered the corridor and followed it back until they reached the intersection with the two tunnels they'd seen racing away into darkness, before they'd found the Concentrator. Eleanor looked in both directions, and both passages appeared identical as far as her flashlight could reach.

"Looks like we have a choice to make," Luke said.

— CHAPTER —
15

"WHICH WAY DO WE GO?" BETTY ASKED. "I'M COMpletely turned around down here."

"I think we want to go north or northwest," Eleanor's mom said. "That would take us in the opposite direction from Copacabana, back toward Puno."

"Any idea which way is north?" Eleanor asked.

"That way." Luke pointed back toward the Concentrator chamber.

Eleanor's mom sent her light down one tunnel, then the other. "How can you be sure?"

"Call it a pilot's intuition," Luke said.

"I'll go with that," Betty said.

"All right, then." Eleanor's mom nodded toward the

tunnel to Eleanor's right. "That would make this west. I suppose that's close enough to the way we want to go. This way is it?"

She led them forward, and they walked for quite some distance down a very straight passage. The walls proceeded uniformly, with very few distinguishing features beyond the subtle grain of the stone, and soon the view was the same looking forward or back, which created the unnerving sensation that they weren't moving at all. But the longer they walked, the more sure Eleanor became that the path would not lead them to a dead end. This tunnel had been made to take people someplace. She just wished she knew where.

"So are we under the lake?" Finn asked.

"I believe so," Eleanor's mom said. "I don't know how this tunnel isn't flooded."

"Inca ingenuity," Betty said.

They walked for an hour.

Then another.

And another.

"I'm not claustrophobic," Eleanor's mom whispered. "But this could drive a person insane."

"That person could be me if we don't get out of here soon," Luke said.

Eleanor couldn't believe how long it was taking them, and she worried whether the batteries in their flashlights would last. The scuff of their steps and the sound of their breathing filled the tunnel until they were all she could hear. Her body felt each and every one of the miles they had walked. She was hungry, and tired, and thirsty. They stopped to rest occasionally, and that helped. In addition to the Sync, the pack Betty had grabbed off the boat held the few snacks they'd brought from the plane. Granola bars didn't fill Eleanor up, but they gave her some strength, and sips from the water bottles gave her relief from her thirst. None of that helped her with the weakness from her connection to the Concentrator, although that seemed to be slowly fading.

After they rounded the fourth hour, Eleanor thought her vision was deceiving her, because the straight tunnel appeared warped ahead. But she soon realized that it wasn't her vision. The corridor was actually changing course, rising up at an angle. After the maddeningly hypnotic journey they'd just taken, Eleanor welcomed any deviation.

The tunnel climbed by degrees for some distance, and then they came upon a stone door much like the one Eleanor had recognized at the Titikala. It even had the same release mechanism. But when Eleanor pulled the little rock from its notch, this door didn't move on its own. Luke had to put his shoulder into it, but once he got it going, the stone rolled away with the same grinding sound.

It was dark outside. They stepped out of the tunnel, and Eleanor sucked in a chestful of cold, fresh air. The plentiful stars and the slivered moon above them alloyed the white clouds into pewter.

"I thought we'd never see the end of that," Betty said. "I can't even imagine what it took to build it."

Luke clapped Finn on the back. "Aliens, you think?"

"No," Finn said, and left it at that. Luke was obviously trying to lighten the mood, perhaps distract Finn from his father and brother's situation, but it wasn't working.

"So where are we?" Eleanor's mom asked, partly to herself.

They stood on a rocky hillside at the base of an escarpment, and not too far below them was the lake. Off in the distance, the Isla del Sol was a thin black streak across the shimmering water.

"Looks like we're on the western shore of the lake," Betty said.

"That island's gotta be twelve, maybe fifteen miles away," Luke said.

Eleanor marveled at the distance, too. They had traveled under Titicaca, using the ancient roads of the Inca. Or maybe the tunnels were even older than that.

Perhaps there was something to Finn's idea that even if the aliens hadn't been directly involved, they had somehow inspired or influenced the people who lived around the Concentrators.

"Now we just need to get back to Juliaca," Eleanor's mom said. "Get on the plane and get out of here."

"What if the G.E.T. found *Consuelo?*" Eleanor asked.

"We never told Amaru about her," Luke said. "The professor told him we'd been in Lima. Smart thinking on his part. Watkins and the G.E.T. know what *Consuelo* looks like, but if they're actively looking for her, let's hope it's in the wrong place."

At the mention of Dr. Powers, Eleanor turned her attention to Finn. He stood apart from them, facing the water, his face slack, emotionless. She had felt a measure of what he was going through when they had decided not to pick up her uncle Jack. But this was different. The G.E.T. wasn't holding her uncle Jack captive. Eleanor walked up beside Finn but kept a respectful space between them.

"We'll get them back," she said.

He kept his eyes forward. "I know."

"I'm sorry," Eleanor said.

"Not your fault. I should've been with them."

"Don't say that."

"Why not?" He looked at her, his emotions still too hidden for her to read. "It's true." Then he turned his back on the lake and walked toward the others.

Eleanor's mom had pulled the Sync from the pack. "No cell signal," she said. "But I've got GPS. It looks like we're not too far from a main road. It's late, but maybe we can pick up a ride there."

She led the way, and about a mile later they reached the road and followed it in the general direction of Puno. The landscape around them was starting to feel familiar, with its fields of grain, white as snow in the moonlight, and the low-swelling mountains on the horizon. Distant lights marked farms and homesteads, and they even saw the occasional pair of headlights, but no vehicles approached them for several miles.

When they did finally cross paths with a car, it turned out to be a truck with a tall, wooden, crate-like bed. The driver, an old man with graying hair and a face that had borne a lifetime of wind and sun, looked very confused, and even a little irritated, after Luke flagged him down and tried to ask for a ride in broken Spanish. But apparently, he was heading to Puno, and Eleanor heard the word alpaca. She had no idea how they must've appeared to him, walking down a road out in the middle of nowhere, in the middle of the night, and she expected him to just drive off.

But instead he nodded with a frown and said, "Yah, yah," and thumbed them toward the rear of the truck.

"Gracias," Luke attempted, and they went around to the back of the bed.

The driver got out of the cab and met them there, where he lifted a couple of thick metal pins and lowered the back of the box. The vehicle was obviously used for transporting livestock, and even though there weren't any animals in it at the moment, the evidence of them was. It smelled of fur, and of the hay that lined it, and of the manure that hadn't quite been cleaned out.

"Gracias," Luke said again, not quite as enthusiastically, and they all climbed into the box.

The driver raised the back and shoved the pins back into place, effectively trapping them inside. Only then did Eleanor feel unnerved. The man could now take them anywhere he pleased, and she suppressed the paranoid thought that he was somehow working for the G.E.T. and Watkins.

The truck emitted a resigned kind of let's-do-this growl and lurched ahead, and everyone in the bed stumbled and reached for something to hold on to at the same time. The smell of old engine exhaust mixed with the animal aroma unpleasantly, though every now and then a clean breeze would find its way through the slats in the box.

It was a bumpy, long ride, and after the hours and miles they'd just walked, everyone soon settled down as best they could to rest. Eleanor ended up sitting in the straw, her back against the rough side of the truck, watching the road in slices and growing very tired. But every time she closed her eyes, she saw Amaru—the fear in his eyes and the blood on his chest—and she thought about his family. Eleanor hadn't made Amaru the promise he had wanted. She had made him a different promise, and she intended to keep it, but deep inside she feared she couldn't, and that made her guilt and grief over Amaru's death even worse.

"You were right," Eleanor's mom whispered.

Eleanor glanced in her direction and found her mom looking at her as though she'd been doing so for a long time. "About what?" Eleanor asked.

"What you said about Amaru. I *would* do the same for you. And more."

They'd been thinking about the same thing, a rare moment of connection, and Eleanor felt suddenly glad, and grateful, at the same time that she still felt guilty, and sad, and scared, a mosaic of emotion that made an unsettling picture.

"His son's name is Lucio," Eleanor said. "He's two years and four months old."

Her mom nodded and smiled. "Lucio."

Nothing more was said, and the moment of connection between them passed away gently on its own. Dawn came, and soon a lattice of sunlight crisscrossed the interior of the truck bed. Not long after that, the truck came to a stop, the engine still running, and Eleanor watched as the driver walked down her side of the bed to the rear of the vehicle, pulled the pins, and lowered the back wall.

Everyone inside rose, and stretched, and winced, then hobbled out of the truck onto the street. Betty tried to offer the driver some money, but he waved both hands before him and wouldn't accept it. Luke helped him raise the back of the truck and secure it, after which they shook hands and the driver got back into his cab and drove away in a cloud of dust and exhaust.

"We need to find water and food," Eleanor's mom said. "Then hire a cab back to Juliaca."

Luke's gaze darted up and down the street. "What we need is to be careful."

"But no one will be looking for us here," Eleanor said. "Watkins will probably just be getting back to the island now. It'll be hours before he discovers how we escaped, if he even finds out at all."

"Might be," Luke said. "But if there's anything I've

learned by now, it's that the G.E.T. has eyes everywhere. We can't afford to take any chances."

So they wandered the backstreets of Puno, watchful for anyone who might be following them, until they found a bakery. They bought some pastries and breads, along with several bottles of water, and moments later, every drop and crumb was gone, and Eleanor felt much better. The cabs were a little harder to come by, but they eventually managed to hire a van similar to the one in which Amaru had driven them, and they were back on the road.

Eleanor recognized some of the landmarks they passed on their way back to Juliaca, including the university at the edge of town. The van took them right to the airport, and as soon as it came into view, Eleanor's body tensed up. They still didn't know if *Consuelo* had been discovered, and if she had, Eleanor had no idea what they would do next.

Luke seemed even more on edge. He got out before the cab had even come to a full stop and marched toward the tarmac. Betty paid the cabdriver, and they all hurried after Luke, walk-running as fast as they could without drawing attention to themselves. Eleanor leaned ahead as they approached the place they had left their plane, craning to see around the corner of a hangar.

And there she was. Parked right where they had left her.

"Oh, thank God," Eleanor's mom whispered.

Luke beat them to the plane and looked her over, circling all the way around and crossing under her belly.

"I don't think she's been tampered with," he said. "But it's not like we have time or equipment to do another sweep for trackers. We need to move and hope for the best."

"Then let's get going, shall we?" Betty said.

So they boarded the plane and took their places. It was hard not to notice the two empty seats, the ones Dr. Powers and Julian usually claimed. Eleanor glanced back at Finn and caught him staring at the vacancies. When he noticed her watching him, he snapped his attention away and directed it out his window.

Luke roused *Consuelo*, radioed the flight tower for clearance to take off, and she labored along the tarmac into position on the runway. Eleanor watched the airfield and the terminal, searching for G.E.T. agents or police cars in a way that was becoming a familiar routine. How many times would they have to take off under threat or with the fear that at the last moment they would be caught?

But moments later, they were in the air, and Eleanor

breathed a slight sigh of relief. If Watkins did know where their plane was, he hadn't found out about their escape in time to stop them. But as they climbed higher into the sky, leaving Lake Titicaca and its Island of the Sun farther behind, the small measure of triumph she had felt in no way compared to the loss.

They had left Dr. Powers and Julian in the hands of the G.E.T..

Eleanor couldn't believe it had really happened; it felt as if it was a decision someone else had made, one she'd read about in a book. But it was *she* who had decided to leave them behind. They all had.

"Mom?" she whispered, hoping Finn couldn't hear her.

"Hmm?"

"What if we missed something?"

"What do you mean, sweetie?"

"What if there actually was something we could have done to rescue Dr. Powers and Julian?"

Her mom didn't answer for several moments. "Self-reflection is a good thing," she said. "Second-guessing is not."

"What's the difference?"

"Self-reflection is about the future. Doing better next time. Second-guessing is stuck in the past. Beating yourself up over things you can't change."

That made sense but didn't really do anything to make Eleanor feel better about the fact that Dr. Powers and Julian were now prisoners. She wondered where they were, what was happening to them. Were they in a jail cell? Were they frightened? Were they waiting—hoping—for rescue, not knowing they'd been abandoned?

"I wish it were different," her mom said. "But . . ." And here she brought her hand down before her as if laying it on a table. "We made the only choice we could with the information we had."

She sounded much more definite than Eleanor felt, almost practiced, but everything she'd said struck Eleanor as false reassurance. Like she was trying to convince herself as much as she was trying to convince her daughter. Eleanor listened to the plane engines for a few moments, no clearer than she'd been before.

"I just . . . ," her mom started, but the strength went out of her voice. "I just hope they're okay."

Now it was Eleanor's turn to reassure. "Watkins said they hadn't been hurt."

"I don't trust him for a moment."

But Amaru had believed Watkins was an honorable man. Right now, Eleanor could only hope that was true.

CHAPTER
16

Very quickly, discussion on the plane turned to where they should go, and what they should do. Eleanor had successfully shut down two Concentrators, which emboldened her, and her thoughts on their plan were clear.

"We go to Egypt," she said. "We find the third Concentrator, and I shut it down. Then we go to the Himalayas."

Just a few weeks ago, the idea of going to Egypt, let alone the Arctic or Peru, would never have crossed her mind, but now she said it as if it were the most obvious choice they could make.

The rest of the passengers on the plane didn't

seem as certain as Eleanor that their next move was to immediately go looking for a third Concentrator— Watkins was clearly onto their plan now, and he would anticipate this move—but they soon came to the shared conclusion that they didn't really have a choice. If they were going to pursue their original mission, even without Dr. Powers and Julian, it was Egypt or the Himalayas, and Egypt sounded like the better choice of the two at the moment.

The only other alternative was to abandon the mission altogether. No one brought up that idea directly, but as Eleanor glanced from face to face, she was pretty sure they were all thinking about it. Why wouldn't they be?

But the Freeze was still happening. The rogue planet was still up there. Two of the Concentrators were still feeding it. Nothing about their situation had changed, other than having achieved a few first successes and getting themselves branded as terrorists. To give up now was to give up on the human race, and none of them seemed prepared to do that just yet.

"As the chauffeur here," Luke said from the cockpit, "I agree that Egypt is the better choice. The Himalayas are twelve thousand miles from here. Egypt is seven thousand, and generally on the way. I'll still need to refuel twice to get there, which, by the way, will just about be the end of my petty cash. We need to fly north, then east. So where should we stop?"

"Cuba?" Eleanor's mom asked.

"Too many eyes there," Luke said. "With all the folks from Florida trying to move south, there are lots of bureaucratic hoops to jump through if we want to land in Cuba."

"Venezuela, then," Betty said.

"Too risky," Eleanor's mom said. "With their oil reserves, the G.E.T. has a huge presence there."

"What about Florida?" Eleanor asked.

"Florida makes sense," Luke said. "Miami. From there, Spain. Madrid or Barcelona. Then on to Egypt."

"My mom lives in Florida," Finn said.

His statement hung in the pressurized air of the cabin for several moments, unacknowledged, but taking up a lot of room.

Eleanor's mom cleared her throat. "I assume the G.E.T. are watching her very closely. In case you try to make contact with her."

"I know," Finn said.

"I'm afraid it would be too risky to try to—"

"Yeah, I get it," Finn interrupted.

Eleanor wanted to reassure him somehow. "It's the same reason we didn't go to get my uncle Jack."

Finn nodded. "Sure. And once you've watched your

dad and your brother get captured, and then abandoned them, not stopping to see your mom isn't really a big deal."

That statement hit the air too, but much heavier.

"Besides," Finn added, "what would I say to her?"

Eleanor had not thought about that, but the minute Finn posed the question, she saw what he meant. His mom would obviously want to know where Julian and Dr. Powers were, she'd want to know about everything that had happened, and Eleanor certainly wouldn't be able to formulate a way to explain it all.

Luke said the flight to Miami would take them a little over nine hours. During the first part of the flight, Eleanor slept some more, as did the others in the cabin. When she woke up, she snacked on some potato chips and another granola bar, wishing she had something to read.

Eventually, she found herself up in the cockpit with Luke.

"Don't you ever get tired?" she asked him.

"I've never needed much sleep," he said. "Back when I was a kid, I had the worst insomnia. Always restless. My grandma used to say I was half firecracker."

"Is that why you became a pilot? So you could keep moving all the time?"

"No," he said. "I became a pilot because I hate

people, and up here is about as far away from them as I can get."

"You don't hate people," Eleanor said.

He opened his mouth as if he were about to argue, paused, and then nodded. "Maybe it's just most people."

"So nice of you to give some of us a chance."

"I never said I was perfect," he said. "What about you? Things any better with your mom?"

"I don't know. I think the whole thing still freaks her out."

"Well, now that I've seen it . . ." But he didn't finish that, and instead asked, "What's it like when you connect with that thing?"

Eleanor stared out the window at the ocean below them, endless in every direction. "It's hard to explain. It's kind of like when you learn something, and it makes so much sense to you, it's like you already knew it, you just didn't know you knew it."

"Hmm," he said. "That kinda makes sense."

"Really? It doesn't to me. I just want to know what makes me different."

"That's natural," he said. "But you ask me, the rest of us should simply be grateful that you are different. If it wasn't for you, we'd still be up in the Arctic right now, trying to figure out what that thing did. Or, you know, dead."

"Thanks, Fournier."

"You're sounding like Betty."

Eleanor smiled and laid her head back against the seat.

A few hours later, they landed in Miami. While Luke refueled and swept the plane for tracking devices as best he could, Eleanor's mom decided to run over to the airport terminal to buy some new clothes for herself and Eleanor. They both still wore the thermal suits from their diving equipment, and the only clothing they had on the plane was their polar gear, the rest of it either lost in the Arctic or left on Amaru's boat. Eleanor wanted to go with her, but her mom worried it would be too risky and insisted she go alone. A short while later she returned with sweatpants, sweatshirts, and T-shirts, the only things she could find, all of them branded *Florida: the Sunshine State!*

For the length of their stopover, Finn sat off by himself, and though Eleanor could guess what he was thinking about, she knew she didn't really understand what it was like for him. After she'd changed into her new clothes, with their new-clothes smell, and they boarded the plane once more, she went over and sat down next to him, much in the same way he had sat next to her in the cargo hold.

"Are you okay?" She knew what a dumb question it

was, how annoyed she'd be if someone asked her in the same situation. But she didn't know what else to say.

"In general, or considering what we've been through?" he asked. "In general, life sucks. But considering in the past couple of weeks we've nearly frozen to death, been shot at a couple of times, and lost my dad and brother, I'm doing pretty well at this precise moment."

"Point taken. I deserved that."

"No, you didn't," he said. But he didn't apologize, either.

"Do you still think you should be with them?" she asked.

"I don't know," he said. "I guess so. But I know how that sounds. My dad would say I'm being *irrational*." He deepened his voice when he said it, imitating Dr. Powers.

"I don't know about irrational," Eleanor said. "But I think I kinda get it."

"It's not that I wish I got caught. I just . . . I wish I was with them, I guess."

Just then Luke rushed on board. "Everybody ready?"

They all took their seats and buckled in, Luke performed his flight checks, and thirty minutes later, they were once again in the air with nothing below them but ocean. Before long, they flew over the United Lucayan Archipelago—a sprawling, dense network of islands, land bridges, saltwater lakes, and waterways. Eleanor's mom said the region was once very different, decades ago, with much smaller islands, like the Bahamas. The falling sea levels had reshaped it.

Their journey across the Atlantic took them nearly ten hours, and during that time they flew in and out of night, so that with the change in time zones they finally reached Barcelona early the next morning. Eleanor, like most of the kids she'd known back home, had never been to Europe before, but she had learned about it in school.

The European ice sheet now completely covered all of Scandinavia, most of the United Kingdom, Germany, and some of France. Spain, still generally free of ice, had received many of the refugees, as had Italy and Greece, though most were now spilling down into Africa, but also the Middle East, where Eleanor's mom believed a war would soon break out between the refugees and the nationals living there. A devastating conflict had already swept through central Africa, ending with the formation of the Union of the Congo Republics, but not before a lot of people had died.

The last thing the world needed was another war.

They didn't stay in Barcelona long—just enough time for Luke to refuel *Consuelo* and take care of some routine maintenance. There was no sign of the G.E.T., and no indication that they were being followed, but that didn't stop Eleanor from worrying. Then they were back in the air, bound for Cairo. They flew over the Mediterranean and its many islands and peninsulas, but when they reached northern Africa, the view below changed from a sea of blue to a sea of beige desert. It wasn't until they neared Egypt that Eleanor saw any green, a long, wide swath of it.

"That's the Nile floodplain," her mom said. She sounded exhausted, which wasn't surprising. "This region has supported human societies for a hundred and twenty thousand years, longer than any other place on earth. Africa is the birthplace of humanity."

Eleanor remembered that the Arctic Concentrator had been in place for at least fifteen thousand years, based on what Amarok's tribe had known about it. "That means the ancient Egyptians might have been around when the Concentrator was . . . installed, or whatever. They might have known about it."

"It's possible that people here did, yes," her mom said. "Though the ancient Egyptian empire as we know it didn't emerge until five thousand years ago."

"So what are you saying?" Eleanor put on mock

heartbreak. "That aliens *didn't* build the pyramids?"

"Sorry to disappoint you," her mom said, but with only a weak smile behind it.

Luke decided to land *Consuelo* at an airstrip outside the Sixth of October City, a little over twenty miles southwest of Cairo. Much like the area surrounding Mexico City, this part of Egypt had become a refugee settlement, mainly for Europeans, and it appeared from the air as if conditions here weren't any better than in Mexico City. There were millions of refugees, densely packed in ramshackle houses that were small and close together. But at least they weren't tents.

"So what's the plan when we land?" Luke asked from the cockpit.

Eleanor's mom pulled out the Sync to look at von Albrecht's map. "The nexus of the ley lines is right over the Giza Plateau, near the pyramids. If what we've come to believe is true, the Concentrator must be somewhere around there."

Everyone agreed, nodding, but said nothing. As Eleanor looked around at her mom, and Betty, and Finn, she noted circles under their eyes, their rounded shoulders. Their journey, from the Arctic to Peru and now here, was taking a toll.

They landed late in the morning without incident. Luke said cargo planes came in all the time to that airfield, because of the refugees, so theirs wouldn't stand out—at least not until someone came looking for them specifically. They deplaned onto the sandy tarmac, the air dry, the sun warm on Eleanor's skin, the horizon flat and featureless in every direction she looked, a mix of sand and grass and fields of grain.

At the airport terminal, they arranged for a taxi van to pick them up and then waited outside. When it arrived, they piled in and Luke asked the driver, a very friendly, middle-aged man named Youssef, if they could be taken to the pyramids.

"No, no." He waved both hands across the air above the steering wheel. "Closed."

"Closed?" Eleanor's mom asked.

"Yes, closed."

"Why?" Luke asked.

"The G.E.T.," he said, and did not sound happy about it. "They block off the whole area. Why? I don't know. No oil there!" He stuck his open hands out in front of him, over the dashboard, his shoulders raised.

If the G.E.T. had closed off access to the pyramids, that surely meant they knew about, and had possibly found, the Concentrator. This was exactly what Eleanor had worried she would find when they arrived. She wiped some sweat from her forehead. Youssef's van was getting uncomfortably warm. He didn't have the air-conditioning turned on, and the windows were all up.

"Could we get close enough to see them?" Eleanor's mom asked.

Eleanor didn't know what good that would do. If the G.E.T. had taken control of the site, would it even be possible to get close enough to the Concentrator to do what she had come to do?

"Yes, yes," Youssef said, and turned the key. "I take you to a good place. Good view. Good food. You will like it."

He pulled the van away from the terminal and onto a two-lane road. As they drove across the desert, they passed several cars, as well as groups of people leading camels. Before long, they reached the refugee community and skirted along its edge, the small, severe structures made of cinder block and seemingly constructed only for basic shelter without giving any thought to comfort. From the look of it, they had no power or running water. People loitered outside them and stood in the doorways, staring at the cars driving past.

"Germans," Youssef said, pointing at the tract, with evident irritation in his voice.

"You don't like the refugees?" Eleanor's mom asked.

He shook his head and pointed a finger at the roof

of his van. "They do not respect Islam. We let them come here, we say you are welcome, we give them what they need to build houses, but we say you will respect Islam. They say they will respect Islam, but they do not."

"You want them to convert?" Betty asked.

"No, no, no," he said, waving his hand. "We do not force on anyone. But this our way." He laid a hand on his chest. "Friday is a holy day. We close our shop and business. Refugees want to open business on Friday, and this is not pleasing. They eat and drink in the open during Ramadan. This is not pleasing. They do not respect Islam. And they have many crimes, also."

"It's worse in Syria and Iraq," Betty said. "Now that Israel has closed its borders."

"Yes." Youssef nodded his head deeply enough that Eleanor worried whether he could still see the road. "That is very bad situation. That is *not* Islam."

Eleanor didn't understand all the politics, and she didn't understand how some people couldn't see they were all one planet facing the same threat—that they needed to work together. But maybe that was actually why things were so contentious here. If people were scared they might lose what they valued the most, maybe that made them try even harder to protect it, drawing lines along the edges of ancient conflicts and resentments. No wonder most people hadn't figured out what was really going on with the Freeze. They were too busy contending with one another.

They left the refugee tract behind and drove into an urban area, lined with shops, restaurants, and movie theaters, with palm trees leaning gently over the street. Youssef took several turns and pulled onto a road that ran along the edge of an open expanse of desert. He then stopped in front of a café and pointed across the front passenger seat.

"There, you see?"

Eleanor followed the invisible line from the tip of his finger, between two buildings, to several triangles stabbing upward from the horizon. She hadn't noticed them, but there they were. Right there. The pyramids.

"You want to eat here, yes?" Youssef got out of the van and walked around to open the sliding door for them. "Good food. Good view."

"Okay," Luke said.

They piled out of the taxi and followed Youssef into the café, where another middle-aged man greeted them with a smile and a slight bow of his head. He wore a black apron around his waist and a white button-down shirt open at the collar, and he and Youssef embraced and kissed each other on both cheeks. They spoke together in Arabic, with smiles and laughter.

Then Youssef turned back toward them. "This is Samir, the brother of my wife."

Samir nodded again. "Welcome. You are hungry. Come, please." He opened his arm inward to his café.

"I'll leave you now," Youssef said. "But Samir will call me if you want a hotel. I will take you to a good one. Anywhere you want to go. You are very nice."

"Thank you, Youssef," Eleanor's mom said.

He left, and Samir shepherded them through the café and settled them at a table on a back patio, shielded from the sun by a white canopy overhead. The spot did have an amazing view of the pyramids, off in the distance, and it occurred to Eleanor that the image before her had likely changed very little in the last five thousand years.

"One moment," Samir said, and after he'd left them, Luke leaned over the table.

"What do you want to wager that hotel Youssef mentioned is owned by his uncle?" he said.

"No bet," Betty said.

"Stop it—it's fine," Eleanor's mom said. "I get the feeling that's how it works here. He seemed like a nice man."

Luke frowned. "So did Amaru—"

"Amaru *was* a nice man," Eleanor said, almost challenging him to dispute it. "He made a bad choice."

"If you say so, kid," Luke said. "That argument doesn't make me feel any better about nice-guy Youssef, though."

"Can we eat something?" Finn asked. "I'm starving."

He sounded like Julian, though Eleanor refrained from making that observation out loud. A moment later, Samir returned with menus, and also two pairs of binoculars.

"For the view," he said, and pointed toward the pyramids.

"Thank you," Eleanor's mom said.

Eleanor grabbed one of the pairs before anyone else could claim it and aimed it out across the sand. It took her a moment to adjust the dial and bring the view through the lenses into focus, and then another moment to land them on something to see.

But she wasn't hoping to get a better look at the pyramids, or the Sphinx. She was looking for the G.E.T.

They were everywhere. Vehicles. Tents. Agents. Every road leading there was blocked off, and dozens of structures had been built throughout the area, like a small city. It was a massive operation, all in and around the bases of the pyramids.

Eleanor brought the binoculars down and looked at everyone else around the table. "We're screwed," she said.

CHAPTER
17

They looked at one another in silence, having each taken a turn with the binoculars and seen the state of things around where the ley lines intersected. They didn't know exactly where the Concentrator would be, but the fact that a small army of G.E.T. agents swarmed the entire site meant they wouldn't even be able to search for it, let alone get close enough for Eleanor to shut it down.

Samir returned, smiling. "What can I bring you?"

"We, uh . . . ," Eleanor's mom began. "We haven't had a chance to look at the menu. What would you recommend?"

"You want me to bring my specialties?"

"That's fine," Luke said.

"Of course," he said, and hurried away.

"Boy," Finn said. "Good thing we abandoned my dad and brother to stick to the mission."

"I'd rather be here," Betty said, "than be back there in G.E.T. custody, thank you very much."

"Well, I'm glad you're happy," Finn said.

"Hey," Eleanor said. "That's not what she meant. I'm pretty sure your dad would *thank* Betty and the rest of us for getting you out of there. So we hit a snag—"

"A snag?" Luke pointed across the desert toward the pyramids. "You call that a snag, I don't even want to see what you'd consider a crisis."

"We'll find a way," Eleanor said, though she had no idea how or what it might be. She looked to her mom for support, but she was looking down, brow furrowed, idly scratching the vinyl tablecloth.

Samir returned bearing a tray of iced magenta drinks. "Karkade," he said. "Hibiscus tea."

He next brought platters of flatbread, hummus, baba ghanoush, with some white crumbly cheese, and falafel, and for the next several minutes, no one said a word. They ate and they drank, and when Samir came back to check on them, the food was already nearly gone.

"You enjoy it?" he asked.

"Very much," Eleanor's mom said.

He smiled. "Very good. I bring you dessert?"

"I'm afraid we're on a budget," Luke said.

"Then please," Samir said. "Dessert is on the house."

"Well, that's very kind of you," Betty said.

He left again, and Eleanor's mom sighed, as much from being full as being discouraged, it seemed. "What are we going to do?" she asked. "We can't get anywhere near the site."

No one answered her. The exhaustion Eleanor had sensed in them back on the plane lingered around the table, made worse by the bleakness of their predicament. But she would not be defeated.

"I think we should at least check it out," she said. "Get a bit closer."

"Closer is dangerous," Luke said. "They've got to know we're coming. I think we can assume Watkins has put the word out, and they'll be ready for us."

"That's why we need a plan," Eleanor said. "Maybe just a couple of us can get close enough to find out if they've discovered the Concentrator."

"Close?" Samir asked. He'd brought them a plate of baklava and some bowls of sweet rice pudding. "Close to what?"

"The pyramids," Eleanor said.

"Ahhh," he said, glancing up toward the horizon. As he turned back toward the kitchen, he said over his shoulder, "The UN thinks it is okay that the G.E.T. takes our history from us."

"I say we do it." Finn took a big bite of baklava. "That's why we're here."

"It might be possible," Luke said. "*Might*. But we can't have more than two of us going. And even then, it seems pretty risky."

"Too risky," Eleanor's mom said. "I'm not convinced."

"Convinced of what?" Eleanor asked, irritation with her mom growing.

"That we can do this."

"So then what?" Eleanor asked. "We just give up?"

"I didn't say that—"

"Yes, you did. But if we don't try, and try now, the mission is a bust. If they haven't found the Concentrator yet, they will eventually, and once they start tapping its energy, that's it. We're running out of time."

"That doesn't mean we should lose our heads and go rushing into something," Betty said.

"Then we don't rush in," Eleanor said. "We get closer, *carefully*, and find out more. Then we make a plan."

"Either way, we're going to be here for a little while," Luke said. "Maybe we should find a hotel and make this plan you're talking about."

"Fine," Eleanor's mom said, and when Samir returned, she asked him if he might call Youssef for a ride.

"He is almost here," he said. "I call him a few minutes ago."

Eleanor looked once more at the pyramids before they left the table and went to wait out in front of the café. The traffic seemed to move through the streets without pattern or rules, or at least none that Eleanor could discern. But no one got in an accident, either, which meant there had to be a method to it. Youssef pulled up, and as he leaped out of his van he smiled at them as if they were the oldest of friends, and his enthusiasm felt genuine.

"You liked the food?" he asked, opening the door to the van. "It is very good, yes?"

"Very good," Luke echoed, the last to climb in.

Youssef scooted around to the driver's side, hopped behind the wheel, and eased the van into a slight gap in the traffic.

"You know a hotel?" Eleanor's mom asked.

"Yes," Youssef said. "Very good hotel. It is my cousin's."

Luke smirked. "You guys sure take care of each other."

Eleanor wanted to jab him with her elbow.

"Oh, yes, of course." Youssef looked back at them in his rearview window. "Family is everything, yes?"

The open and earnest way in which he said it drove the smirk from Luke's face and brought silence to the vehicle.

"Yes, it is," Finn said.

Eleanor leaned forward. "Could you drive us closer to the pyramids first?" Her mom whipped a glare at her, but Eleanor knew they needed more information and kept going. "We know they're closed. We just want to get a closer look."

"Certainly," Youssef said.

"What are you doing?" Luke whispered.

"Let's just see," Eleanor said. "If it looks bad, we don't even have to get out of the car."

The others accepted that, grudgingly it seemed, and the cab drove them through the chaotic streets, and again Eleanor witnessed the disparity between the refugees who had nothing and the wealthy who had everything. It took some time, but eventually they reached the pyramids, which rose up like mountains above a chain-link G.E.T. fence.

Youssef brought the vehicle to a stop some distance from a large throng of people. They carried signs printed with GET OUT G.E.T., and they shouted before the gates of the encampment. There were at least a hundred of them, while dozens of guards stood watch on the other side of the fence, armed with guns and stationed at regular intervals.

"Protesters," Youssef said. "They march every day."

"Looks like the G.E.T. has a lot of security because of it," Luke said, looking at Eleanor.

"Yes," Youssef said, shaking his head.

But Eleanor and everyone else in the car knew what that meant. Because of the protesters, the high level of security meant it really would be impossible to get into the site and search for the Concentrator. They had come all the way to Egypt for nothing.

"Uh, guys?" Finn said.

He nodded toward one of the nearest guards, who was looking right at them and talking into a radio.

"I think we're ready to go to our hotel," Betty said. "Quickly."

"Very good," Youssef said.

He pulled away from the encampment, and Eleanor looked through the back window, watching as the guard with the radio rushed away from the fence.

It was now safe to assume that not only was the encampment impenetrable, but the G.E.T. knew they were here and would be out looking for them. Perhaps her idea had been reckless, after all.

"Do not worry," Youssef said. "I'll take you to hotel. Then I bring someone to meet you."

"Who?" Eleanor's mom asked.

"A niece of Samir," he said. "He heard you talk about the pyramids, and he called her. She is a . . . I don't know the word. She studies the pyramids."

Eleanor looked at her mom. This could be good for them. This niece could somehow help them get closer to the Concentrator site. But it could also be bad for them, if she turned out to be affiliated with the G.E.T. Eleanor reassured herself that Youssef and Samir clearly didn't trust the G.E.T., and hopefully neither would a relative of theirs.

A few minutes later, they pulled up to a nice-looking hotel, quite new, made of white stone and glass, with round archways that grew wider before they closed at the top. Youssef walked them in and spoke with the concierge at the front desk, then told them he would return in one hour with Samir's niece and to meet them in the lobby. Then he left, and Eleanor's mom checked them in, crowding into just one room this time.

"We really need to watch what we spend," she said. "Our money won't last forever."

But the room was large, with two wide beds, angular furniture of modern and sterile design, and a carpet with no pile that still felt thick and plush.

"So who do you think this niece is?" Luke asked.

"I have no idea," Eleanor's mom said.

"Do you think it's safe meeting with her?" Betty asked. "I feel like the fewer people know that we're here, the better."

"You're right," Eleanor said. "But she could be someone who can help us get onto the pyramid site. We're going to need all the help we can get. And we've been lucky with the people we've met so far."

"Have we?" Finn asked. "How do you know they won't turn on us the way Amaru did?"

"Intuition," Eleanor said.

"Alien intuition?" he asked. "That's worked out well."

Eleanor was about to fire back at him, but she noticed that Betty, Luke, and even her mom didn't seem to have noticed Finn's jab, or weren't nearly as bothered by it as she was.

Luke threw himself down on one of the beds. "Whoever she is, I'm taking a nap until she gets here." Almost as soon as he finished saying it, he was snoring.

Finn shouldered his backpack. "I'm going for a walk."

Eleanor's mom reached out for him. "I really don't think you—"

"I just need a few minutes to myself, all right?" he

snapped, then softened. "I'm going to check out the hotel. That's it, I promise."

Eleanor just stared at the wall. She would probably have wanted to go with him, had he not just made that alien comment.

Her mom nodded. "Okay, but don't be long."

"Yeah," Finn said, and left the room.

"That poor boy," Betty said. "What do you think is going on with Julian and their dad?"

"That depends," her mom said. "The G.E.T. put out that bulletin you read back in Fairbanks, calling us terrorists. But we don't actually know if they've pursued any criminal charges. Are there warrants for our arrest out there? Or are they worried we'll talk if the authorities take us in?"

"So you think the G.E.T. is just keeping them prisoner?" Eleanor asked. "They're not in a jail cell?"

"I doubt it," her mom said. "The G.E.T. is above the law at this point. If Watkins does what Skinner did with us, he'll first try to convince Simon to sign on with the Preservation Protocol."

"I can't see Dr. Powers doing that."

"I can't either," her mom said.

But Eleanor wasn't so sure about that, based on some of the comments Dr. Powers had made. All that talk about going from offensive to defensive.

The room had a television, and Eleanor turned it on to pass the time while they waited. The channels were mostly in Arabic, so she didn't understand much of it, but the images kept her distracted. At one point, she landed on a news program, and it showed aerial footage of the G.E.T. encampment near the pyramids.

"Mom, look." Eleanor leaned forward and scanned the image for something relevant or useful. There were plenty of vehicles and several large structures and tents, with smaller ones between them, arranged in a loose grid. None of them appeared at first glance to be more significant than any other. But as she watched, she noticed most of the agent activity clustered around one particular tent. Two rows down and three in, toward the middle of the site. Eleanor pointed at it and said to her mom, "That one, maybe?"

"Perhaps," her mom said. "There seems to be something going on in there."

The show cut away to an anchor talking into a microphone, a crowd of those angry protesters behind him, and Eleanor leaned back again.

Finn returned a short time later. "Luke still sleeping?" he asked as the door shut behind him. "Are we meeting Youssef soon?" His voice sounded lighter than when he'd left. Maybe the time away had helped him calm down.

"Yes," Eleanor's mom said. "We should probably go down."

Eleanor walked over to Luke and shook his arm. "Hey, lazybones."

He opened his eyes and stretched his arms upward, climbing out of what seemed like a pretty deep nap. "Okay, I'm up," he said, and when he got to his feet, he smacked his mouth a couple of times. "So, we ready for this?"

"Ready as we'll ever be," Betty said.

They left the room and walked down to the lobby, which was carpeted with enormous, intricately patterned rugs, while fronds and plants reached out from so many corners it gave the impression of a greenhouse atrium. They found a group of low, cushioned benches arranged in a semicircle and claimed them while they waited.

Some minutes later, Youssef strode into the lobby, eyes up and scanning. With him was a young woman in her twenties, wearing khaki cargo pants, a long-sleeved, white button-down shirt, and a teal head scarf that covered her hair and her neck. She was quite beautiful, with a narrow face, smooth features, and lips that pulled slightly downward without looking as though she were frowning.

Eleanor and the others rose from their benches as

Youssef spotted them and nodded the woman in their direction. As they approached, Eleanor noticed a name badge clipped to her jacket, but she couldn't read it from so far away.

"Hello!" Youssef said. "You like my cousin's hotel? It is good?"

"Yes, very nice," Eleanor's mom said.

Youssef beamed and then said, "Please, I am honored to present Nathifa, the niece of Samir. She is a . . ." The word seemed still to evade him, and he turned to the woman for help.

"I'm an archaeologist," she said. "It's a pleasure to meet you." She extended her hand to shake with Eleanor's mom, and Betty, but not Luke, and then they all sat down on the benches. "Samir called me and told me you were interested in seeing the pyramids?"

"Yes," Eleanor's mom said. "But we didn't mean for him to go to so much trouble. It was only something we mentioned in passing."

Nathifa offered a knowing smile and nodded. "Well, that's Samir. I'm sure you noticed that he takes care of every customer of his. It's an important point of pride for him."

"Yes, we did notice that," Betty said.

"And the pyramids are a source of pride for me," she said. "I'm sorry for the current situation."

"Not your fault," Luke said.

"Actually," Nathifa said, "in a manner of speaking, it is."

"How so?" Eleanor's mom asked.

Nathifa moved her lapel to reveal her name badge. "I'm a part of the team there."

Her badge bore a large G.E.T. logo.

Eleanor's whole body went cold and rigid, and for a moment no one spoke. They had flown halfway around the world and walked right back into the hands of the enemy.

"Oh—" Eleanor's mom said. "I, um . . . Is that so?"

"Yes, though I'm more of a consultant," Nathifa said. "They have their work, and I have mine. I'm there to make sure they don't damage our national heritage."

"I see," Eleanor's mom said.

So she wasn't actually a G.E.T. agent. That made Eleanor feel a bit better, but she still wondered how much Nathifa knew about everything. An archaeologist might even know about the Concentrator. "Why are the G.E.T. there in the first place?" she asked.

Nathifa shrugged. "They're digging for something that is 'relevant to global energy interests.' My team is just there to assist with the excavation and make sure they don't disturb any of the ruins or artifacts, wake any mummies, that sort of thing."

Eleanor suddenly wondered if the power of the Concentrator might have indeed brought any mummies back to life. Nathifa must have noticed her expression and chuckled. "I'm only kidding."

"But have they found anything?" Eleanor asked.

"That is technically classified," she said. "You probably saw yourself they are still digging, which means I can't take you to the site, unfortunately. It truly is closed to the public. But as a favor to Samir, I'm here to answer any questions about the pyramids you might have."

"What do you say to people who think aliens helped build them?" Finn asked.

Eleanor wanted to kick him.

"Aliens?" Nathifa's downturned lips *did* appear to be frowning then. "I usually say it is historical arrogance to assume that the ancient Egyptians couldn't have built them on their own. Not to mention a little more than crazy to believe that aliens actually landed on our planet. Isn't it?"

"Humph," Luke said.

"So there's no way we could get closer to them?" Eleanor asked.

"I'm afraid not," Nathifa said. "Is there a special reason why you want to?"

"No," Eleanor said, shrugging casually. "We just . . . hoped to see them."

"Of course," Nathifa said. "You have traveled far?"

"Yeah."

"Where did you come from?"

"We were in Italy," Eleanor's mom said.

"Really?" Nathifa said. "Where?" Her frown still hadn't gone away, and her tone was a bit harder than before.

"Florence," Betty said. "Quite a lovely city."

"Is that so?" Nathifa said. "Are you sure you weren't in Peru?"

Eleanor nearly gasped. *She knows.*

Youssef looked a bit confused by the conversation, while Eleanor's mind scattered in fear. No longer a statue, she wanted to run.

"N-no," Eleanor's mom said. "Why do you—"

"Because I know who you are," Nathifa said, her eyes darkening. "And I know why you're here."

18

ELEANOR LOOKED AT HER MOM, AND LUKE, AND BETTY. They were just sitting there, perhaps too stunned to do anything else. But Eleanor felt they had to get away, now, while they still had a chance. Her body screamed at her to move.

Eleanor's mom swallowed. "What do you—"

"This isn't the place to discuss it," Nathifa said.

"I do not know what you are saying," Youssef said next to her. "What is this?"

"Oh, it is nothing to worry you," Nathifa said to him. "Please thank Samir for calling me when you see him?"

"Of course." Youssef blinked and nodded. Then he

spoke in Arabic with her, and Nathifa replied to him in Arabic, and Youssef nodded again and rose to his feet.

"I leave you now, but here is my number." He handed Luke a card. "Call me, please, if you want me to drive you." A few more good-byes followed that, and then he left.

Nathifa leaned closer to them and lowered her voice. "I have another van coming. It will take us somewhere we can talk."

"Hold on," Luke said. "You're crazy if you think we're going anywhere with you."

"Please," she said. "You must."

"No, we mustn't," Luke said, rising. "And unless you brought a few of your friends from the G.E.T. with you, it looks like you're outnumbered, pal."

"I have not told the G.E.T. you are here," she said, motioning for Luke to sit again. "And I won't. I promise. There is someone who would like to speak with you, and I'm here to take you to him. But it's not the G.E.T. You must trust me."

"The last person we trusted pointed a gun at her head." Luke nodded toward Eleanor.

Even then, in that moment, Eleanor's mind flashed briefly to the sight of Amaru's bleeding chest, and she shut her eyes tightly for a moment.

"And he was working for the G.E.T., too," Betty said.

"I am *not* working for them," Nathifa said. "That's what I'm trying to tell you. You must understand, I've only cooperated with them to keep an eye on what they're doing."

Eleanor wanted to trust her but hesitated.

"We know what you are looking for," Nathifa said. "And we know where it is."

"We?" Luke said.

"Where what is?" Eleanor asked.

"*It*," Nathifa said.

Eleanor and Luke shared a look. "Does the G.E.T. know . . . where *it* is?" Eleanor asked.

"Not yet," Nathifa said. "Please, there isn't much time. If I was working with them to catch you, they'd be here already, and you'd be in custody, no? There is a van waiting right outside, and we can go someplace where we can talk. Will you come with me?"

Eleanor looked at her mom, and her mom looked at Luke and Betty. Luke scratched his beard but nodded. Betty cocked her head to the side and raised her eyebrows, but she seemed to be agreeing.

"Very well," Eleanor's mom said.

Nathifa rose to her feet. "Thank you."

The others slowly stood and followed her. On the

way, Eleanor surveyed the other people in the lobby, and then the street, searching for any sign of a trap.

Nathifa was right. There was a van waiting in front of the hotel. She opened the doors, looking up and down the street, and ushered them in. Finn climbed in first, followed by Betty, and then Eleanor's mom. As Eleanor climbed in, she glanced toward the front to get a look at the driver, and in that same moment heard her mom whisper, "My God."

Luke stopped halfway inside the van. "What is it?"

Eleanor's mom stared at the driver. "You're Johann von Albrecht."

The driver was a slender man, with long gray hair pulled back tight in a ponytail, and wide, thick glasses in gold frames. "Pleasure to make your acquaintance," he said, with a slight German accent, and a nod of his head.

Luke climbed the rest of the way into the vehicle, and then Nathifa took the front seat. She gave von Albrecht a nod, and he pulled into the afternoon traffic somewhat less competently than Youssef had.

"You are Samantha Perry, if I am not mistaken," von Albrecht said.

"I am," Eleanor's mom said. "This is my daughter,

Eleanor. And this is Luke Fournier, Betty Cruz, and Finn Powers."

"Dr. Simon Powers's son?" von Albrecht asked.

"You've heard of my dad?"

"Naturally."

"How?" Finn asked.

"I am working for the G.E.T.," he said. "Or rather, I was."

The situation they faced seemed to have changed dramatically in the past few moments, and Eleanor struggled to decide on the question she wanted to ask first. To begin with, it was obvious now that Nathifa had known who they were through her G.E.T. connections. Youssef, on the other hand, hadn't seemed to understand what was going on, but had Samir? After all, it was he who'd alerted Nathifa to their presence. When Eleanor asked Nathifa about that, she shook her head.

"No, he asks me to come talk with tourists about the pyramids at least once a week," she said. "He's tried to get me to give lectures at his café. Usually I tell him I don't have the time, but when he described you, I had to find out if you were the fugitives we've been warned about. The moment Finn mentioned aliens, I knew who you were."

Eleanor glanced back at Finn, and he hung his head.

"You are looking for the telluric vortex machine, are you not?" von Albrecht asked.

"Yes," Eleanor's mom said. "But we call them Concentrators."

"Concentrators?" von Albrecht said, and then repeated the word a few times, listening to himself. "That is a good name. Watkins calls them the Trees of Life."

"Nathifa said you've found it?" Eleanor asked.

"No," von Albrecht said. "But we know where it is."

Eleanor didn't know what the difference was, but there was a more important question to ask first. "How close are the G.E.T. to finding it?"

"Not close," Nathifa said. "They believe it is located at Giza."

"But we have your map," Eleanor's mom said. "That *is* where the telluric nexus is located."

"I was wrong," von Albrecht said.

"Then where the hell is it?" Luke asked.

"The Valley of the Kings," Nathifa said. "Three hundred miles up the Nile."

"Your map is three hundred miles off?" Betty said.

Von Albrecht pushed his glasses farther up his nose. "Mapping telluric currents is no simple matter, madam."

"So where are we going now?" Eleanor's mom asked.

"A warehouse," Nathifa said. "You will not be discovered there, and we can explain everything."

The van crawled through the city, past shops, mosques, houses, and hotels, and even an open-air bazaar. They eventually came to a stop outside a tall gate. Nathifa gave von Albrecht a key card. He swiped it through an electronic station, and the gate opened to admit their vehicle, then closed behind them. After they'd climbed out of the van, Eleanor noted the thicket of barbed wire atop the wall that enclosed the courtyard in which they'd parked. Stacks of wooden pallets and crates filled the corners, along with chunks of masonry.

"This way," Nathifa said, and led them to a low door in a building that rose three or four stories above them, one with a flat, barren facade and tall, imposing windows.

The door had another electronic lock, which chirped and blinked with a swipe of the card, and the door opened. Nathifa led them in, with von Albrecht following at the rear. The interior was somewhat dark and hazy, the only light falling inward from the windows up near the rafters. But Nathifa threw a switch, and a formation of fluorescents buzzed to attention, illuminating a dozen or so rows of freestanding shelves that ran the length of the building, three or four tiers high, stuffed with boxes and crates.

"What's in all those?" Finn asked.

"Historical artifacts," Nathifa said. "Property of the Ministry of State for Antiquities."

"Mummies?" he said, and Eleanor couldn't tell if that idea excited him or frightened him.

"No. The warehouse climate isn't controlled. Most organics are far too delicate to store here. This is mostly ceramics, sculptures, that kind of thing. From all periods, so you'll find stuff from the Old Kingdom, the Ptolemies, the Romans, all of it."

"Wow," Eleanor said.

"I'm surprised you still care about all this," Betty said.

"What do you mean?"

"No offense." Betty made a gesture toward the door. "But the refugees out there will tell you the world is ending, and some might argue this is a waste of resources."

"There are some in my own government who argue that," Nathifa said. "Because of them, my department has almost no budget left. Many of us volunteer."

"Why?" Finn asked.

Nathifa looked at von Albrecht. "It seems to me that if the world really is coming to an end, it is more important than ever to preserve who we were. To leave something behind."

That made sense to Eleanor, though it didn't seem to satisfy Betty, whose toughened skin showed her disagreement in its creases. But Betty was also the type of person who had voluntarily gone to work the Arctic oil fields, and as Eleanor had come to know her, she believed that choice to have been motivated as much by the desire to do something that mattered to her in the face of a dying earth as it was by a desire for profit. It was the practical choice, and it seemed that to Betty, this warehouse of historical artifacts couldn't be less practical.

"Come," von Albrecht said, and he strode toward a work area against one wall of the building. There were several tables mounted with magnifying glasses the size of dinner plates, and spread with a feast of small statues, vases, and fragments of both. Von Albrecht assembled a ring of rolling office chairs in the space between the tables and motioned for them all to sit, and once they had, he asked, "What are they like?"

"What are what like?" Eleanor's mom asked.

"The Concentrators."

"They're . . . how do I even describe them?" Her mom looked up at the ceiling. "They're about ten meters tall, with branches that span the same distance. They do resemble trees . . . but they have strange physical properties that defy human perception."

"So they are extraterrestrial in origin?" he asked.

Her mom nodded. "The evidence is conclusive."

He sighed. "When the G.E.T. came to me, they said they had found a way to harness the earth's telluric currents in order to keep us alive. I was excited, and I worked with them to identify the places on the planet with the highest energy potential. They had already found the first Concentrator in the Himalayas, of course, only I didn't know it then. They were only using me to look for more of these . . . machines. They intend to tap the devices themselves, not the telluric currents, which is an insane proposition. We know so little about them. When I realized the true purpose of the G.E.T. here, I left and went to hide among my refugee countrymen. But I have maintained contact with Nathifa."

"So they have control of the Himalayan Concentrator?" Eleanor's mom asked.

That would make shutting it down very difficult, and perhaps impossible. It might even make what they were trying to do in Egypt pointless. But Eleanor believed they still needed to try.

"Yes, they have control of it," von Albrecht said. "But from what I hear, it is very different from the ones you describe. Much larger. Perhaps it is the master, connected to and in charge of the others."

"Do you know about the rogue planet?" Eleanor's mom asked.

"Yes." Von Albrecht's back hunched forward, as if he were deflating. "Yes, I know about the dead world."

"But do you know they're connected?" Eleanor asked.

"What are connected?" he asked.

"The Concentrators and the planet."

"What? No, they . . ." But von Albrecht stopped then and exchanged a glance with Nathifa. His eyes went to the floor, where his gaze seemed to roam absently for several moments while he worked something out in his mind, and then he looked back up at Eleanor, his eyes wide. "It is a predatory world? Can this be?"

Eleanor nodded, relieved that he believed her.

"It all comes together," he said. "That is where the energy is going."

"Yes," Eleanor's mom said.

"So it's not dead after all. Questions I had not previously been able to answer." He held up two fingers. "Where did the machines come from, and where is the energy going? You have answered both. And now . . ." He pushed his glasses up, squinting, working more things out. "The Concentrators must be stopped," he said. "Or the earth is doomed."

"We're trying to find them to shut them down,"

Eleanor said. "I already stopped the one in the Arctic, and the one in Peru. Now we're here."

"You shut them down?" Nathifa said. "How did you do that?"

Eleanor felt reluctant to reveal the answer to strangers, considering how her own mother had reacted to it, but if they were to help each other, von Albrecht and Nathifa would find out anyway. "I have a kind of connection with them," she said.

"Fascinating," von Albrecht said. "They say the same about Watkins and the Himalayan Concentrator."

Watkins could connect with a Concentrator? While something about that reassured Eleanor—she wasn't the only freak—it also meant she shared something singular with her enemy, and that made her feel even less comfortable with her mysterious ability. Who . . . what . . . was she?

"But if she can shut it down," Nathifa said to von Albrecht, "that would ensure the G.E.T. never find it."

"What do you mean?" Eleanor's mom asked.

"They're looking in the wrong place," Nathifa said. "Sooner or later, they will realize it, and they will go searching elsewhere. But if we have already shut it down, there won't be any telluric energy for them to trace."

"How'd they come to be looking in the wrong place?" Luke asked.

Von Albrecht smoothed his hair. "It was my mistake. My calculations did not account for the ingenuity of the ancient Egyptians. It seems they not only found the Concentrator, they harnessed and manipulated its energy. They turned the Nile into a conduit, sending power up and down the length of their empire. The pyramids were their power plants, a secret they guarded jealously from their enemies, so we lost all record of it. The Egyptians, in a sense, rewired the telluric currents across this whole region, and that's why I thought the Concentrator would be on the Giza Plateau. But that's only where they sent the energy. The source is upriver, in the Valley of the Kings. We don't know exactly where, but it's there."

"And the G.E.T. doesn't know?" Betty said.

"We have kept that information from them," Nathifa said.

"Then we can do this." Eleanor felt more hopeful than she had since they had landed here. "We can stop it."

"You are certain you can shut it down?" von Albrecht asked.

"Yes. I've done it twice now."

"Then we should go soon," Nathifa said. "I heard the G.E.T. saying Watkins is on his way here."

"He is?" Finn said. He turned to the rest of them.

"If he has my dad and Julian with him, maybe we can rescue them!"

"Slow down, there, kid," Luke said. "We're not staging some jailbreak—"

"What? But—"

"We haven't forgotten about them," Eleanor's mom said. "Believe me. But we have to wait until the time is right. I know it's hard—"

"Do you?" Finn said. "You keep saying that, but I don't think you do."

"They're right about one thing, Finn," Betty said. "It isn't the right time. We don't know for sure if Watkins even has your dad with him. And even if we do rescue them, it's only going to serve to let them know we're here. Either way, we need to make a plan."

Finn brought his hands inward and folded his arms.

Eleanor's mom turned back to Nathifa. "So how do we get to the Valley of the Kings?"

"By boat," she said. "That will be the fastest way. We should leave tonight."

CHAPTER
19

THE SLUGGISH NILE RIVER LOITERED ALONG ITS REEDY banks, only three hundred feet or so across, the moon's reflection in it quivering and shy, the black water flecked with the city's lights. As Eleanor and the others had made the journey toward it through the city, Nathifa had told them how, before the Freeze, the river had been wide and deep enough for cruise ships to ply tourists up and down its length. Now, glaciers to the south in the high African mountains held on tightly to the water that once flowed freely.

After parking the van, Nathifa and von Albrecht led their party to a small dock where a rented boat waited for them. The craft was a pontoon style very similar to Amaru's, which reminded Eleanor of his smiling face at the helm, but also of the blood pouring from his chest. The suddenness of that memory seized her breath and caused her to gasp silently. As she took a seat on this boat that was not Amaru's, but seemed somehow haunted by him, she wondered how—or if—she would ever escape his ghost. She could not even say if she truly wanted to.

"How long will it take us to get there?" Luke asked. He carried a few duffel bags full of equipment they'd brought from the warehouse.

"It will take us twenty hours to reach Luxor," Nathifa said. "From there, the Valley of the Kings is only a few miles away."

"Twenty hours?" Betty said. "I suppose we'd better get comfortable."

"What about the G.E.T.?" Eleanor's mom asked. "Will they be looking for you?"

Nathifa scoffed. "They will be glad I'm not there looking over their shoulders. I did leave a message that I am ill. Trust me, no one will give me a second thought."

Finn sat down next to Eleanor and mumbled, "I wish we could at least wait to see if Watkins has my dad and Julian with him before we go."

"I know," Eleanor said. "We'll find out when we get back."

His eyes were red when he looked at her. "I know *you* mean that." But then he looked at Eleanor's mom and Luke and Betty. "But I don't know if they do. What if they want to just leave them behind again?"

Eleanor wished she could promise him they wouldn't do that, but she also didn't want to break that promise later, so she stayed silent.

Von Albrecht and Nathifa stowed the duffel bags and packs in a compartment at the bow, and then Nathifa pulled the boat away from the pier. The rotors gurgled in the water behind them, and once they were out in the middle of the river, Nathifa pushed the throttle and they picked up speed.

It was a bit strange traveling this way at night, like being on an aquatic treadmill; the boat had a spotlight aimed ahead of them, but Eleanor couldn't tell if the motion of the brown water through its light was the current moving past them, the forward movement of the boat, or both. The city along the banks gave the only clear sign that they were actually plowing south up the river.

Von Albrecht kept watch from the prow for any obstacles in the water, and Eleanor's mom joined him. They started talking about the Concentrator and its energy signatures, and the conversation quickly reached a level of technicality that drove Eleanor away. She turned to Finn, but he had withdrawn to the back of the boat, watching the water, while Luke had already lain down on one of the bench seats with folded arms and fallen asleep. So Eleanor went to sit near Nathifa.

The woman stared ahead, the wind buffeting her head scarf where it draped loose about her neck, and Eleanor couldn't tell if her expression was grim or simply resolute. Neither was Eleanor sure if she should fully trust Nathifa or von Albrecht. It seemed this conspiracy had the power to make good people do bad things, and somehow make bad things seem good. It turned people against each other who might otherwise be allies.

"Why are you helping us?" Eleanor asked her, trying to speak loudly enough to be heard over the motor but quietly enough the others couldn't hear.

Nathifa paused a moment, looked at Eleanor, and said, "The first reason is simply that I hate the G.E.T. digging around in our historical heritage, and I want them gone. I don't know why the UN has given them such power."

"Do you know about the Preservation Protocol?" Eleanor asked.

"I've heard of it. Just rumors."

"It's real," Eleanor said.

Nathifa blinked and turned her gaze to the flowing water. "That is . . . unsettling."

"You said first reason," Eleanor said. "Is there a second?"

"The second is that I agree with Dr. von Albrecht. He knew those *things* should not be used. Now we know they must be stopped. So I do this for my family. My parents and my sisters. My . . . friends."

Amaru did what he did for his family, too, though that motivation led him to make a very different choice. The more Eleanor thought about this whole conflict, the more complicated it seemed, and the less willing she became to judge anyone for how they responded to it.

"What about you?" Nathifa asked. "How old are you?"

"Twelve," Eleanor said.

"Twelve," Nathifa said. "And why is a twelve-year-old doing this?"

It was a harder question to answer than it seemed. Jenna and Claire, Eleanor's friends back home, certainly wouldn't have come this far. They wouldn't have stowed away on Luke's plane in the first place. The truth was that Eleanor had made her choices without stopping to think too hard about them. She had simply acted in the moment, doing what she thought was right. The G.E.T. had to be stopped not because they were evil, but because Eleanor knew their chosen course of action to be wrong: the Preservation Protocol, choosing who would survive and who would freeze, keeping secrets from the world for its own good. Everyone deserved to make their own choices, not to have those choices made for them.

"I want to save everybody," Eleanor finally said.

Nathifa nodded.

"You mentioned your parents and sisters," Eleanor said. "I guess you're not married?"

"No," Nathifa said, her demeanor becoming sad and distant. "In my country, it is forbidden to marry the person I want to marry. So I will remain unmarried until it is allowed. My parents find this very distressing."

"Who do you want to marry?" Eleanor asked.

Nathifa shook her head. "I should not say."

Though curious, Eleanor let the question go.

They traveled upriver for several hours, through a darkened countryside of farms and fields, in the pockets of which glowed periodic cities. Occasionally, towering shadows hulked along the banks. Nathifa said they were old abandoned ships, cargo vessels and cruise liners that could no longer navigate the shrunken river and had been left to rust.

As the night deepened, Eleanor grew tired and lay down on one of the bench seats. Luke woke up just as her eyes were about to close, and he took a turn keeping a lookout, while von Albrecht took the ship's wheel from Nathifa. Eleanor then slept, and when she next woke, Nathifa was back at the helm, while von Albrecht dozed nearby, and the sky had just barely crossed the border between night and day.

A few hours later, they stopped for fuel in a small town, but they did not leave the boat and were soon back on their way. As they traveled up the river, Finn grew even more sullen, and every so often he would turn around and stand at the back of the boat, staring down at the wake they'd left behind them. Eleanor's mom and Betty tried to console him, and even Luke made an attempt, but Finn rebuffed and ignored them. But then von Albrecht approached him. Eleanor sat close enough to hear what he said.

"My father was an architect." Von Albrecht smoothed his hair back. "He was very famous. He left his mark. Even though he died when I was but a little older than you are, I never felt that he was gone. Everywhere I looked, I saw his life's work, his buildings, and I heard an echo of his voice in my head. I still do. His monuments ask me what I have done. What mark have I left?"

Finn turned away from the water and looked at von Albrecht. "How do you answer them?"

"I have always looked away from them in shame," von Albrecht said. "I have left no mark. I have been mocked my whole career. No one has given me any respect, until quite recently. You know this, I am sure."

Finn nodded.

"But this," von Albrecht said. "What I am doing right now, here on this boat? This is important. More than anything I have done. After this, I will no longer look away in shame."

Finn's posture had slackened, just a bit, as though someone had loosened his strings.

"You will see your father again," von Albrecht said. "When you do, he will ask you what you have done since he last saw you, because that is what fathers do. I wonder, what will you say?" Von Albrecht then clasped his hands behind his back and walked back up to the front of the boat.

Finn stood there, alone, staring at his feet for a minute or two. Then he cast one more glance down the river before showing the water his back, and came to sit next to Eleanor. "So let's get this done," he said.

"We will," she said.

"You know what's weird?"

"What?"

"I'm mad at Julian. I have been this whole time."

"Why?"

"Because he's there with my dad and I'm not."

"I don't think that's so weird."

"Everyone says I'm just like my dad. But Julian is the one he's proud of."

"He is proud of you," Eleanor said. "I've seen it."

"He *will* be," Finn said.

Whereas the others, including Eleanor, had been trying to reassure Finn, Von Albrecht had simply challenged him. Eleanor had to admit that it had worked.

The day passed mile by mile, and the river flowed into monotony, the villages and farms all appearing similar to one another by the afternoon. Most towns had their own bridges, and as the boat crossed under them, sharp-winged birds dove from their nests in the girders and sliced the air around them, chirping and scolding. Stilted ibises patrolled the shore, stabbing the water with their long beaks, and Eleanor even glimpsed an enormous Nile crocodile sunning itself on the muddy shore, indifferent to the passage of their boat.

"There aren't many of them left," Nathifa said. "It's getting too cold."

"He looks like he's keeping plenty warm," Luke said.

"No," Nathifa said. "It's too cold for the eggs. They incubate in the sand, and almost none of them hatch now. But the mothers keep laying them and guarding the nests long after their young should have been born. It's very sad."

"They guard their nests?" Betty said. "I've never thought of crocodiles as especially maternal."

"Oh, yes," Nathifa said. "A mother will watch the nest for three months and then protect her young for two years."

Eleanor agreed with Nathifa. It was very sad. But this was happening all over the world, and there were hundreds and maybe even thousands of species that were already gone. Extinct. With thousands and thousands more in danger. In all the worry over human life, sometimes Eleanor forgot about the rest of the earth's inhabitants. They suffered too. And when they were gone, no one would remember.

A few hours later, the evening sun reached that point where it lustered the world; the water, the reeds along the bank, people's eyes and skin, all of it seemed to glow from within. They reached the city of Luxor, and from the river Eleanor glimpsed the columns and walls of its ancient temples rising up above a fringe of palm trees. Nathifa guided the boat to a dock on the opposite shore from the ruins, and they unloaded the packs and duffel bags from the forward compartment.

"How will we get to the Valley of the Kings?" Eleanor's mom asked.

"Taxi," Nathifa said. "Then camel."

"Seriously?" Finn asked.

"It is a priceless archaeological site," von Albrecht said. "The government closed it to tourism several years ago. Motor vehicles are restricted. It's three miles into the Theban hills, and I'd like to get there before dark. So, yes, camels."

They were unable to find a van large enough to take them all and ended up in two cars. Eleanor searched for but saw no evidence of G.E.T. presence here, at which she felt relief, as the taxis drove them through town, then out of it into farming country and across a wide irrigation canal. They then turned onto a road that followed the waterway for a mile or so north before another turn onto a winding road. As they proceeded along it, toward a range of hills, they passed another temple on the left.

"That is the mortuary temple of Seti the First," Nathifa said.

"What's a mortuary temple?" Finn asked.

"A memorial to commemorate the reign of a ruler," she said.

"So it's not where they turned them into mummies?"

he asked. "Where they removed their brains and internal organs and everything?"

She smiled. "No, it's not."

Not far beyond the temple, they arrived at a gated road with a small building adjacent to it. Several camels roamed a paddock nearby, grunting and grazing. The taxis stopped to let them out in front of the gate, and Nathifa approached the building as a guard wearing a kind of police uniform emerged to greet her. They spoke in Arabic, and she showed him her badge, gesturing toward the rest of them as they waited. The guard finally nodded and walked around toward the paddock as Nathifa returned.

"He'll saddle the camels for us," she said. "We should make it before dark."

"What did you tell him?" Eleanor's mom asked.

"You are archaeologists from the United States," she said. "I'm here to show you the tombs. My badge said the rest."

The sun was flirting with the horizon by the time the guard brought their animals around, and it was getting quite cold. Eleanor had never been near a camel before and hadn't realized how large they were, well over six feet tall at the shoulder. Everything about them seemed big: their yellow teeth, their wide hooves, their makeup-commercial eyelashes that had to be three inches long. They also smelled terrible, like acrid urine, and manure, and some other animal odor she couldn't identify. The guard set about strapping their packs and duffels to the animals' saddles.

"You'll need to ride two to a camel," Nathifa said.

"Are they safe?" Eleanor's mom said, standing some distance from them.

"Oh, perfectly safe," von Albrecht said. "Just don't insult them. Camels hold grudges."

The guard used a spoken command to get the animals to fold their long legs and kneel, and then divided the riders up according to size. Eleanor ended up with Luke, and Finn ended up with von Albrecht. Betty rode with Eleanor's mom, and Nathifa took a camel to herself. Eleanor slipped her foot into the stirrup and climbed onto the saddle, while Luke did the same behind her.

"Just a warning: lean backward as they stand," Nathifa said.

Eleanor did, and was glad for it, because the camel stood up one end at a time and nearly toppled her to the ground. Once up, she marveled at the height of her saddle, the ground below seeming very far away.

The guard then roped the animals all together in a single column, with Nathifa at the head, and they set off.

"They know the way," Nathifa said. "Just settle back and enjoy the ride."

"That god-awful smell makes it a bit difficult," Luke said.

Eleanor had to agree with that, but she enjoyed the ride nevertheless. Some distance past the guard station, they entered a shallow canyon and lost the sun. The road carried them through the cold and shadowy recesses of washes and gullies, winding deeper and deeper into the hills. In the failing light, the geology around Eleanor had a pale, rocky, almost lunar quality, far enough from the waters of the Nile to remain barren and desolate. She felt grateful the camels knew the route, because she would have quickly become lost.

After they had ridden for a bit, they arrived at a tattered, haunted encampment. Large canvas tents stood in various states of disrepair, some with holes and torn pieces fluttering in the breeze, some fallen down around their broken metal skeletons. Without a command or warning, the camels knelt down, and once again Eleanor nearly hit the sand below her headfirst. After the riders had all dismounted and unstrapped their gear, the camels stood and returned the way they had come.

"They really do know the way, don't they?" Betty said.

"Even if they are out of practice," von Albrecht said, glancing about. "Look at the state of things. When was the last time anyone was here?"

"It has been several months," Nathifa said. "No funding."

"What is this place?" Eleanor asked.

"A camp for archaeologists and other researchers," Nathifa said. "We'll take one of these tents for the night, and then begin work tomorrow. Come."

She led them to one of the better-looking tents and untied the flaps over the doorway. Inside, by flashlight, they found a dozen cots, a couple of folding tables and chairs, and a rug on the ground barely visible through a layer of sand that had apparently blown in. Everyone claimed a cot and lay down. Eleanor's emitted a bleating sound as the synthetic fabric stretched beneath her. Luke's actually buckled, crashing him to the ground, and he had to choose a new one. Von Albrecht pulled some thermal blankets out of the duffel bags and handed them around.

"Do you sense anything?" her mom asked.

"No," Eleanor said. "We must not be close enough yet."

She lay on her back, pulled the blanket up to her chin, and stared up at the ceiling of the tent. A hole to the right of just above her head held a swatch of stars.

Eleanor stared through the opening a few moments and then closed her eyes. Tomorrow, they would begin the hunt among the pharaohs' tombs for the Concentrator. Thought she couldn't feel it yet, she knew it was out there, somewhere close by.

CHAPTER
20

ELEANOR WOKE TO THE SOUND OF ZIPPERS AND OPENED her eyes. Her mom, von Albrecht, and Nathifa were reaching into the packs and duffels and laying out the instruments and equipment on the tables. There was a laptop too, but when Finn reached for it, Nathifa waved at his hand.

"That's a G.E.T. laptop," she said. "We shouldn't use it. I probably should not have brought it with us, but I wasn't thinking."

"Is it connected to their network?" Finn asked.

Eleanor wondered why he would ask that.

"Not at the moment," Nathifa said. "Let's keep it that way, okay?"

Eleanor rose from her cot and walked up to stand beside her mom, stretching her arms up above her head. "What's all this for?" she asked.

A moment passed before her mom looked up. "To get us a bit closer to the Concentrator, so you can pinpoint its location."

Eleanor recognized one of the devices as a telluric scanner, a piece of equipment she'd seen up in the Arctic.

"How is it you can sense them?" von Albrecht asked.

Eleanor looked at her mom. "We don't know."

"Is it safe for you?" Nathifa asked. "This . . . connection?"

Eleanor nodded. "Sure. I've done it—"

"We don't know if it's safe," her mom said. "We don't know what it is or how it works. Truthfully, I'm very uncomfortable with it."

"But we've talked about this before," Eleanor said, more to her mom than to Nathifa. "We don't have any other options. Do we?"

Her mom said nothing.

"*Do* we?"

Still her mom didn't answer, and Eleanor realized the matter would probably never be settled. Her mom would never accept this about her, and Eleanor discovered she was more okay with that than she would have thought.

Nathifa looked back and forth between them, then turned away. "Right, so . . . I think we're ready to begin scanning."

Eleanor's mom brushed her hands together. "Good. Let's do it."

She, von Albrecht, and Nathifa each picked up a scanner and walked out of the tent, where Finn, Luke, and Betty were waiting. The valley reached away from them toward a high, pyramid-shaped mountain peak, the morning sunlight striking its eastern face. The canyon walls rose up on either side of them, gradually sloping in some places, leaping vertically in others.

They proceeded as a group along the valley floor, down a wide path with branching side trails that stretched toward shadowy doorways set right into the rock.

"Each of those is a tomb," Nathifa said. "I think it's perhaps best to begin scanning here. It's likely the ancient Egyptians would have discovered the Concentrator while digging out one of these."

"How many are there?" Finn asked.

"Sixty-three that we know of. There are likely still more waiting to be discovered, but considering everything that's happening now, I don't know that we'll ever find them. Just think—if the Freeze continues, there will be dozens of tombs, a record of an entire civilization, floating though space on a dead, frozen rock."

"Not if we can help it," said Eleanor.

They passed many of the tombs, but the telluric scanners they carried gave no indication of where the Concentrator might be.

"How big are the tombs?" Finn asked.

"Some have but one chamber," Nathifa said. "Others have many. The one known as KV5 has one hundred twenty rooms. It was built for the sons of Ramses the Second."

"Incredible," Eleanor's mom said.

"Yeah, but what about the Great Pyramid?" Luke asked. "For a tomb, it's even—"

"The pyramids are not *tombs*," von Albrecht said. "They never were. They were used to gather and store the earth's telluric currents concentrated here."

Luke held up his hands. "My mistake, doc."

"Speaking of currents," Betty said, "are you getting any Concentrator vibes, Eleanor?"

She shook her head, reminding herself that it had taken time, and some dangerous underwater exploration, to find the Concentrator in Peru. Locating each one had proven a unique challenge; it was clear that whoever put them here didn't want them to be easily discovered. Eleanor hadn't necessarily expected it to be easy here in Egypt either. But at least she was fairly certain no diving equipment would be needed.

They passed tomb after tomb, dozens of their rectangular entrances, and Eleanor felt nothing. The telluric scanners still hadn't picked up any traces of current, either. When they reached the foot of the pyramid-mountain at the end of the valley, it appeared they had run out of tombs.

"What now?" Finn asked.

"There is one more tomb," Nathifa said. "Some say it is the oldest tomb in the valley. It is very odd."

"Sounds like we should've started with that one," Luke said.

Nathifa narrowed her eyes at him. "It is also the farthest from the camp, and we would have passed the others anyway. It is called KV39. It's up there." She pointed up the mountain, into the nook at the head of a wide ravine.

"What makes it odd?" Finn asked.

"You'll see."

So they climbed. The path they took was rocky and narrow, winding up and up. When Eleanor looked back down behind them, she could see the valley below, with its network of tombs, and it made sense to her that, like the Inca, the pharaohs would have been drawn to this place. The Concentrators radiated a power strong enough to resurrect Amarok and his tribe, after all. And it sounded like the Egyptians had an even deeper connection with its power.

That was when Eleanor felt it. A gentle jolt through the soles of her shoes. The hum. They were getting close, and Luke was right. They should have started with the old, odd KV39.

When they reached it, the recessed opening appeared far less grand than the entrances below it, almost more of a cave. The tomb was isolated up here as well, far from the others that huddled so tightly together on the valley floor.

To reach the entrance, they had to shimmy down a rocky slope into a gully. The tomb's narrow opening reminded Eleanor of the cave she'd entered under the waters of Lake Titicaca, except that something about this place felt more sinister. But the hum had only grown stronger as they had neared it. Eleanor opened her mouth to tell everyone, then shut it, unwilling to speak.

But this is what you're here to do, she told herself. Yet she couldn't bring herself to say anything, not yet.

"Not very inviting, is it?" Luke said.

"Top marks for understatement, Fournier," Betty said.

"I just don't want to get cursed," Luke said.

"Is there a mummy in there?" Finn asked.

Nathifa chuckled. "No, it's empty. Archaeologists have long assumed it was looted thousands of years ago, and they don't even know who was buried here. They once believed it was Amenhotep the First, but many now doubt that."

"Whoever it was," Eleanor's mom said, looking back down the ravine, "they liked their privacy."

"I am getting some mild telluric signatures," von Albrecht said, frowning down at his device. "Eleanor, do you sense anything?"

Eleanor opened her mouth again to speak, but nothing came out. Once more, something in her simply refused to say yes, as though a fail-safe had been tripped, and now she knew what it was.

The tomb before them led to the Concentrator—Eleanor had no doubts about that. What she doubted were the people around her, specifically Nathifa and von Albrecht. She had been tricked into leading Amaru to the Concentrator in Peru, and that had resulted in his death and the capture of Dr. Powers and Julian. She wasn't about to make that same mistake again. She needed time to think.

"Nuh—" She coughed. "No, nothing."

"We should investigate it, nevertheless," von Albrecht said.

No one seemed to want to be the first to enter KV39. It was Nathifa who finally pulled out a flashlight and led the way, but her steps were slow and tentative. Von Albrecht followed her, and then Luke. Eleanor went next, with her mom behind her, and then Finn and Betty pushed forward into the darkness.

Just inside the entrance, they found a steep, crumbling stairway that descended through a chamber. The walls and ceiling were rough-hewn and unadorned, not at all how Eleanor imagined an Egyptian pharaoh's tomb would appear. There were also several disconcerting cracks that suggested to Eleanor that the whole place could collapse at any time.

They descended the staircase, their breathing and movement filling the chamber, and when they spoke, it was in whispers for fear of disturbing . . . something.

At the bottom of the steps, they passed through a narrow portal, and on the other side of that entered another downward-sloping chamber. But this one had no stairway, only a decrepit wooden ladder Eleanor would not have trusted for two rungs.

"Be careful," Nathifa said. "One at a time."

She went first. The ladder creaked and quivered but somehow held. Each of them followed after her in turn, and at the bottom they stood in a room whose walls were the color of chalk and much smoother than those they'd passed. Ahead of them, another stairway dropped away into the darkness. To the left, there were two passages, one that led straight forward, and another that doubled back in the direction of the entrance.

"Which way do we go?" Eleanor's mom asked.

Eleanor knew. The hum came from the stairway in front of them. But she said nothing, and von Albrecht checked his telluric scanner.

"That way," he said, and pointed in the same direction Eleanor had silently identified.

This stairway was much narrower and steeper, with deeper steps, and Eleanor used her hands to climb down backward. They were now deep underground, and Eleanor found her heart rate rising. Whether that was from claustrophobia, though, or her nerves about misleading her friends, she couldn't tell.

The chamber at the bottom was perhaps twenty feet long and twelve feet wide, with a ceiling several feet above Luke's head. But it was a dead end.

Eleanor was confused. The hum was definitely louder down here.

"You sure you're reading that thing right, doc?" Luke asked.

Von Albrecht checked the telluric scanner again and then said, "Dr. Perry, will you please confirm?"

"Of course." Eleanor's mom took her own scanner, made some adjustments to its dials, studied it, and then compared it with von Albrecht's. "Yes, this is where the signal leads."

"What about you, kid?" Luke said. "You still coming up empty?"

Eleanor could only bring herself to nod. She would find a time and place to tell him the truth when they got back to the camp.

"You mean we came here for nothing?" Finn said. "My dad might be back in Cairo right now!"

"No, not for nothing," Eleanor's mom said. "It's here. We're just missing something."

"Perhaps we should explore the rest of the tomb," Nathifa said. "To be certain."

They all agreed with that and climbed back up the staircase. For safety's sake it was decided that only von Albrecht and Nathifa would go, while the rest of them waited in the central chamber above. Eleanor didn't mind. She already knew the Concentrator would not be found elsewhere, and as a pharaoh's tomb, KV39 had disappointed her. There were no paintings of the Egyptian gods, no hieroglyphics, no artifacts, no golden sarcophagi. When von Albrecht and Nathifa returned from their expedition, they reported that both passages, though much longer, had also ended in dead-end chambers.

"I don't understand," von Albrecht said. "The nexus is here. It must be."

"Unless you got your map wrong again," Luke said.

Von Albrecht smoothed his hair back. "I did *not* get it wrong."

"Perhaps we should return to the camp," Eleanor's mom said. "Run another check on the data. Maybe we're missing something."

Everyone agreed, so they climbed out of the tomb and then made their way down the pyramid-mountain. Eleanor glanced back at the opening, still unsure if she had made the right call in withholding what she knew. She needed to talk to someone about it. The one person she knew she could trust.

Back in the tent, Eleanor's mom, von Albrecht, and Nathifa pored over his calculations and conclusions, double-checking and triple-checking at every step. While they were occupied with that, Eleanor pulled Luke outside and told him that she had actually sensed the Concentrator back at the tomb.

"Why didn't you say anything?" he asked.

"I just . . ." She was still figuring that out for herself. "Everyone is trying to save something, right? Amaru wanted to save his family. Nathifa wants to save her Egyptian history. Von Albrecht wants to save his reputation." She moved on to even harder thoughts. "Even Finn just wants to save his dad now. I don't know . . . how to trust them."

"Ah." He closed his eyes. "What about your mom?"

Eleanor shook her head. "She has made it very clear she doesn't even want me doing this. She wants me to stop."

"Well." Luke looked down at the ground and moved some dirt around with his boot. "I think she'd want to know."

"I am not telling her. That's final."

Luke looked at her for a long moment. "She'll be furious with us both. But I'll let this be your call."

"I can do it without her, or the others. But I'd love your help."

"Best option is tonight, when they've gone to sleep." He bent his head to make eye contact with her. "How're you holding up? With Amaru and everything. You okay?"

Eleanor almost pulled out her prefabricated, flat response—*I'm fine*—but decided against it. "It's hard," she said. "I still see him when I close my eyes. It feels like everything changed in Peru. Amaru died, and we left Julian and Dr. Powers behind."

"It is hard," he said. "There's no rule book for this kind of thing. Hard things have to be done. Hard decisions have to be made. And I don't think it's going to get any easier."

Eleanor hoped he was wrong, but she also knew it to be a false and desperate hope. If she let herself believe she wouldn't have to make hard decisions, that meant she might not be ready for them when they came.

"But we'll get it done," Luke added.

"Yes," she said. "We'll get it done."

S everal hours later, Eleanor's mom declared von Albrecht's data valid and reliable, his conclusions sound. The ley line nexus was in or near the Valley of the Kings, and since Eleanor hadn't corroborated the signal they had encountered in KV39, it was determined to have been an anomaly, and they planned to do some further exploration the next day.

"There is the West Valley," Nathifa said. "It has only five tombs, but it will be worth exploring with the scanners."

If Eleanor had told Nathifa the truth about what she

had sensed, it might have changed that plan. A pang of guilt struck her, and she wondered how she would tell them the next day what she had done. Her mom would be furious, of course. Finn and Betty might feel a little betrayed, and no doubt Nathifa and Von Albrecht would be very disappointed. Eleanor would just have to deal with all that when the time came. Assuming she was successful in the first place.

It was after midnight when she and Luke finally felt satisfied that Nathifa and von Albrecht and the others were asleep, and outside the tent, the valley was cold and nearly featureless in the darkness. They used flashlights to hurry back through the valley, past the dozens of tombs Eleanor now tried unsuccessfully to ignore, convinced at times that if she looked, there would be eyes in the doorways looking back.

The mountain path was a bit more difficult to navigate at night, even with the flashlights, but they picked their way up the ravine and before long stood once more above the opening to KV39.

"You expecting me to go first?" Luke asked.

Eleanor pushed past him and climbed down into the draw. "Why would I expect that?"

Luke skidded down behind her and they entered the tomb, which it turned out did not look very different than it had earlier in the day. Dark was dark.

They descended the stairs, and then the ladder, and then the second set of stairs, until they stood once again in the bottom dead-end chamber. The hum was still there, confirming to Eleanor that they were getting closer. The room must hold some secret.

"What now?" Luke asked.

"We should check for a hidden door or something," Eleanor said. So the two of them crept along, scanning, scraping, rubbing. Eleanor got so close to the wall that the dust on it made her sneeze.

Finally Luke whispered, "Over here."

Down low, on his hands and knees, he showed her a seam in the wall—the outline of what appeared to be a small door, three feet wide and two feet high.

"Does it open?" Eleanor asked.

Luke pushed hard against it. "Not easily. Hang on." He rolled onto his back with his feet pointed at the wall, and then he kicked straight against it. With the impact, more dust broke free from the walls and the ceiling, while a spiderweb of cracks appeared across the stone door.

"Keep trying," Eleanor said.

Luke kicked again, and then a third time. With the fourth, the wall shattered inward, broken to pieces, and Eleanor realized it wasn't stone, but a couple of inches of some kind of cement or hard plaster that had simply been smoothed to look like the rest of the wall.

Luke shone his flashlight through the new opening. "Another tunnel. A long one."

"Only one way to go, then," Eleanor said. "I'm having déjà vu."

"Let's just get this over with," Luke said. "And I will go first, whether you expect me to or not." With that, he got down on his belly and shimmied through the little doorway.

Then Eleanor got down and followed. The feeling of claustrophobia that rushed through her wasn't quite as bad as it had been in the underwater cave. On the other side, she climbed to her feet and found herself in a narrow passageway.

"Now, that's more like it," Luke said

Eleanor's earlier disappointment turned to awe. Paintings and hieroglyphics covered the walls in brightly colored, carved relief. A procession of animal-headed Egyptian gods held court down the length of the corridor, surrounded by other figures, vanishing beyond the limits of their flashlights' reach. Some of them carried what Eleanor guessed to be lightning bolts in reed baskets and boats, and they surrounded the image of a tree, which she assumed represented the Concentrator.

"Oh my God," Eleanor said.

"You mean *gods*, don't you?" Luke said.

"I mean this is incredible," she said. "Could we be the first people in thousands of years to see this?"

Eleanor found that thought almost frightening in how small it made her feel. In the years between the sealing of that wall and Luke's breaking of it, the Egyptian empire had long since fallen, and dozens of nations had risen and fallen since. In the vastness of time and space, in the cavalcade of human communities rising and vanishing, life's evolutions and extinctions, it was hard to believe that any of it mattered. Von Albrecht was trying to leave his mark, like his father, but the problem with marks was that they eventually faded.

But Eleanor wasn't doing this to leave a mark. Hardly anyone would ever know what she had done, anyway. She was doing this simply to survive.

"Let's go," she said. "The Concentrator is this way."

⟶ CHAPTER ⟶
21

THE CORRIDOR STRETCHED ON FOR SEVERAL YARDS AND then stepped down another stairway. In addition to the gods, whose names Eleanor didn't know but whose jackal, ibis, and alligator heads looked familiar, the walls bore depictions of Egyptian life. Rows of identical workers harvested wheat and fished the Nile with nets from shallow boats, charged into battle riding chariots, and held court before a figure on a throne. Floor-to-ceiling panels of hieroglyphics gave Eleanor the impression of walking through a book, or a papyrus scroll.

The passage continued a regular descent, hallways

followed by stairways, followed by hallways, followed by stairways.

"We must be under the mountain by now," Eleanor said.

"You notice it kind of looks like a pyramid?" Luke asked.

"Yes," Eleanor said.

"Kind of a coincidence," Luke said. "Maybe they built the pyramids at Giza as a kind of tribute to the mountain where the energy came from."

"Maybe," Eleanor said.

"If you think about it, it is pretty incredible, though. That they were able to use the Concentrator's energy. Maybe that explains how their empire lasted for so long."

"Maybe," Eleanor said again. It seemed the Egyptians had basically done what Watkins hoped to do. They had harnessed the energy of the Concentrator. But then, they didn't have to worry about a rogue world, or the whole earth turning into an ice cube. And they weren't sacrificing the rest of the planet to ensure their survival.

Eventually, the corridor bottomed out and they reached a doorway. Through that they entered into an improbably cavernous chamber, with a ceiling more than fifty feet high, supported by thick columns in regular formation, and distant walls far outside their sphere of light. Even their voices seemed to get a bit lost in there. Every surface was decorated with the same kinds of artwork and writings. Eleanor wondered how long this would have taken to create, and what it all meant—whether any of it might be the instruction guide for how to run the ancient Egyptian power grid. The humming was more forceful here, too, and coming from a direction up ahead of them.

"This way," Eleanor said.

They set out across the chamber, and before long they lost sight of the doorway through which they'd come and were surrounded on all sides by retreating columns.

"Keep track of the exit," Luke said. "It would be easy to get turned around in here. Every direction looks the same."

Eleanor wondered how big the chamber actually was, and whether its size and features were a part of how the Egyptians harnessed the Concentrator. When she posed this idea to Luke, he stopped and took another slow glance around them.

"You know, it almost has the feel of a capacitor network, doesn't it?" he said.

"Uh, sure?" Eleanor said.

"No, it does," he said. "For storing power and stabilizing output. A giant capacitor network, or maybe an array."

Eleanor wrinkled her brow. "That just went completely over my head."

"Capacitor is like a battery, only it doesn't store energy for a long period of time. A capacitor charges and discharges fast. Most electronics use capacitors, to make sure things run smoothly. Usually, they're small. This is—"

Something moved off in the distance. The sound of a foot dragging along the stone floor. Or at least, that was what Eleanor imagined, but when they both shone their flashlights in that direction, they saw nothing.

"Rats?" Eleanor asked. "I'm sure they're down here. Right?"

"Big rat," Luke said.

Eleanor turned back toward the direction of the Concentrator's hum. "Let's just keep going."

As they moved forward, the hum grew louder, and louder, until Eleanor knew it must be very near. A hundred yards on, an open space appeared in the columns, and the chamber floor reached the edge of what seemed to be a large chasm. When they got closer, Eleanor realized it wasn't a chasm but a kind of broad, circular amphitheater.

Down at the base of its terraced steps, at its center, stood the Concentrator.

The device very closely resembled the other two Eleanor had seen, with a black trunk rising up to its twisted, angular branches, and the structure defied perception in the same perplexing manner that the others had. Eleanor stood at the top of the amphitheater for a moment and then began the short descent to it. Luke followed, and when they reached the bottom, he picked something up off the ground.

"What's that?" Eleanor asked.

"A sword." He held it out to show her. It had a curious, almost question mark shape, its tarnished blade straight near the hilt, then curved like a sickle. "There's more of them," he said, pointing at the ground, and he was right. There were a dozen or so of the swords strewn about.

"Well, that's a bit concerning," Eleanor said.

"Makes sense to me," Luke said. "They would have wanted to guard this thing, right?"

"I don't mean that," she said. "I'm wondering why the guards would have just abandoned their weapons here. Like they left in a hurry or something."

"Never held an actual sword before," Luke said, testing its weight, swinging it in casual arcs.

Eleanor turned her attention back to the Concentrator

and quickly found its control console. "Let's do what we came to do," she said.

"Be careful, kid," Luke said.

Eleanor nodded and placed herself in front of the console. Then she laid her hand against it, awaiting the familiar sensation of something inside reaching back, touching her hand, her skin, picking at her nerves. What she felt instead was the aggressive force of something seizing her by the arm, almost painfully, and it didn't let go. She gasped.

"What is it?" Luke said.

"Nothing. It's under control."

But it wasn't. Eleanor felt locked in a battle with the Concentrator, and she knew that if she gave even a fraction of ground, the thing would break her. This one seemed . . . angry. If that was possible. She couldn't let it into her mind. But if she didn't, she wouldn't be able to establish the connection she needed to shut it down.

"What in—?" Luke shouted.

Eleanor tore her eyes from the control panel and looked up. At the top of the amphitheater, several impossibly narrow figures shambled down toward them, with raisin-like faces gaunt enough to reveal the contours of their skulls, their eye sockets empty pits beneath their ragged, deteriorating headdresses. Scaled armor covered their chests, while their sinewy arms showed through wrappings of cotton.

Mummies?

"I guess those guards never left!" Luke said.

The Concentrator threw itself against the gate of Eleanor's mind, seizing upon the moment of her distraction. She fought it back, her arm shaking, her hand going white against the console. She had to ignore what was going on around her, even though there were mummies descending upon them from all sides of the amphitheater now.

"Did . . . did the Concentrator do this?" Luke asked.

"It must have!" Eleanor shouted. "It . . . preserved them, like the one in Alaska."

"Not exactly how I pictured that Amarok guy," he said, glancing about nervously.

But this was different. These were mummies, which meant most of their brains and organs were gone. They were just animated shells.

When the first of them reached the bottom of the amphitheater, it extended its bony hands to grab for Luke, but he swung the sickle sword and cleaved its arms off. When that didn't stop its advance, he swung two-handed for the neck, and the mummy's head shot sideways, bounced to the ground, and rolled away. With that, its body slumped to the ground in a heap.

"Easy enough," he said. "I got this, kid! Do your

thing!" He charged another mummy. It took him a few more swings, and a few more severed limbs, before he'd hacked away enough pieces of the thing to stop it. "Kid! Shut it down! Hurry!"

Eleanor returned as much of her attention to the Concentrator as she could. She didn't know what made this one different from the others. Perhaps the Egyptian manipulation of its energy centuries before had somehow strengthened it, triggered its defenses. Or perhaps it was simply created that way. But she had to find a way to defeat it.

She tried relaxing, letting down her own guard just a bit, but each time she did, the awareness in the Concentrator rushed her, like something shoving her aside and grabbing the steering wheel of her mind, and she struggled to push it back.

The mummies kept coming, and Luke kept chopping them down around her. "Any time now, kid!"

Eleanor cursed herself. They had come all this way, and now it was up to her to do what no one else could. What good was her ability now? If she couldn't use it to stop this thing, then it had no purpose, and that meant she really was nothing but a freak.

She still didn't know what to make of the anger she felt burning within the Concentrator, if it could be called anger. Eleanor was attuned enough to the language of the Concentrator to know the awareness in there loathed her—or rather, loathed people. Humans. All of them, and especially the ones who had enslaved it thousands of years ago.

"Look out!" Luke shouted.

Eleanor glanced over her shoulder. A mummy had almost reached her, its claw hand but inches away, its face a rictus of mindless drive. Before she could react, Luke's blade came down, taking the arm with it, and then he went for the head and sent it flying.

"Remember the guy who talks to llamas, kid," he grunted, reminding Eleanor of their conversation in the cockpit of his plane. "You are what you are. You can do this."

The awareness in the Concentrator rammed her again, throwing her head back as her mind shook with the force of it, and her body stiffened. She wanted to retreat, to find some far corner of her thoughts and hide there until the invading consciousness had moved on. She had only her memories to use as a shield—her friends back home, her uncle Jack, the swell of purpose she'd felt when she'd found out her mother was lost and she had gone to find her, the quiet moments she'd shared with Finn. But these thoughts only kept the Concentrator's aggression at bay. She had to gather the strength to face this thing and beat it.

Like Luke had just said, she had to be what she was. But what was that? She was Eleanor, sweetie, Ell Bell, kid, a friend, a girl, a person—there was no way to hide any of that from the Concentrator's hate and aggression. But then it occurred to her that she must be something else, too. The something in her she didn't understand, the something that made her unique, that allowed her to connect with the Concentrator in a way no one else—except, perhaps, Watkins—could. She had to bring forward that part of her. She had to show the Concentrator what she was afraid to show everyone else.

A mummy's arm landed on Eleanor's foot, but she ignored it.

I am not a freak.

I am different.

I am who I am.

She closed her eyes and pushed up against the Concentrator's awareness with the thought, *I am like you.*

She felt its wall of resistance weaken, and in an act that terrified her, she let hers down by the same degree. *I am like you,* she repeated in her mind. *I am not one of them, I am like you.*

When she finally got to a point where she felt she could trust the awareness, she let it in, and it wriggled up her nerves to her mind with the desperation of something frightened and alone. And as she merged her thoughts with it, she realized why.

This Concentrator remembered.

The other two hadn't, at least not in a way Eleanor experienced, perhaps because they were devices of a lesser order, or perhaps because they had been treated differently by the humans who had found them and worshipped them.

The Egyptians had tortured this one. In their study of it they had burned it. They had stabbed it. They had dug up its roots, which they wrenched, and twisted, and broke, bending them to their will. And the Concentrator had felt all of it.

This was not just a machine. It was alive, in a way. A tree, with memories in its roots.

The pain it revealed to Eleanor nearly overcame her, and she found herself pitying this wretched thing, in spite of what it was doing to her world. But she indulged in that for only a moment and then did what she had come to do. She took hold of the Concentrator's battered roots, and carefully, ever so gently, she eased them into a position where they could do no more harm. And then she took the alien awareness, at peace for the first time in millennia, and brought it to her chest. Then quickly, before it knew what was happening, she killed it.

The Concentrator shut down, and the hum ceased, and the terrible silence that followed carved a hollow into her mind. Eleanor felt an even greater weakness than she had with the last, and collapsed to the ground just as Luke struck a final, heavy blow to a mummy, sending it sprawling.

"You okay?" he shouted, rushing over to her. "Kid, you okay?"

"I'm okay," Eleanor whispered. Dessicated mummy parts littered the ground around her. She wiped at her face and was surprised to find her hand wet with tears. "I . . . yeah. I'm fine."

"You don't look fine. Is it done?" Luke knelt beside her, his face smeared with dirt and sweat.

"Yes," Eleanor said.

"Then let's get out of here. This mummy killing ain't even fun anymore."

But Eleanor didn't know if she could walk. She could barely hold herself upright in a sitting position. "I don't think I can. . . ."

Luke sighed. "Okay, then." He reached his arms beneath her knees and around her back, cradling her, and then lifted her up with a grunt. Then he labored up the steps of the amphitheater to its ridge.

"Do you remember which way the exit is?" Luke asked. "I've gotten turned around."

"I think it's that way," Eleanor said, pointing in a direction that felt right to her.

"You sure?"

"I'm sure."

He nodded. "Well, you haven't been running around playing whack-a-mummy. Let's go for it."

Eleanor heard a sound to her right. She whipped her flashlight around as a mummy leered out of the darkness. "Run!"

Luke took off in the direction Eleanor hoped was right. The chamber seemed more endless on the way back, nothing but pillars, and Eleanor was beginning to wonder if she had been wrong. But Luke kept running, breathing hard, and then he was just trotting along, then he was only walking under the strain of her weight. But soon she saw the dark shadow of the doorway up ahead.

From there, it was a steep climb back up through the mountain, stairway after stairway. Luke would never be able to carry her up that.

"I think I can walk now."

"You . . . sure?" he said, panting.

"Let me try."

He set her down gently, and she tested the weight on her legs. They didn't give out from under her, and she took a few steps. Some of the weakness had faded.

"I can do it," she said, even though she wasn't sure.

"Okay." Luke looked relieved and led the way, setting their pace. Eleanor's legs wobbled before they'd made it very far, and her muscles wanted to give out before they'd reached the top. The dragging, shuffling sounds of the mummies followed after them, while the almond-shaped eyes of the painted Egyptian gods stared at them from the walls.

"Here it is," Luke finally said, out of breath and bent over, clutching his knees in front of the secret doorway. "You first, kid."

Eleanor's legs were happy to clock out for a moment or two, and she dropped to the ground and crawled back through into the chamber of KV39. Then Luke came through, and they allowed themselves to rest for a moment, sitting on the chamber's floor.

"I think we need to block the opening," Eleanor said.

It wasn't hard to find the rubble to do it, just exhausting to gather it from the crumbling stairs and carry it back. After a few trips, they had filled in the gap with tightly packed stones. It wouldn't take a person very long to excavate the opening, but Eleanor figured a brainless mummy would have more trouble.

They left the tomb and emerged into the cold night air, which chilled Eleanor everywhere she'd been sweating. She took a deep breath, and she laughed. Luke looked at her in surprise for a moment, but then he started laughing too.

"Mummies," Eleanor said. "I just . . ." She shook her head, her eyes wide, her mouth hanging open, nothing to say except "Mummies," again.

"Come on," Luke said. "We should get back before the others wake up and notice we're gone."

They half walked, half stumbled back down the ravine and crossed the valley to their tent. As they approached, they turned off their flashlights and quieted their steps and other sounds, to avoid disturbing those sleeping. Luke ducked inside first. Eleanor was already halfway through the entrance when she noticed the black helicopter hunkered down in the shadows a short distance away.

"Welcome back," a familiar voice said from inside the tent. "I am Dr. Pierce Watkins. I was beginning to fear we'd lost you."

CHAPTER

22

A LIGHT SWITCHED ON, AND ELEANOR FELT A FIRM HAND against her back pushing her the rest of the way into the tent. Her mom, Finn, Betty, and von Albrecht sat side by side on two of the cots. Two G.E.T. agents wearing paramilitary uniforms stood behind them, holstered pistols at their sides. Nathifa stood near the table where the scanners and instruments had been laid out, her mouth downturned in its usual way, her eyes sad, and Eleanor noticed the G.E.T. laptop there was running.

"Come in, please," Watkins said, standing next to Nathifa, his hands clasped behind his back. "Sit down, won't you?"

The man behind Eleanor gave her another shove, and she stepped farther into the tent to stand with Luke. The scene before her actually felt more surreal in its way than fighting the mummies had. Eleanor's triumph at finding and shutting down the Concentrator still pulsed through her, even as she realized they had just been captured, their mission incomplete.

"Oh, sweetie, thank God," her mom said. "Where have you—"

"I'll do the talking for now, Dr. Perry," Watkins said.

"What you're doing is illegal," Betty said.

"Is it? Taking saboteurs into custody?"

"Saboteurs?" Eleanor said. "Not terrorists?"

"Of course not," Watkins said. "I know you do not intend to inflict harm on anyone, in spite of what happened to Skinner. But it seems you have made it your mission to disrupt the G.E.T.'s Preservation Protocol. So yes, I think, saboteurs."

"What happens to us now that we're in your custody?" Luke asked.

"That is entirely up to you," Watkins said.

"In that case," Luke said, "I think I'll be going."

He turned back toward the tent opening, but the man who had pushed Eleanor inside stood in the way, blocking it. He wore a uniform like the other two guards but exuded a much greater authority. His silver hair was shorn close, and he had the muscled neck of a bull, with deeply tanned skin, and Windex-blue eyes. Luke stepped right up to him and said, "You gonna move, or what?"

"I'm afraid leaving is not one of your options," Watkins said. "I think you'll find Mr. Hobbes here quite capable of elucidating that."

Luke hadn't taken his eyes from the man Hobbes. "That a fact?" he said.

No part of Hobbes moved, except his lips. "That's a fact."

"So what options do we have, then?" Eleanor's mom asked.

"That is precisely what I would like to discuss," Watkins said. "I had just begun to explain things to your mother and friends here when you surprised us all by returning. Were you successful? Did you find the Osiris Tree?"

"Osiris Tree?" Eleanor said. "I don't know what you're talking about. We just felt like a nighttime walk."

Watkins chuckled. "How charming you are. Yes, the Osiris Tree. So named for the legends connecting Osiris to the Egyptian Tree of Life. Did you know that nearly every culture and religion in the history of the world has a Tree of Life myth? I believe that is due to the ancient presence of the . . . what do you call them? Ah, yes, the Concentrators, around the world."

"It's a name that describes what they do," Eleanor's mom said.

"True," Watkins said. "But I prefer to think of them as the Trees of Life they are."

"How charming you are," Betty said.

"I ask again," Watkins said. "Were you successful in finding it?"

"No," Eleanor said.

"No?" Watkins frowned. "Pity. But no matter. Nathifa assures me this is the correct site, and it shall be found. As I have demonstrated, I'm very good at finding things. We will move our operation down here from the Giza Plateau, beginning tomorrow. The protesters there were becoming troublesome, at any rate."

Eleanor's suspicions had been confirmed the moment she'd walked into the tent and seen the laptop, but Watkins had just removed all doubt. Nathifa had betrayed them. Eleanor had been right not to trust her. But von Albrecht, sitting next to her mom, looked as defiant as the rest of them did. Was it possible he wasn't a part of the deception?

"And what happens to us?" Eleanor's mom asked. "What happens to my daughter?"

"Yes, let us return to that," Watkins said. "What happens to you? If you cooperate with our requests, you will enjoy our protection. I believe you've earned your place among the planet's elite, after all. If you refuse to comply, however, there will be a series of escalating consequences that correspond to your level of opposition."

Escalating consequences sounded pretty terrifying to Eleanor, especially in Watkins's refined voice.

"So what do you *request?*" Luke asked.

Watkins brought his hands up before him, almost in an attitude of prayer, fingertips touching his chin. "Quite simple. You will sign the Preservation Protocol and assist us in saving humanity."

"But you're only saving *some* of humanity," Eleanor said. "What about everyone else? You're just going to let most of them die?"

"I see your point," Watkins said, nodding. "And it is fair. But let me put it another way. Imagine you are trapped on an island and have just watched some of your friends get captured by your enemy. You have a very difficult decision to make. If you stay, you will surely be captured as well—your mission a failure. On the other hand, if you escape, you might succeed, but you will be abandoning your friends, perhaps never seeing them again. What do you do?"

Eleanor narrowed her eyes. She could tell what he was doing.

"Oh, pardon me," Watkins said. "What *did* you do?"

Eleanor looked over at Finn, who hadn't said a word since she had returned with Luke. He was staring at the ground. "That was different," she said.

"Was it?" Watkins asked. "How?"

"They made a choice," she said. "Dr. Powers and Julian, they knew what we were trying to do, and they came along willingly. The people of earth, though—they have no idea what you're doing. You haven't given them a choice."

"And because it was their choice," Watkins said, with reptilian coldness, "you left them to die?"

Eleanor swallowed. She was certain he was bluffing, trying to scare her, but either way, it was working. A sudden terror punched her in the stomach. What if he *had* killed Dr. Powers and Julian?

"Please understand," Watkins said. "I believe you did the right thing, escaping from the Isla del Sol. I admire you for it. That was the best decision you could make under very difficult circumstances. The earth faces a similar dilemma. It is our island in space, and we must decide who will escape the fate that awaits us. All or none is not a rational approach. We can and must save *some*. And given that we cannot provide each person with that choice, someone needs to make it for them."

The reality of the situation was finally sinking in for Eleanor. What did it matter that she had just shut down another Concentrator? The mission was over. A failure. They had been captured anyway, which meant they had abandoned Dr. Powers and Julian for nothing, to a fate she truly didn't know.

"Did . . . did you kill them?" she whispered.

"Of course not," Watkins said. "They are in Cairo."

Eleanor almost let out a sob of relief, and Finn finally looked up from the floor.

"I don't take human life unnecessarily, Ms. Perry. I adore human life. The sanctity of human life is what the Preservation Protocol is built upon. I won't let anything—not a second ice age, nor a rogue planet, nor a small girl with world-saving delusions—keep me from preventing its extinction." Dr. Watkins then turned to Eleanor's mom. "But I believe I made my point, yes? I notice Dr. Perry has been quite silent. Mr. Fournier as well. Would either of you like to voice an objection?"

"There are other ways," Eleanor's mom said. "Other avenues to explore before we start using these things to harvest what energy the earth has left."

"That is exactly why we need you," Watkins said. "The best minds on the planet have already joined together to confront this. If you have a better idea for a solution, by all means, come with me and present it."

"Yeah," Luke said. "You guys have been really open to that so far—"

"*Ideas*, Mr. Fournier!" Watkins shouted. "Not *actions*! You have all taken it upon yourselves to act for the entire world! Does that not strike you as the height of arrogance? Taking away the very *choice* you seem so adamant to provide? Who do you think you are to assume you know better? And I don't mean better than me or Skinner. I mean better than everyone else in the world."

"There *was* no one else!" Eleanor said. "We were there, and we did what we knew was right. And I would do it again."

"How do you choose?" Eleanor's mom asked.

"Choose what?" Watkins said.

"Who survives and who dies?"

"The selection process within the Preservation Protocol is still under development," Watkins said. "Perhaps that is an area where you would like to help?"

Eleanor eyed her mother, wondering what she was doing.

"Selection process?" Luke said. "When in the history of the human race have those two words ever meant anything good?"

334

"Never," Finn said.

"That is because it has always been a function of tribalism and rivalry," Watkins said. "But in this case, the world is coming together for a greater purpose."

Luke folded his arms. "Sounds like classic dictator-speak to me."

"So how will you choose?" Finn asked.

"I just told you," Watkins said. "The process is still under development, but I can assure you it will be fair and impartial to—"

"Will it be the rich people?" Finn asked. "The ones who can buy their way in?"

"Of course not," Watkins said. "That's—"

"You want smart people, though, right?" Finn rose from the cot to his feet. "Are you going to give IQ tests?"

"That is—" Watkins had gone red. "That is not something—"

"What about criminals?" Finn asked. "You don't want them, do you? I mean—"

"Young man!" Watkins shouted. "Criminals have already demonstrated they are unfit for society, have they not?"

"*Unfit?*" Eleanor said.

"Yes," Watkins said. "Unfit."

"That's a word with as many definitions as there are people," Luke said.

"And that means it's not exactly impartial, is it?" Finn said. "You're deciding who fits, and who doesn't."

Watkins stared hard at him. "I see you have your father's keen intellect. I'm impressed."

"You think I care?" Finn said. "You think you can bring up my dad and—"

"Would you like to see him?" Watkins cocked his head to the side. "The helicopter is waiting outside. We can be in Cairo in a little over two hours."

That shut Finn's mouth.

"I suggest we all go," Watkins said. "This tent is far from comfortable. Some time away from the debate would do us all good, I think. We can resume talks after we've landed and eaten breakfast."

No one argued with him, but then again, Eleanor knew that as friendly as Watkins sounded, he was leaving them with no choice. He held the end of the golden chain.

Nathifa moved to pack up the equipment, but Watkins told her to stop. "You will stay here," he said. "Resume your search. I will send support staff as soon as we land."

"Yes, Dr. Watkins," Nathifa said.

Though Eleanor wasn't surprised at the woman's betrayal, it still hurt. Amaru had betrayed them to save his family. She suspected Watkins must have some leverage over her beyond her passion for archaeology. Nathifa, like everyone else, probably had people she wanted to save. Family. Friends. With millions of people barely hanging on in refugee camps, that was an inevitability. And it would only get worse.

Hobbes and the other two armed guards marched them all from the tent and across the short distance to the helicopter. It was large enough inside to carry all of them and more, a military-style aircraft with mesh benches that pulled down from the wall. After they had all strapped in, Hobbes climbed up into the cockpit and fired up the engines. The propeller whined above them, and soon the whumping sound it made drowned out all others and felt like a sack over Eleanor's head. They lifted off the ground, and as the helicopter flew away, Eleanor caught one last glimpse of the Valley of the Kings, and the tent with a solitary figure standing in the light of the doorway.

The next two hours passed far too slowly. The bench Eleanor sat on dug into her hip bones at just the wrong places, and the mesh straps were unyielding. It was too loud to talk to anyone, but Eleanor didn't know what they would say anyway. She certainly didn't want to have a conversation in front of Watkins.

But the flight eventually came to an end, and it

was dawn when they finally landed on the Giza Plateau, near the pyramids.

They stunned her with the weight of their presence, and the power in their simplicity and perfection. They did evoke the pyramid-mountain under which they had found the Concentrator, and Eleanor agreed with her mom that must have been intentional on the part of the pyramids' builders. But what boldness and audacity they must have possessed—to re-create a mountain range.

"That thrill you're feeling never goes away," Watkins said. "Come, please."

Again, polite, but it wasn't a request, and they followed him through the G.E.T. encampment of tents they had seen earlier. Watkins led them to one of the larger ones, and inside they found a well-appointed office space, not at all like the tent they had left last night, complete with partial walls, cubicles, desks, filing cabinets, and other furniture, and beneath it all a temporary floor of rubber tiles.

Watkins led them to a conference room with a long table surrounded by high-backed chairs. "I'll have some breakfast brought in," he said. "Please wait here." And then he and Hobbes and the other two guards left.

Everyone was quiet at first, and then one by one

they took seats around the table and stared blankly across it at one another. It didn't matter anymore who was right and who was wrong. They were prisoners now. Prisoners were always wrong.

"What on earth were you thinking?" her mom nearly shouted. "Going off alone! Without me!"

Eleanor had known she would be angry. "I did what I had to do," she said.

"And you!" Her mom pointed a finger at Luke. "What gives you the right to take my daughter—?"

"No right, ma'am," Luke said. "But you know how your kid can be when she's made up her mind."

"It wasn't his idea," Eleanor said. "It was mine. If you're going to be angry at someone, be angry at me."

"Oh, I am," her mom said. "Do you have any idea how worried I was?"

"You don't need to worry. That's what I've been trying to tell you this whole time. But you won't listen to me."

"Did you guys find it?" Betty whispered. It was the first thing Eleanor could remember her saying since they'd left the Valley of the Kings.

Eleanor assumed they were being listened to but also figured it didn't matter now. Nathifa would probably guess where they had gone, and even without her scanner, it wouldn't be hard for them to find their way down to the Concentrator now that the only thing blocking the secret entrance was a conspicuous pile of rocks. "Yes," she said. "I shut it down."

Betty nodded, and there was a catch in her voice. "That's good."

"Are you okay?" Eleanor asked her.

"Nope. But there's nothing to be done about it, is there?"

"No," von Albrecht said. "There is nothing. We tried and we failed. But I, most of all, because it was I who trusted her."

"So did we," Eleanor's mom said. "And we, more than anyone else, should have learned our lesson by now."

The door opened then, and Dr. Powers walked into the room, followed by Julian.

"Dad!" Finn shouted as he leaped to his feet.

"Finn," Dr. Powers said, pulling his son into a tight hug that lasted for several moments, and when they parted, Julian grabbed Finn and hugged him too, pounding his back.

"I was afraid I'd never see you again, Finn," he said.

"Me too," Finn said. "I was so worried."

"We're fine, son," Dr. Powers said. "They've treated us fairly, from the moment they took us from the island."

"I didn't want to leave you." Finn reached an arm around Julian's shoulder. "But we had to."

"You did the right thing," Dr. Powers said. "I'm proud of you."

There was something about Dr. Powers's tone that Eleanor found disconcerting. He had the measured hesitancy of someone with bad news they're just waiting for the right moment to share. But Finn didn't seem to notice anything amiss and beamed at his father.

The door opened again, and Watkins walked in. "Ah, I missed the reunion. But I trust you're all happy to see one another safe and sound?"

"Very happy," Dr. Powers said. "Thank you again."

"Good," Watkins said. "Breakfast is on its way, but in the meantime, I thought we might resume our talks."

"Do we have a choice?" Eleanor's mom asked.

"Sam," Dr. Powers said, "a lot has changed. You need to hear Dr. Watkins out."

"Dad," Finn said, stepping away. "What're you—"

Dr. Powers pulled him close again. "Just listen, son."

"I don't understand," Eleanor's mom said. "Simon, don't tell me you—"

"Our plan was flawed," Dr. Powers said. "Based on a false assumption."

"But we've stopped them," Eleanor said. "Three of them."

Watkins bent his ear forward with the tip of his finger. "Excuse me, stopped them?"

Eleanor glowered at him. "The Concentrators."

"Oh, my dear." Watkins shook his head. "I'm sorry, but you didn't stop them. Well, not permanently."

"What do you mean?" her mom asked.

"Your daughter turned them off, certainly. But what has been turned off can be turned back on. The Inca Tree has already resumed operation. We should be ready to harvest energy from it in a matter of weeks. We're still digging the Arctic Tree out from under the ice, but that is only a matter of time and persistence."

He was lying. He had to be. The Concentrators weren't just turned off—they were dead. Eleanor had felt them die as she killed them.

"It's true, Sam," Dr. Powers said. "Our plan was never going to work. Please. Listen to us."

— CHAPTER —
23

I F WHAT DR. POWERS AND WATKINS HAD JUST SAID WAS true, then she had no idea what it meant for her, for her mom, for Uncle Jack, for her friends. For the refugees—in Tucson, in Mexico City, in Cairo. For the entire earth.

"Might I have a word with Eleanor alone?" Watkins asked.

"Not a chance in hell," Luke said.

"It's okay," Eleanor said. "Really." She supposed she should probably be frightened by the request, but she wasn't. Watkins, the man, didn't actually scare her. It was Watkins, the architect of the end of the world, who scared her.

"Why do you want her?" Eleanor's mom asked.

"I think she and I can come to a better understanding if we are able to talk freely."

"She's a kid," Betty said. "Why do you need to come to any understanding with her?"

"She knows the answer to that," Watkins said, turning and eying her meaningfully. "Don't you, Eleanor?"

Eleanor got to her feet. "I'll be fine."

Watkins opened the door for Eleanor as she came around the conference table. "Shall we, my dear?"

She stepped through, looking back over her shoulder at her mother as Watkins closed the door, and then followed him back through the office tent to the exit. A moment later she found herself outside, once again beneath the pyramids. Watkins looked up at them, shielding his eyes from the sun.

"Let's take a closer look, eh?" he said, and guided her through the tents of the G.E.T. encampment toward the largest of the structures, the Great Pyramid.

As they approached it, Eleanor could see just how enormous the stone blocks were from which it had been built, each of them over four feet tall, and the closer she got to the structure, the more massive and imposing it became.

"They estimate it contains over two million blocks," Watkins said. "Placed one at a time, twelve stones an

344

hour, day and night, for twenty years."

"It's unbelievable," Eleanor said, and meant it, even when she compared it to Concentrators, and Amorak's tribe, and the mummies. "Can I climb it?"

"The Egyptian government would tell you no," Watkins said. "But what does their opinion matter anymore? I've wanted to myself, to tell you the truth."

Together, they mounted the first step and then climbed up onto the next, and the next. There were times when Eleanor couldn't find any foothold and had a very hard time pulling herself up. The angle of the pyramid's slope was quite steep, too, so that the higher she climbed, the more she feared falling. The wind that clawed up and down and back and forth across the stone didn't help. They had just reached a point high enough to look down over the entire camp when Watkins stopped.

"That's about it for this old man," he said, and sat down. "We've really only just started."

Eleanor couldn't even see the peak from where she stood. To even think of climbing the entire way utterly exhausted her. She still felt some of the linger-ing weakness from shutting down the Concentrator.

"I brought you up here for a reason," Watkins said. "Do you know what that might be?"

"Not a clue," she said.

He chuckled. "I wanted you to see what man can do. What we can achieve. What we can conquer. There is no limit to human ingenuity, and this pyramid is a monument to that."

Eleanor shrugged. "Okay."

"I know you and your mother believe it is dangerous to utilize the Trees. But I have faith in our dominion. We have mastered the air, the sea, the earth. We have mastered the interior of the atom, and the vastness of outer space. We will master this dark energy, too. But I need your help to do it."

Eleanor couldn't help herself. She laughed. "You think I'm going to help you?"

"I do," he said, and went reptilian again, cold and unknowable. "Because I know what you are."

The laughter plummeted from Eleanor's voice, and for a surprised moment, words evaded her. "Wh— I don't— Who I am?"

"Not who," he said. "*What.*"

Before last night, and her confrontation with the last Concentrator, his statement might have terrified her. But since she had embraced that part of her, whatever it was, she found she no longer needed so badly to understand it. The drive to do so had been motivated by fear, and she was no longer afraid.

"You know what I am?" she asked.

"Yes."

"Then what am I?"

"I will only tell you if you help me."

"That's what this is about?" Eleanor said. "A bribe? That's all you got?"

"You—you do not want to know?"

"Of course I want to know," Eleanor said. "But I don't *need* to know." And she wasn't about to let Watkins think he had any kind of power over her.

He licked his lips and frowned. "I underestimated you. That is not a mistake I often make."

Eleanor shrugged. "Guess you don't know me as well as you think you do."

"But I don't think I've underestimated how much you love your uncle Jack."

The quietly menacing way Watkins said it robbed Eleanor of what strength she still had, as if a wind could have stripped her from the pyramid's face. Was he threatening to hurt Uncle Jack? Had he already done so?

"What we won't do for the people we love, eh?" Watkins said.

"H-have you done something to him?"

"I've brought him here, to Egypt."

Eleanor looked down at the encampment. "Uncle Jack is here?"

"Safe and sound."

She felt a sudden elation but quickly suppressed it, angry that Watkins had found a way to get to her, and worried this was some kind of trap. He could easily be lying. "I want to see him."

"You will. He is like you, you know."

"What do you mean?"

"He shares your ability. Though it would seem yours is phenomenally strong."

What was Watkins saying? That Uncle Jack could also connect with the Concentrators? "He can—?"

"Yes. It would seem the trait is most common in males. A recessive, X-linked gene, like color blindness. But every so often, a female does manifest it."

Eleanor had always assumed, without really questioning it, that the ability had come from the Donor, her unknown father. But Watkins seemed to be suggesting it had come from her mom's side. If Uncle Jack had it, maybe that explained why she had always felt closer to him than she had to her own mom.

"I sensed it, you know." Watkins took a deep breath through his nose, nostrils flaring. "All three times, I sensed it when you shut them down. A sudden weakness. With the last, I could barely move. I thought I might be dying. I'm sure your uncle Jack felt it as well, along with everyone else on the planet who has the trait."

348

"How—?"

"We are connected to them. And I'm sure you've noticed, the weakness gets worse each time. What do you think will happen to you and the rest of us when you shut down the last one? What will happen to your uncle?"

Eleanor tried to speak, but her mouth had gone dry. She hadn't even considered that she might be affecting others, let alone Uncle Jack. And Watkins was right—the weakness was getting worse each time, and he seemed to be suggesting that she could be doing real harm to other people. But how many people, and what kind of harm? She wondered what would happen when she shut down the last Concentrator. How bad would the weakness get? Could people die? And how much of what Watkins was saying could she even trust?

"How do you know all this?" Eleanor asked.

"I already told you. I know what you are. And if you want to know more, you will assist me." He got to his feet. "But now, it is time to return. I wouldn't want to concern your mother, and I'm sure you would both like to see your uncle Jack."

He said nothing else as they scrambled back down, and by the time Eleanor's feet touched the sandy ground, her hands were scraped raw by the stone, and her emotions had been scraped raw by what Watkins had just revealed. They returned to the same tent from which they had left, and Eleanor found that breakfast had arrived while she was gone. There was a big bowl of fruit, cheese, and a platter of breads, some of them sweet. Tension wound those at the table into a knot, and Eleanor could tell they'd just been arguing about something. But whatever it was didn't matter to her.

"Mom," she said, "they have Uncle Jack here."

Her mom tilted her head, as if she didn't believe she'd heard correctly. "What?"

"It is true," Watkins said. "He should be here momentarily."

Eleanor turned toward the door, putting aside her fear and uncertainty for the moment, focusing only on the joy. She bobbed a little, anticipating as the moments ticked by. He was here. Her uncle Jack, who'd always taken care of her, who cooked the best food on earth, who understood her better than anyone. And then she saw him through the Plexiglass, walking toward them, escorted by a guard.

"Uncle Jack!" Eleanor cried as he came into the room. She rushed him and threw her arms as far around his large frame as they would reach, which wasn't very far. His long arms completely enveloped her, and he smelled the same, like aftershave and a hint of something baked, and she was crying.

"Ell Bell!" he said, kissing the top of her head.

"Jack!" Eleanor felt her mom's arms come around them both.

"Samantha," Uncle Jack said. "I've been so worried about you both!"

Watkins cleared his throat. "I'll leave you to have your reunion. I'm sure there is much to discuss." Then he turned and left the room.

Uncle Jack pulled away so he could look Eleanor in the eye. "Do you have any idea what you put me through, young lady? Running away like that?"

The last he'd known, Eleanor's mom was missing in the Arctic and Eleanor had gone to find her. "I know, I'm so sorry," she said. "But I found her and . . . there is so much to tell you!"

"That's what I gather," Uncle Jack said. "But that Watkins fellow hasn't told me much. The G.E.T. basically said you were both here and put me on a plane. What are you doing in Egypt? Who are these people?"

Eleanor looked at her mom, and then together they introduced everyone and gave a brief account of all that had happened, including the Concentrators and the rogue planet. Uncle Jack listened without reacting in any way, and when they were finished, he sat there for a long time without saying a word.

Finally he spoke, staring at the conference table. "What you're telling me sounds too incredible to—"

"But you believe us, don't you?" Eleanor said.

He looked over at her. "Of course I believe you. But more than that, I'm proud of you."

That was exactly what Eleanor wanted and needed to hear, and she wanted to hug him all over again. That was what she had been missing. Someone who understood her.

"So what happens now?" he asked.

"Now?" Dr. Powers said. "Now we have a decision to make."

"A decision you appear to have already made," Eleanor's mom said, which seemed to be a reference to whatever she and the others had been arguing about before Eleanor came back from the pyramid.

"What are you talking about?" Eleanor asked.

"Well, let's see," Finn said. "My dad has apparently signed on to the Preservation Protocol since I last saw him, and now he's trying to talk the rest of us into it."

"What?" Eleanor said. "I can't believe this."

"What did you think would happen when they caught us?" Julian said. "Look around. You think we have a choice?"

"I have a choice," Luke said. "So do you. But I guess it's easier to pretend you don't."

"What choice would that be?" Dr. Powers asked. "I have placed my sons in harm's way, and for what? All our efforts haven't changed a thing. Do you know of another way to stop the Concentrators? In addition to being a pilot, have you become an expert in telluric currents since I last saw you?"

Von Albrecht knew more about telluric currents than anyone there, but he had been silent for a long time. "What do you think about all this?" Eleanor asked him.

He pushed his glasses up the bridge of his nose. "I think I will not be a part of this Preservation Protocol. This is not the mark I want to make. It is wrong, and I would rather freeze out there than send someone else to die."

"Amen," Luke said.

"But we can change it," Dr. Powers said. "From the inside. We can make it better—"

"Oh, come on," Luke said. "Do you hear yourself? Do you know how naive that sounds?"

"Naive?" Dr. Powers said, raising his voice. "You think I'm naive?"

"Either that or you're not as smart as I thought you were," Luke said, raising his.

"You better watch your tone!" Dr. Powers said.

"Or what?" Luke said.

Eleanor wanted to cover her ears to shut out the conflict. This was not how things were supposed to be. They had started out as a team, with a common purpose, and now they were fragmenting, and Eleanor straddled the fault lines. She understood what Luke and von Albrecht were saying, because that was how she felt, too. She had made a promise to Amaru to save his son, and she intended to keep it. But she didn't know how. She didn't know how to stop the Concentrators anymore, and she didn't know what effect that might have on others. She wasn't even worried about herself. But Uncle Jack was sitting there, and Eleanor didn't know how to tell anyone else about this. Her mom would see it as a confirmation of everything she'd feared.

Dr. Powers was still shouting. "I will not be threatened by some ignorant bush pilot!"

"Ignorant?" Luke yelled back.

"Shut up!" Finn shouted. "Just stop it, all of you!"

That brought quiet into the room, which lasted a few moments, and then Watkins returned.

"We have some decisions to make," he said. "Hard decisions, I'm afraid, but necessary ones."

"I've made mine," Dr. Powers said.

"Simon . . . ," Eleanor's mom said.

"Indeed you have, Dr. Powers," Watkins said. "And you, Dr. Perry?"

"I haven't made any decisions," she said.

"No?" Watkins said. "I'm surprised you would put your daughter in such danger."

Eleanor froze, while her mom frowned. "What are you talking about?"

Watkins glanced at Eleanor with a hint of a smile and that same meaningful look. "She knows."

Helplessness and rage set Eleanor quivering. She knew how her mom would react to this. She knew what this would mean.

Her mom turned toward her, and so did Uncle Jack. "Sweetie, what is he—?"

"Allow me to explain," Watkins said. "Shutting down the Concentrators comes at a dangerous price for your daughter, Dr. Perry. A price for many people, including your brother, who shares her ability. Perhaps the ultimate price, if they're all shut down."

"What are you saying?" Eleanor's mom grabbed her hand. "Is this true?"

Eleanor couldn't speak.

"It might be," Luke said quietly. "I had to carry her part of the way out of that tomb."

"Mom," Eleanor said. "Please, don't—"

"I knew it." Her mom closed her eyes and shook her head. "I knew it all along, and I didn't stop you." She opened her eyes and looked at Eleanor with a fierceness that almost frightened her. "Well, I will not allow you to endanger yourself anymore."

"Mom, please. We'll find another way."

"What other way is there?"

Eleanor didn't know. She didn't know how she could shut down the Concentrators if doing so meant hurting Uncle Jack, or anyone else. Watkins had twisted things around so much, she wasn't even sure what was true. But the one thing she did know was that the Preservation Protocol was still completely wrong.

"Please, Uncle Jack," Eleanor said. He would understand. He knew her better than anyone. "Tell her."

"Ell Bell, listen to me." He cupped one of her cheeks with his broad, warm hand. "I still don't quite understand what's happening here, but I know I don't like this Preservation Protocol any more than you do. If I knew of a way out of this, I'd take it. They've got us over a barrel."

It was as though the bottom had fallen out of the room, and the walls had rearranged themselves. No one spoke. Eleanor was too stunned to make sense of where she sat now, but she wasn't in the same place she had been a moment ago.

"An accurate assessment, Mr. Perry," Watkins said. "Thank you. And now—"

Hobbes entered the room, interrupting him before he could finish. "Sir, there's a situation developing. We need to get you out of here. Now."

CHAPTER

24

"SITUATION?" WATKINS SAID. "WHAT KIND OF SITUATION?"

"I'll explain on the way," Hobbes said. "Let's move."

"They are coming with me," Watkins said, pointing at Eleanor and her mom.

"Yes, sir. What about the others?"

"Watkins," Dr. Powers said. "We had a deal."

Watkins squinted at them. "So we did. I suppose we should bring the others with us."

A slight twitch beneath Hobbes's left eye was the only sign of irritation he displayed. "I'll have two cars brought around. Wait here." He left the room, speaking into his wrist.

"I truly have no idea what this is all about," Watkins said.

Eleanor believed him and wondered what could possibly be happening that might pose a threat to him or the G.E.T.

"But not to worry," Watkins said. "I'm sure it will be fine. I've yet to encounter a problem for which Hobbes is unprepared."

The agent returned a few minutes later, beads of sweat on his brow. "We're clear, but the window is closing. Let's move out."

"You heard the man," Watkins said.

Everyone rose from the table and proceeded out of the conference room, through the tent, and outside into the sun. Eleanor smelled smoke. Then she saw it, a thick column rising up on the far side of the encampment, and she heard the roar of a large crowd. Hobbes opened the doors of two black SUVs parked in front of the tent.

"I want Eleanor and Dr. Perry with me," Watkins said.

"Uncle Jack, too," Eleanor said. "Or I'm not getting in." She wasn't going to be separated from him again.

Watkins rolled his eyes. "Fine, the uncle as well."

Hobbes nodded and ushered Eleanor, her mom, and Uncle Jack into the backseat of the rear vehicle, with

Eleanor on one side of Uncle Jack and her mom on the other. Luke and Betty went with von Albrecht, Dr. Powers, and his two sons to the forward car. Hobbes shut all the doors and then climbed into the driver's seat of Eleanor's SUV, speaking into his wrist again, while Watkins took the front passenger seat next to him.

"Proceed to route alpha forty-one," Hobbes said. "Let's roll." Once they were moving through the encampment, he seemed to relax a little and glanced back at them in his rearview mirror.

"Can you explain the situation now?" Watkins asked.

"Local mob," Hobbes said. "They started mobilizing about an hour ago. Preliminary assessment this morning determined it was just another protest, one of the usual. Nothing to worry about. But the climate took a hostile turn. They broke down the gates and set fire to a couple of our tents."

"Good lord," Watkins said. "Was anyone hurt?"

"Not yet," Hobbes said. "Egyptian security forces are on their way. They'll have the mob dispersed soon. But in the meantime, it wasn't safe for you to be there."

"I see," Watkins said. "Well, I trust your judgment implicitly, Hobbes."

The SUVs reached the edge of the encampment,

where the rioters weren't as numerous. But Eleanor saw them staring and shouting at the vehicles, making hurried calls on cell phones. Armed guards opened a gate, and the vehicles plowed through, then charged forward into the streets of the city at a speed that made Eleanor nervous, bouncing down narrow roads, scattering pedestrians and animals. After hearing the way Youssef and Samir had spoken about the G.E.T. presence at Giza, she wasn't surprised to hear the protest had turned violent, and she hoped it wouldn't get any more dangerous or destructive than it already had.

"Where are we going?" Eleanor asked.

"Secure location" was all Hobbes would say.

"And why did you want us in your car, specifically?" her mom asked Watkins.

"It was Eleanor I wanted," he said.

"What? Why?"

"You don't realize how useful she is."

Eleanor's mom leaned forward. "What do you mean?"

"Why are we slowing?" Hobbes said into his wrist.

Eleanor looked ahead of them and saw the forward vehicle's brake lights, and ahead of that car, an approaching mob of men that had completely filled the street. It seemed the protesters on their cell phones had quickly organized a roadblock.

"Back up, back up!" Hobbes ordered, but when Eleanor craned her neck, she saw that another group had closed in behind them.

They were trapped.

Hobbes got on a radio and spoke loudly in Arabic, while Eleanor watched the crowd squeezing in on them, anger evident on their faces and in their voices as they chanted things she couldn't understand. Her heart pounded in her ears and throat.

"It's going to be okay," her mom said. "Stay calm."

"Indeed." Watkins swallowed. "Hobbes, what's the plan here?"

"Security forces on their way," he said. "Six minutes out."

The crowd had completely surrounded them, and Eleanor flinched at the first pounded fist against her window. More pounding followed, against the hood, the doors, the windows.

"Six minutes?" Watkins said. "Will we even last six minutes?"

"Let's hope so." Hobbes pulled a pistol from his holster and brandished it, which sent some of the rioters scattering away, like a receding wave, only to have the mass of people crash up against the car again with renewed strength.

Eleanor had lost sight of the forward vehicle and

hoped Luke and Finn and the others were safe. She avoided making eye contact with any of the people right outside her window, keeping her gaze trained straight ahead at the back of the seat in front of her.

"We should be safe in the vehicle," Hobbes said. "It's armored and bulletproof. Just sit tight—"

Something smashed against Watkins's window, a brick or a stone, and he yelped.

"Sir!" Hobbes shouted. "Get down!"

The impact had left the shatterproof glass frosted white, fractured in thousands of pieces, but intact. But then someone smashed Eleanor's window, and then her mom's. Eleanor couldn't see out them anymore, could only hear the repeated bashes, again and again, until the claw of a crowbar poked through, leaving a sliver of clear light that widened with each successive impact.

"Hobbes!" Watkins shouted. "The girl!"

Hobbes pivoted in his seat to point his gun at the opening in Eleanor's window, but then her mom screamed as they broke through her side. Hobbes swung his gun in that direction.

"Careful where you point that!" Uncle Jack shouted.

When they breached Watkins's window, Eleanor knew it was hopeless. The gap in her mom's window was now big enough for an arm to reach in, toward the lock. Uncle Jack reached for it, roaring as he seizing it with both hands.

But then a second hand slipped into Eleanor's window, and before she could react, it had unlocked her door. She screamed as the mob wrenched it open, and several men clawed inside and pulled her out.

"Eleanor!"

She felt Uncle Jack grasping for her, his hands slipping away, and then she saw him charge out of the vehicle toward her as the mob carried her, but he was quickly surrounded and cut off. Hands gripped her arms tightly, and she was surrounded by angry faces of men she didn't know.

A gunshot split the air, echoing off the rising walls of the narrow street, and the mob recoiled from Hobbes, who stood by the vehicle with his pistol aimed upward. Watkins stood behind him, her mom next to him.

"Stand down!" Hobbes shouted over the sudden silence.

The mob replied with renewed shouts of anger but kept some distance from the SUV. Uncle Jack was still trying to fight his way toward Eleanor, buffeted on all sides by the protesters. But now that Watkins had exited the vehicle, the rioters seemed to be directing most of their fury in his direction, and Uncle Jack eventually reached her side.

"Let her go!" he bellowed at the men holding her, and they did.

Sirens wailed in the distance, and the rioters reacted to that with another pause, like they were all taking a collective breath. Then something at the edge of Eleanor's sight caught her attention, someone waving, and she turned to look.

It was Youssef. He stood a little back, out of the thick of the mob, waving at her and *smiling*.

She couldn't help it. She waved back.

He motioned for her to come toward him, to go with him. Eleanor shook her head, but he didn't give up.

"Who is that?" Uncle Jack asked.

"That's Youssef," she said. "Our taxi driver."

"What does he want?" Uncle Jack asked.

Youssef's waving had become more urgent, and he started shouting something Eleanor couldn't quite understand. But he kept repeating it over and over. It sounded like "escape," but she didn't know what he could mean by that until she saw Samir standing behind him. With him were Luke, Finn, and von Albrecht. They had left the forward car, and they were waiting for her. She had to make a choice. She believed there was a way to set it all right somehow, but she knew she wasn't going to find it with Watkins and the Preservation Protocol.

"We have to go with them," she said to Uncle Jack.

"Go?"

"You said if you knew a way out of this, you'd take it."

"But—" He looked toward Eleanor's mom as the sirens drew closer, and some of the rioters began to disperse.

"She won't understand," Eleanor said. "You have to trust me, Uncle Jack. It's now or never."

He frowned for another moment of indecision, and then nodded. Then he helped push their way through the surging crowd toward the others.

"Hurry!" Samir called to them. "This way!"

When Eleanor and Uncle Jack reached them, Luke gave her a relieved nod, and Finn smiled. Over her shoulder and over the roar of the mob, she heard her mom screaming her name. But Eleanor didn't turn to look.

"Let's go," she said.

Samir then blazed a path for them through the throng, with Youssef coming behind them, and one street over they all reached the edge of the mob and found a van waiting for them.

Youssef hopped into the driver's seat. "Get in, get in!" So they piled into the vehicle, and Youssef turned the key and floored it, shooting off in the opposite direction from Watkins's SUVs, leaving Samir waving good-bye to them from the street.

"Took you long enough to get the hint, kid," Luke said to Eleanor.

"I had no idea," Eleanor said. "How did—"

"It was Nathifa," Betty said.

"What? How?"

"She wasn't the one who got on the laptop," Finn said. "It was me. I was trying to find out about my dad. When she realized what I had done, she told me to act like it was her, no matter what. She said that was the only way she could stay free and help us."

"So she didn't betray us?"

"No," Finn said. "She rescued us."

"She call Samir," Youssef said. "She said we need big G.E.T. protest. This is an easy thing, because everyone *hate* the G.E.T. And then she tell us where to watch to get you out."

"Wow," Eleanor said. "She . . . she's my hero."

"Mine too," Uncle Jack said. "And I've never met her."

"Where is she now?" Eleanor asked. "Will she be okay?"

"She be okay," Youssef said. "We take care of her."

"And what about us?" von Albrecht asked. "Where are we going?"

"To my plane," Luke said.

They reached the airport without incident, but across the desert they could still see smoke rising from the G.E.T. camp near the pyramids. *Consuelo* waited for them on the tarmac, faithful and ready as always. They thanked Youssef, told him to thank Samir and Nathifa, and said good-bye. Then they boarded the plane, and this time, Eleanor took a seat next to Uncle Jack, and as Luke prepared for takeoff, she asked Finn if he had said anything to his dad.

"When?" he asked.

"When you left him back there."

"Oh," he said. "I just told him that everyone fits. No matter who they are."

Eleanor nodded. "I think that's true."

Luke called back to them from the cockpit. "We're just about ready, kid! Let's get this show on the road. Where we going?"

Eleanor had no idea. She didn't know how to shut down the Concentrators without paying a painful price. But she wasn't ready to give up. Not yet. She looked around the cabin at Uncle Jack, and Finn, and then she looked at von Albrecht.

"Didn't you say the first Concentrator that Watkins found was the master of the others?" she asked him.

"Yes," he said.

"Then that's where we're going," Eleanor said. "To the Himalayas."

ACKNOWLEDGMENTS

I want to thank the many people who have helped me see Eleanor through the next chapter of her adventure. First, Donna Bray, for introducing me to Eleanor in the first place. Jordan Brown has continued to provide invaluable insight and guidance, as well as friendship. My agent, Stephen Fraser, has offered unceasing encouragement and support, not to mention reliable movie recommendations. The love of my family and friends remains one of the greatest gifts in my life, for which I am endlessly grateful. And finally, I would like to thank Jaime, for whom words fail me in expressing my love and appreciation.

MATTHEW J. KIRBY is the author of the acclaimed middle grade novels *The Clockwork Three*, *Icefall*, and *The Lost Kingdom*, as well as one book in the *New York Times* bestselling series Infinity Ring. He was born in Utah, but with a father in the military he has lived in many places, including Rhode Island, Maryland, California (twice), and Hawaii. As an undergraduate at Utah State University, he majored in history. He then went on to earn MS and EdS degrees in school psychology. Matthew currently lives in Utah. You can visit him online at www.matthewjkirby.com